STAND UP! DELIVER

by

Sandra Amberg

DORRANCE
PUBLISHING CO
EST. 1920
PITTSBURGH, PENNSYLVANIA 15238

Dorrance Publishing Co
585 Alpha Drive
Pittsburgh, PA 15238
Visit our website at www.dorrancebookstore.com

ISBN: 978-1-4809-9039-5
eISBN: 978-1-4809-9061-6

Chapter One

March – Names

Sister Margaret Sorenson no longer felt guilty as she left the casino, her pockets ten dollars lighter. After following the prescribed route to holiness for most of her long life, she felt she needed a detour once in a while.

At age ninety-two, Sister could be easily recognized from a distance by her snappy gait and the large-framed reading glasses she wore dangling around her neck on colorfully constructed cords. During a previous interminable Dubuque January, cooped up inside, she found herself among the convent crafters in the sewing room sorting through vibrant scraps. Experimenting with different color combinations while biding her time for breaks in the winter weather, she found that making something useful soothed her restless soul. She gifted them to every sister with reading glasses, donated them to the gift shop, and laid in a lifetime supply for herself. Always passionate in her pursuits, it took her a while to apply the brakes.

Margaret liked traveling the roads of life, loved a map to show the way, but was unafraid to take a road "less traveled." She relished her life in the convent and spent fifty years of it as a teacher from elementary school through college. The education she had was something most girls of her time, growing up in a large family of ten children, could never have hoped for. She was the nun who was out on the playground with the kids for every recess, and not to supervise, but to play! She liked people and had a good ear for listening.

Her eyes still sparked the same brilliant blue as they had when she joined the convent seventy-one years ago. They had withstood the wear and tear and occasional tears of time.

Her thick, wavy white hair was the beautician's awe. Sister so appreciated the weekly opportunity at the convent to get her hair fussed over. She had never liked wearing the wimple, hot on her head, making her scalp sweat in the summer and itch in the winter.

She was petite, slim, with straight as an arrow posture, a sharp dresser. The secondhand store at the convent was blessed with a lot of stylish castoffs. She liked to browse there at least once a month.

"Sparkle and bling are my thing." She would quip to comments on her pizazz. She had an eye for color and an optimism that things looked good if you stood "tall" and enjoyed life.

When teased about standing "tall," the spine of her 4'11" (and shrinking) body would straighten, and she would quote T.S. Elliot saying, "If you aren't in over your head, how do you know how tall you are!"

This would be followed by a hearty laugh and a headshake. "Believe me. I have been there. In over my head! Yes, indeed."

When she was eighty-nine she had been invited to be interviewed by a public high school psychology class on aging.

"Why do you seem so happy?" they wanted to know.

"Genetics. I come from a very salubrious family. If you don't know that word, write it down. S-a-l-u-b-r-i-o-u-s. It means to promote health and well-being. Oh, and we are mostly sanguine also. That's s-a-n-g-u-i-n-e., tending toward positivity. One way to be happy and healthy is to look for the best in everything, trust in God, and don't worry." Oops! The teacher in her was always at hand. "Just remember to smile a lot. It helps." She added to cushion her slip.

"Sister Margaret," asked a very serious young man in the second row. "Who has influenced you most in your life?"

"Oh, heavens, many people. My parents mostly. Some of my other sisters. But I think, my namesake, Saint Margaret Clitherow Middleton.

We are a lot alike in our daring thinking. Not so much in the courage area. I hope I never have to have that tested like she did."

"What do you mean?"

"Well, she was persecuted in the 1500s because she hid Jesuit priests when the Church of England was harassing, torturing, and killing Catholics. Pretty scary time. Got herself martyred for that."

Sister noticed movement as they sat taller in their desks. A few who had been sagging in their seats after lunch, were now alert and ready to take notes.

"How did that happen, Sister?" asked one of the former slouches. He wanted a gory story, and she would give it to him. Sometimes she wished she had chosen someone a little more cowardly to emulate. The *brave* bones in her body had a lot of cracks.

"Well now, because you are high schoolers, I'll tell you. I wouldn't tell this to younger ones.

You see, like I told you, Margaret was sentenced to death because she was providing hiding places for the Catholic priests. The government authorities hired two men to kill her, but they chickened out and instead paid four beggars to do the job.

Now that is something for you to study in a psychology class. Think about that. You are poor, so will take money to torture and kill someone. To feed your kids? Yourself?" She shivered. "What kind of decision is that to have to make? I like to think that Saint Margaret would have fed those poor men if they asked."

She paused and wiped her eyes. "You think torture is bad now? Well, I tell you, we don't have much on those murderers of olden days. Burned at the stake, roasted, all manner of inhumane treatment. It always makes me upset to tell this story."

She took a deep breath. "They made her take off her clothes. Then they put a blindfold on her and made her lay on the ground on her stomach...on a pointy rock. After ripping the front door off her house, they positioned it on her back and piled it high with rocks. Well, you can imagine, young woman, mother of four, left there for six hours to die in pain."

The classroom was subdued. "One other thing I want to say. Don't dwell on stories like this. Admire the person for their courage and then go out and make a difference happily. Be positive. My motto is **STAND UP! DELIVER**."

Yes, she thought to herself, she planned to do it until she died. Life was a time of living and delivering.

•   •   •   •   •

Marilyn Sewell had a secret and each year it seemed to weigh heavier and heavier on her mind. At this point, gravity was taking its toll, pulling her deeper into it. Would she ever extricate herself? What would be the cost? She had reconstructed her life thirty years ago when Carolyn was born, and now her daughter was pressing her more than ever, wanting to know who her father was. Did she dare to open that coffin and let all the worms out? Was it safe?

To top that off, three years ago, Carrie moved with her family to Dubuque, Iowa, the residence of the motherhouse of the nuns who had helped her escape the misery and terror of her former life. One of them had passed away years ago. She wasn't sure about the other. Dubuque wasn't that big of a place. If Carrie ever met that nun, it would be the end of her secret. Marilyn could feel the fuse burning its way toward an explosion.

•   •   •   •   •

Carolyn Marilyn Sewell Donovan (Carrie). What a name! She liked her first name. The sound was lyrical. Her second name was her mother's, so although the rhyme made it sound "dorky," as her son Connor would say, she was fond of it, as she was fond of her mother, the woman who provided her with a good life even as she struggled as a single mother to finish her education, become a librarian, and raise a lively daughter.

Sewell. Now that was the clinker. Her mom was mute on the subject of her father. Carrie's favorite book as a teen had been *Black Beauty*, written by Anna Sewell. Was it a coincidence? Carolyn liked to believe that maybe Anna was her grandmother and had a son who was Carrie's father who just happened to love horses and animals like she did. In fact, as a child she devoured the books on the shelves devoted to animals, spending long summer hours reading and helping her mom in the rural library in northern Kentucky.

She and her mom were close. They called each other often, e-mailed, and texted.

And yet, Carrie really had no idea about her mom's life pre-Carolyn Marilyn. It was as if they were aliens that had landed their spacecraft in the hills of Kentucky one night to start their life on planet Earth. Even Uncle Donald and Aunt Katie, who she loved dearly, were not her real relatives.

People often said that she and her mother were more like sisters. They looked almost as if they had been cloned. One of her favorite photos was with her mom on a cold sunny day standing along the Mississippi River at Dubuque.

Life was good. She seemed as "normal" and contented as most, maybe more. She was a bit of a dreamer. But the idea to identify her biological father was constantly like an itch that she couldn't reach. Her mom assured her that she didn't know who her father was, that Carrie was loved by many and should be content with that. Not only did her mom refuse to tell Carrie about her own father but also would say NOTHING about Carrie's grandparents! They were another mystery.

It was all so weird. Had her mom been a prostitute? No, she couldn't believe that of the shy, studious, devoted mother and respected librarian. She was actually very religious and went to church, albeit different churches. "To give them equal opportunity," she always qualified. Carolyn knew that her mom was giving her the run-around.

When Carolyn learned about "rape" somewhere along her growing up years, she ventured to ask her mom if she had been raped. She shuttered to think of it. Was her father a criminal? A beast? Her mom avoided the question, which to Carolyn was the same as an affirmative answer.

"Don't worry. You shouldn't worry about that, Carolyn," Marilyn would say. "You are my wonderful, precious girl...," listing all her daughter's attributes in a lengthy litany that had Carolyn distracted by the time her mom ran out of breath.

Carolyn knew she couldn't have been adopted because she and her mom were practically mirror images of each other: blond-brown hair, light brown eyes, and freckled noses.

She had done her own futile background search after marrying Bob and had run into a dead end.

Thank goodness for Bob. Bob was solid and steady. They had met shoveling manure. She smiled at the truth of it. Both were freshmen at the University of Louisville, and for the four years of college, they worked on weekends and some nights at one of the better equine establishments in the area to supplement their tuition and education.

She had fallen in love with her handsome gypsy-man in Mucking 101, when he offered to dump the wheelbarrow on her first day. That and the fact that horses responded so positively to his voice and presence, really impressed her. From the beginning, she pictured him as the perfect father for the children she hoped to have. Fathers seemed to be uppermost in her mind at that time and now in her profession.

Carrie didn't think Bob noticed her. Shoveling manure is not too conducive to romance, and they were both concerned with fitting into college life. She loved Bob's dark brown, expressive eyes; his thick, black, unruly hair; his large, capable hands.

She didn't know until sophomore year and Grooming 201 that he was an exceptional lover. Their first kiss happened under the neck of a hot-blooded thoroughbred. They were brushing and talking history, one on either side of Telling Tales, when the tall animal raised its head and they were face to face. Whew! The sparks flew. From that time on, they were a pair.

Their relationship got her wondering about her dad again. Who was that mystery man? Just recently, in her capacity as a caseworker with foster care and adoptive families, she had met Sister Margaret Sorenson, a volunteer on the Foster Care Review Board.

"You look so familiar," the nun had said to her after the monthly meeting. "Do I know you?"

"I don't think so. I am Carolyn Sewell Donovan." She shook Sister's hand. "We've been living in Dubuque for 3 ½ years now. We moved from Louisville."

That had led to the conversation that revealed that they both had connections in Kentucky. Sister Margaret had a younger sister, Katie, age eighty-nine who was married to Donald Bergfeld. They lived in Mayville.

"My God!" Carolyn remembered muttering. "I have an Uncle Donny and Aunt Katie Bergfeld who live there. What are the odds?"

Then Sister Margaret's face had turned almost as white as her hair. Carolyn could practically see a proverbial lightbulb hovering over her head. Sister had sat down hard. Luckily, there was a chair behind her. Carolyn had gotten her a glass of water while someone else had fanned her with a folder. The woman had been visibly upset.

"I might know your mom." Sister Margaret said when she gained her composure. "You look just like her."

But there was no time to talk, as Carolyn's boss called for her to respond to a home emergency and she had to leave. She needed to find Sister Margaret and delve into that.

• • • • •

Robert Carlos Donovan stood on the wide front porch and once again marveled at the scene before him, a gift from David Donovan, a distant cousin many times removed who Bob hadn't even known existed.

The sloping lawn stretched a short distance to the chain-link fence, which he had erected when they moved in four years ago. The fence wasn't high enough to obstruct the view of the moods of the Mississippi since the house sat on the land's highest point. He would never tire of gazing across the rolling Father of Waters to the low-lying shores of the state of Wisconsin.

In the summer the view was lush. Now, in early March, there was a chill in the air, and the water was high, flooding some of the lower islands across the river, but not covering the steel ribbons of train rails that mimicked each other below his bluff, on the Iowa side and, across the water on the Wisconsin side.

He could almost feel the trees holding their breaths, awaiting that whispery resurrection green of new spring growth, giving the shoreline a hopeful demeaner after the white-grey of winter. The dam below was opened wide, letting the melt-off through. I am a contented man, he thought, high and dry.

He often experienced being in sync with nature in a special way. Maybe it was his gypsy heritage. The feeling encompassed his heart and soul.

Earlier that morning, after checking on their mare, who was due to foal in a couple of months, and before heading off to teach history at the local high school, he had sat on the front porch, with his coffee, enjoying the view of a grey cloud settled on the river, a slow moving old ghost drifting under the sunrise along the flow. He was living a charmed life with a thoughtful and passionate wife, who was caring and nurturing, and who also loved genealogy and history just as he did. They really clicked, and thanks to the generosity of Bob's deceased cousin many-times-removed, were shortly to begin a new venture that they were both excited about, raising Gypsy Vanner horses.

Bob and Carrie had a thing about names. Maybe it was their interest in genealogy. Bob was named after his own grandfather, who had moved from New York to Kentucky to work as a hand on a fancy farm that raised thoroughbreds. He had worked himself up to manager. Bob's middle name was for his *abuelo* Carlos Dominguez, his maternal grandfather, who had labored alongside Cesar Chavez fighting for workers' rights in California.

Carolyn's middle name was for her mother. Unfortunately, that is all they knew about her family history. She wanted a genealogy, one that didn't begin and end with her mother. Sometimes she said she felt incomplete, and that made his heart ache for her.

There was very serious consideration when Carolyn and Bob named their children. **Connor Alexander Donovan**, age six was named after Bob's great-great-grandfather, an Irish "tinker" who came to New York in the early 1900s looking for a better life for his wife and three children.

Bob cherished the copy of a sepia photo he had framed and sitting in a prominent position on the shelf in the living room as a reminder of his roots. It showed his ancestor in county Cork, sitting beside a son and daughter on the driver's seat of the typical gypsy caravan. It was decked out with intricate carving and even had windows on the side. A home on wheels.

In front of the *vardo*, or house on wheels, was hitched one of the horses favored by the Romany people of England and Ireland. Bob's own great-grandfather was crouched next to the horse. It was a combination of Clydesdale, Shire, and Dale pony. Just recently, that type of horse had been officially named as a distinct breed, Gypsy Vanner. The horse was becoming an overnight sensation. It was also raising the status of Romany people.

Bob wished he knew more about his ancestors from Ireland. He did know his great-grandpa had been quite a horseman and, his great-grandma, somewhat of a mind reader, a skill she struggled to keep under wraps lest she be thought odd, or even worse, a witch.

The only photo Bob had of her was a little 2x3 that was found in his great grandpapa's pants pocket when he died. Some relative had recovered it and made a copy. She was slim with thick, black hair and eyes that looked a little dazed. Her name was Agata.

Connor's middle name was Alexander, for Bob's great interest, Alexander the Great. A history major in college, Bob had written his thesis on the military genius. He marveled at what Alexander had accomplished in a short life, although he was cognizant of his ruthlessness also. What kind of man would name so many cities after himself? He told Connor of the favorite horse of the Greek conqueror. Connor would often pretend he was riding Bucephalus, Alexander's famed horse. He and his dad had traced all the travels of Alexander on a big map in Connor's room.

Then there was their darling **Annie Oakley Donovan**. That name was Carrie's idea. Three-year-old Annie felt she knew her namesake, sharpshooter Annie Oakley, like a real sister. Her mom read her children's books about the super heroine of American history, and she constantly told Annie stories, not only of the feats, but also about the person, a soft-spoken, talented, respected woman, who set standards for herself and lived up to them. Carolyn was a proponent of women's rights. She wasn't boisterous about it, just subtle and persistent. In her own job. Observing others in situations like her mother's, she saw too many women trying to keep afloat in a world that wasn't very forgiving.

She loved to have Annie curled up on her lap as she told her of this other little girl living a hard life in Greenville, Ohio; and how she learned to ride and shoot, never missing a target.

Living in Kentucky, near Ohio, Carolyn was an Annie Oakley fan and big into girls being good at something.

Bob enjoyed watching Annie and Connor spending hours trying to outdo each other with stories about their namesakes, although Annie was at a disadvantage because of her age. And, whereas Connor had two superheroes to talk about, she had only one.

Their play often revolved around their namesakes. They galloped through their Dubuque, Iowa acreage, Annie on her favorite pretend horse, Target, and Connor riding Bucephalus. They kicked and whinnied through the pastureland behind the house, charging and shooting, driving their caravan, a red Radio Flyer wagon, all the time keeping a running dialogue between the two of them.

Bob and Carolyn had a beautiful little family. If only his wife had some knowledge of her background. He sensed that was always at the back of her mind. There seemed to be no way they could get Marilyn, her mother, to reveal anything. Maybe it was for the best. Maybe it would be worse knowing.

Just recently, Carrie had told him about an incident with an elderly nun who said she knew her mom. He had encouraged her to contact the woman, but she was somehow reluctant until she discussed it with her mother first. For some reason, she wasn't rushing it. Perhaps she was weighing whether the results of knowing were worth it.

•　•　•　•　•

Brenda Schmidt's divorce was finalized. The papers were signed and in one month, her four horses, the chickens, her two sheep and two highland beef cows as well as her prize-winning angora bunnies would be set adrift. She would be receiving $500.00 a month for 25 years or until Kyle or she died. Now she needed to sell her animals or find a place for them. She loved her animals, but a job was her next priority.

Twenty-eight years together, half of them spent in bitter battles, in front of the kids and behind the scenes; while they milked cows, baled hay, grew organic, planted, and canned, picked berries, and fished. Their passion for each other produced five kids quickly, but when it died, life was still busy, but empty. Emotionally, she and Kyle were miles apart.

Brenda would admit that she wasn't the easiest to live with, always having new ideas for improvement which her husband promptly shot down. He didn't want to step past the status quo, afraid to take a risk. He drank a lot, and winter was a time of dark depression for him. He refused to get help.

She was a bit scattered. A friend had suggested that maybe she was attention deficit. She complained a lot about her life but stuck it out until the youngest went off to college. The marriage was over long before, not working for either of them. He already had a girlfriend which really ticked her off. Yet it shouldn't, because she would love to have a guy she could enjoy spending time with.

Well over a year had passed living in limbo with her oldest daughter Jenny, Jenny's husband Eric, and little Sally and Calvin, her only grandchildren. That year was spent waiting for the divorce settlement and taking care of her two grandchildren while Jenny and Eric were off to work the evening shift. They were helping her out. She was helping them out. And, she was gaining weight. Midlife had attacked her with a vengeance. She was missing the outdoors, the satisfaction of seeing things grow and eating the fruits of her labor, riding her horses, shearing the sheep, making angora mittens for gifts. She was in a creative doldrum and her body was reflecting it.

In the mornings, she liked to get away from all the commotion generated by active one and two-year-olds. Her absence also gave the family some space and privacy for a bit. Usually she headed to the farm to take care of her animals. She and Kyle avoided each other.

One morning it was below zero, way too cold to spend too much time outdoors. She was used to the cold on the farm and knew how to dress with her coveralls, boots, and heavy mitts. But she had anticipated the weather and had seen to the animals the day before.

Today she took her car and decided to spend the morning at the casino, have a free coffee and drop some coins in a slot, very few coins as she had very little money. Just buying medical insurance was keeping her near poverty.

She happened to sit down with her coffee next to a little old lady still bundled in her long down coat, probably chilled from coming in from outside.

"Having any luck?" Brenda asked the elderly lady. Brenda liked talking better than playing, especially with adults. She didn't see enough of them.

"Yes, indeed." The woman replied good naturedly. "The sun is shining, my car is running, I'm warm and hopeful. I do this twice a week, Tuesdays and Thursday after I teach." She offered her hand. "Margaret Sorenson."

"Brenda Schmidt." She shook the lady's hand. "I don't usually come here, but I need some thinking time. I'm living with my daughter's family and really need to get my own place and a job."

"Down on your luck? The casino isn't the place to come."

Brenda laughed. "No, I only brought five bucks. Just going to sit, have a free coffee, and slowly bet ten cents and think about what I'm going to do with all my animals and how I can find a place to live and a job."

Like a worn-out water heater that bursts, spewing its contents in all directions, Brenda told the woman about her current situation; her interests in living green; cooking and conservation; her frustration at not being able to make an impact anywhere, or use her talents. When it was all laid out she felt relieved. Then she realized what she had done, and her face turned bright crimson.

"Oh, cripes! I didn't mean to dump all this crap on you. Please forget it all. Have fun. I'll move to another machine."

"Oh, no, don't move," Margaret told her. "I have to go anyway to catch the late lunch group. And, do you know what, Brenda Schmidt? I might have an opportunity for you. Why don't you give me your phone number and I'll give you mine?" She dug in her pocket and handed over a wrinkled card: Sister Margaret Sorenson SFA, St. Francis on the Hill, Dubuque, Iowa.

Brenda stared at it. "My God! Are you a nun?"

"Yes! Seventy-one years last count!"

"This is so embarrassing. You must think I am quite a whiner! I don't know what came over me."

"Oh, don't be, embarrassed. I think I can help you. I just have to do some thinking on this and talk to a few people."

"Well, do you have a pen? I can write my phone number on my napkin."

Sister Margaret unzipped her deep coat pocket, rummaged around until she found a pen and handed it to Brenda. "Oh yes, I think I have something for you to do, Brenda. Something you might enjoy. The

Man up there must be looking out for you!" She gazed skyward and pocketed Brenda's napkin. The bulky coat made for the best filing system. No big purse to drag along everywhere.

Brenda watched her leave, back straight with a purposeful step. Was that hope she was feeling? She pressed a button and her machine started dinging. Looking up there were five wild horses in a row. She had won $30.00 on ten cents. An omen? Maybe there was a future for her. What was that nun doing in a casino anyway?

• • • • •

Sister Margaret was excited when she slipped into the convent's little Chevy compact. The sisters had just had a brainstorming session the night before on how to revitalize their facility, what with all the aging sisters. An idea was brewing. She felt like she was about to STAND UP! DELIVER. It was so invigorating.

• • • • •

Jill and Brian Jacob came as a pair. They were soul mates, connected by mutual love and struggle, both with hopeful and giving natures. Right now, times were a bit tough. They had just spent quite a lot of money that they didn't have because they dearly wanted children. After four years of marriage, they were finding nothing was working. The diagnosis: Unexplained Infertility. The doctors just didn't see any reason why they couldn't have children.

They were both farm kids who fell in love in high school. They were fifteen when Brian told Jill he would marry her someday. That day took place right after high school graduation. Both were eighteen years old with no desire to go on to higher education and no prospects of farming.

Brian loved the outdoors. He was always on the go and an ace at fixing machinery. But he wanted to do it in the field where it broke down or in the drafty machine shed with the door wide open. His favorite spot to sit, was on the rusty red Farmall that sputtered its way up and down the windrows pulling the baler in the summer. In the winter, with the scoop attached, he inhaled the crisp air behind the cloud of snow he pushed to the sides.

His dad was itching to buy a new John Deere tractor with enclosed cab and a GPS but not Brian. He understood machine parts, not all the new computerized gizmos. Deep in his soul, he seemed more connected to his grandfather's generation and didn't have much faith in his ability to figure out all this technology stuff. He had just purchased his first cell phone, a disposable flip phone. He wanted to be able to keep in touch with Jill in emergencies.

Dad would have loved his help on the farm, but his older brother Brad had been working for his dad now for two years and had decided that he would like to keep that place. Brian didn't begrudge him that. Brad did a good job and was a hard worker. Brian needed to find a niche of his own.

After some looking, he landed a job in manufacturing snowmobile and tractor treads. It was a bit over minimum wage, no benefits and one week's vacation the first four years. It was repetitive and boring. Some days he felt that being confined eight hours a day was driving him nuts.

He and Jill lived in such a bad neighborhood, that he didn't want to risk going for a walk after dark when he got home. But the rent was what they could afford. He also didn't like working a different shift than Jill, who had to come home at 11:30 at night. He always stayed awake looking for her, with the porch light on. Sometimes she had to park down the street. That was the reason he got his flip phone, so she could call him before she drove the ten minutes from her job to home.

Jill had taken a high school class on being a certified nursing assistant and immediately started working for the Sisters of St. Frances at the convent infirmary. On the second shift she helped to feed, bathe, and brush the teeth as well as to comb the hair of the older sisters who were unable to care for themselves. She made beds, cleaned bathrooms and bottoms, and answered call lights. It was very basic work. Just recently she had taken the class to get certified to dispense meds. She had gotten a little raise.

One of the perks of the job was that everyone was so nice. She thought she was doing something worthwhile, taking care of older women who had dedicated their lives to helping others and now were helpless. Someday she hoped to be a full-fledged nurse but right now she and Brian were struggling to pay the rent for a shabby one-bedroom apartment in an iffy section of town.

Now they had the bill for the infertility tests. What were they thinking to go through that hassle? And no insurance. They were only twenty-two years old and had years ahead of them. They couldn't even afford a child now!

• • • • •

Sister Margaret loved her pet project from 9:00–11:00 on Monday, Wednesday, and Friday mornings when she didn't go to teach at the Enlightenment Center. She would visit the ill sisters in the convent infirmary, and with their permission, write the stories they told her about their lives in the sisterhood. These were to be gifts to their relatives when the sisters passed, as most of them would spend the final days of their lives in a skilled care unit.

These stories were a way to remember them in their eulogies. It was a way for surviving family and friends to see them as individuals. Not only did the sisters enjoy it, but it boosted her spirit to hear about the obstacles they had overcome in the "olden" days, how they had served in the community, the funny mistakes they made, how they loved their Lord. Her goal was more to show their humanness than to shower them with accolades.

Sister Margaret had taken a computer class before she retired from teaching and kept files for them. At times, when they didn't feel like talking, she would read them some of the amusing stories they had told her. It lifted their spirits.

One Wednesday morning Sister Margaret was visiting with Sister Vi who was actually younger than she was. They had worked together at Holy Saints Grade school in the 50s. While they were talking, a young CNA entered. Sister Margaret didn't recognize her.

"Well, Vi," Sister Margaret said to her friend. "it looks like you have a new gal to administer to you."

Sister Vi gave the young CNA a big smile of greeting. The girl was carrying a glass pitcher of ice water.

"Good morning, Sister Vi. I bet you're surprised to see me here at this hour."

"Jill, yes! This is my friend Margaret."

Sister Margaret held her hand out to Jill's free hand. "Sister Vi and I were just talking about her life story. She's telling me about her experiences and I'll record them. I've never seen you before."

"Good morning, Sister. I'm Jill Jacob. Lilian is out with the flu today so I'm filling in. I usually work the night shift. Sister Vi and I know each other," she said with a big smile, a few strands of curly brown hair escaping her scrunchie.

"It's wonderful what you're doing, Sister Margaret. Did Sister Vi tell you about the time before she went to the convent? Every year she got three new dresses at the beginning of the new school year and one was red. She was so thrilled that she started prancing down the road on her way to school, wearing her new red threads." Jill started an exaggerated sashaying around the bed raising the water pitcher high and holding her uniform trousers with the other hand. Sister Vi and Sister Margaret started to howl with laughter at the performance.

"Anyway, who should see her in her new red frock, but a big old bull in the field next to the road. He started snorting and pawing, steam coming out of his hairy ears and enraged nostrils. He made a charge at her, crashing into the fence. Luckily, the rails were sturdy and only cracked and sagged a bit. She took off running and didn't stop until over a mile down the road at the schoolhouse!"

They were all laughing so hard, tears were running down their faces, each with a picture of the scene in their mind. Sister Vi started to cough.

"Oh, sorry Sister Vi. Here, let me help you sit up, and when you get your breath, I'll give you a sip of water. Okay?"

Sister Margaret noticed how competently and gently Jill helped Sister Vi. She was still smiling when she took her sip of water.

"Jill, you are a card," Sister Vi panted.

"Love you Sister," Jill kissed the top of her head. "I'll be back with your lunch shortly."

She turned toward Sister Margaret. "It was nice to meet you, Sister."

"Jill, when you get finished with your shift at 3:00, would you have any time to talk with me?" Sister Margaret inquired.

"Sure, Brian doesn't get home until almost six. He's my husband. He has a half hour drive from work. I'm going to fix a special supper. We don't usually get to eat together. But, since I'm working this shift, we can share a meal!"

"Could we meet in my room? I'm in the West Wing, number 223. I won't keep you long since you have special plans. I'll be waiting for you."

• • • • •

At 3:20, just about the time Margaret was ready to give up on the girl, Jill showed up at Room 223 West. She looked like she had been crying.

"Sister Margaret," she sniffled, "I'm sorry I'm late, but Sister Vi passed this afternoon. I feel just terrible. Maybe if I hadn't started her laughing this morning, she wouldn't have gotten that coughing fit. She had a weak heart. I should have known better. She was such fun. I loved that woman."

Sister Margaret held out her hands, pulled the tall girl into her arms and found herself crying along with her.

"Oh, how happy I am for Sister Vi. Wouldn't we all like to die laughing or with happy thoughts on our mind? She was eighty-nine years old, Jill. She had a heart condition. It isn't your fault. It's your gift that she was happy."

"Do you think so? I'll miss her."

"Believe me. She was so peaceful and happy when I left her."

That's the way I would like to go, Margaret thought to herself. To die happy. But not yet. There was too much to do. She would keep at it as long as she could. STAND UP! DELIVER.

She sat the girl down on the couch. "Jill, this afternoon, I wrote the story you acted out so well. I've added it to others that she has told me. She was quite a story teller. I'll make a booklet and we'll give it out at her funeral. There will be one for you too. Vi had so many great experiences."

"Thank you, Sister Margaret."

"Jill, I have an idea. You are married, correct?" She had looked that up in the files after lunch and noticed her address and the fact that she was married to Brian Jacob.

"Yes."

"Do you like kids?"

"Oh, yes, Sister! In fact, Brian and I really hope to have children someday." And then she opened up like a faucet. She proceeded to tell their story, the fact that they just couldn't seem to have children but also that they probably shouldn't at this time in their lives, given their marginal jobs. She told of her dreams of becoming a nurse but unable to afford it with the living expenses and how Brian didn't hate his job but was going crazy being cooped up all the time, and how he really wanted to work outdoors, how he had so many skills with machinery and farming, and how she was really worried about him.

"Well, Jill. I want you to be positive. I have something in mind that I hope might please you and Brian and make a difference for many other people too I'll let you know if…no, make that when I work it out. Jill, you're a lovely person."

Jill left a little dumbfounded with all kinds of emotions coursing through her brain.

Sister Margaret stood up. She was about ready to deliver.

Chapter Two

Late April - Connections

Sister Margaret taught at the Enlightenment Center every Tuesday and Thursday morning. It was a community place where people from other countries could come to learn English and study for citizenship. An hour of gambling followed at the nearby casino. No, she never walked the beautiful river walk across the street or stepped into the renowned museum that sat along the Mississippi or rode the popular river excursion boat. Sister Margaret pushed the buttons and watched the reels spin on the slots. She enjoyed the mindless activity, a break from her busy life. She liked the kaleidoscope-like color flashing in the dimly lit place with the cushy carpeting under her feet.

There was also free soda, which she never drank otherwise. Actually, no one but her confessor knew that she spent two of her precious hours a week gambling with the $10.00 she carried in a pocket. She loved to see if she could make it last for the hour. She no longer confessed it.

She had dumped the guilt she felt the first three times or so when she had decided it to give it a try. There were a lot of nice old ladies there. It seemed to be a good therapy for her, slowing down her active mind, taking it to la-la land. The busy ideas stopped running around and colliding in her brain. They settled down side by side to ferment. It was during these peaceful times that problems just seemed to untangle by themselves. It kind of reminded her of a popular saying at one time: *Let go and let God.* This enabled her to let go. She wasn't sure where God fit into the equation, but it worked for her.

She always returned home renewed, most often her pocket lighter, but also her mind. She jokingly referred to it as her retreat. And this morning she had her plan. It would all come together on Sunday afternoon.

There was a phone call she dreaded to make, but knew she had to. She would make three other phone calls that she believed would change lives, for the better.

The past three weeks she had been jockeying between her regular duties and talking with the board of the convent, checking on laws, making some calls to employers. If this worked, she would be following the way of Saint Margaret, STAND UP! DELIVER. She always thought of that in capital letters because it got her moving. Now it was time to deliver.

· · · · ·

Carolyn loved doing dishes on Saturday mornings. It was a quiet time to meditate because she didn't have to rush off to work. The window over the sink looked out on the backyard which was surrounded by all manner of trees. Large blue spruce draped heavy needled skirts to the ground providing a great hiding place for the bunnies and the kids. Conner and Annie were out there now in their rubber boots. Palm Reader was in the corral following them along the fence line. Bob was mucking out her stall. The mare was due to foal sometime in early May.

Huge oaks dropped hatted acorns each autumn, providing entertainment for Connor and Annie, who would turn them into cartoon characters with a Sharpie marker. They also liked to enhance the faces of people appearing in the newspaper, laughing hysterically at their silly alterations of mustaches and warts.

A prolific walnut tree challenged her back and muscles to harvest its bountiful fruit each fall. She had figured that out though, husking the nuts by driving over them with the truck, using gloves on fall evenings taking the husks off as she watched the kids running around the yard. Hanging mesh bags of the hard nuts in the barnage to dry out. Whacking them with a hammer when she was worrying over something at work or home, shelling by the fire in winter. It took a lot of work to process those healthy treats. She had some small 8-ounce jars she loved to fill and tie with colorful ribbons for 'thank you' gifts. The smiles from the receivers more than made up for the hard work.

And then there was her favorite tree, the weeping willow. It was a monster of a mess to clean up in the fall, but, the perfect place to spread a blanket for a summer picnic, the lawn sprinkled with leafy shadows. Even the kids like to watch the shadows on their arms and faces. She felt she had died and gone to heaven at this moment. It wasn't her style to take things for granted. Life had taught her that. They were so fortunate to be able to enjoy all of this.

She was thinking about her absent father and tight-lipped mother and Sister Margaret who had fainted when she met her at the FCRB last month. Before Carolyn had to leave in a hurry, Sister had said, "I think I know your mother. You look just like her." She needed to talk to her again but was afraid she had upset her last time.

As she was thinking this over, the phone rang.

"Hello?"

"Hello, this is Sister Margaret Sorenson. May I speak to Carolyn Donovan please?"

"Hello, Sister. This is Carolyn."

"Oh, great. Do you remember, we met last month at the Foster Care Review Board meeting?"

"Of course, I do. How are you? I was just thinking about you."

"Well, I am just fine now. But I need to talk to you, and some others, Carolyn. I have some information for you, and a request. Could we meet at the convent, St. Frances on the Hill on Sunday afternoon at 3:00? It is really important. Will you ask Bob to come too, and the children?"

"Of course, Sister. Can you give me any idea of what this is about?" How did she know about Bob and the kids?

"Two things really, adoption opportunity and your mother. I think I know her. That's all I would rather say on the phone."

"Yes. We can come. Thank you, Sister." A shiver went up her spine.

"Why don't we meet at the old chapel entrance. It is straight ahead as you come up the drive."

When she clicked off, Carolyn sat down in the chair next to the table, the phone still grasped in her hand. She was shaking.

•　　•　　•　　•　　•

Brenda glanced at the kitchen clock. The grandchildren were shopping with Jenny and Eric was cleaning out the gutters. Brenda had made her bed, thrown in a load of wash and finished the breakfast dishes. She fixed a cup of organic green tea and sat down with a magazine about greenhouses.

She had a lot of ideas about what she would do if she had one. Of course, she needed a place to live and someplace for her animals. It all seemed like an impossible dream as she was practically destitute. It would be heart breaking if she had to sell them. She told Kyle she would let him know this week. If they weren't milk cows, he wasn't too interested in animals.

And Jenny and Eric were talking about the fact that the little ones really needed their own rooms pretty soon. She tried not to take up a lot of space, but a year was a long time to live with your kids. The other four were in college or living with friends while they established their jobs and lives. The youngest, Carl, still lived at the farm with his dad and helped with the milking.

What had happened to her? She had been so competent on the farm. She could do it all, the milking and gardening. She had built a pond by herself and learned to shear the sheep, and butcher. That is, all except her chickens. For some reason they were more like her pets. Discouraging.

The dryer buzzed just as her phone rang.

"Hello."

"Hello. Is this Brenda? This is Sister Margaret." When there was no response immediately she added, "From the casino?"

"Oh, my! Sister. How are you? I didn't expect to hear from you."

"You didn't? Well, now, I can understand that, an old nun playing slots, saying she is going help you solve some of your problems. But I think I might be able to help."

"Really?"

"Yes. Could you meet with me tomorrow at 1:00 in front of the old chapel at my place? Just come straight up the drive, you can't miss it."

"Well, sure I will. I have applied for a number of jobs since I saw you but no luck. I am a farmer, Sister. I've been on the farm too long. Now I'm a middle-aged woman with no marketable skills. It's very discouraging. I so hope you can find something for me to do for you. And Kyle says I have to get my livestock out by next Sunday or he is selling them. He'll give me the money, but that's not the point. I am really hurting. Sister. And my kids are going to be on the day shift soon and talking about getting the little ones into day care for social-ization. I think they are getting tired of having me around. I don't blame them. I think that they resent that their kids behave better for me. Oh, cripes! I am doing it again. Why do I always burden you with all my problems?"

"Who knows, but I am happy to listen. I am hoping you will like my idea. Will you meet me there at 1:00 then?"

"Yes! Definitely! I am so curious. And hopeful."

• • • • •

Brian and Jill inhaled the sharp April air. It still had a bite this early on Saturday morning as they walked one of the trails in the Mines of Spain. The creek on their right was full with winter melt and the rocky hill to the left was beginning to green up. Jill could see that Brian was bit by bit relaxing. They stopped to watch a heron across the water, who was standing at attention in the shallows by the opposite shore. It was as still as a yard ornament.

"Is it alive?" Jill asked him.

"I sure hope so. It is hard to tell."

At that moment, there was a flash of action. The long-legged bird had swooped and was returning to its original spot. It had a small fish hanging from its mouth.

They looked at each other, amazed.

As they continued down the path, Brian noticed saplings about two and a half feet high, standing like pencils with sharpened points.

Jill pointed across the creek. "Look, Brian."

"That is so strange. What in the world?

"Awesome. I never saw that before but it has to be beaver. Don't you think?"

Across the water was a large dome of sticks that appeared to be anchored on top of the water. They looked at each other with big grins. Jill took the cell phone out of her pocket and snapped a picture. "This place is incredible."

"That turned out really good," Brain said, looking at the photo. "This is such a good way to spend the morning." Brian took his wife's hand and pulled her close for a kiss. "I need to get out in the open like this. I feel so much better."

She put her arms on his shoulders and locked eyes with him. "I know you do. It makes me so sad that you have to be cooped up so much working that job."

"Well, I am keeping my eyes and ears open. There has to be something for me out there. And Jill, we're very young. I just have a feeling that someday we'll have our own kids and a house. But sometimes I get so discouraged."

"I know. But like you say. We have time. I told you about the conversation I had with Sister Margaret, the day that Sister Vi died. I just have a feeling that she is up to something. She was asking me all about you and I told her how good you are with machinery. And how we wanted kids, but I couldn't get pregnant."

"Didn't you say she was ninety-some years old. Is she a saint or something, Jilly? Going to make a miracle?"

"I want you to meet her sometime, Brian. She is a dynamo. The other sisters really seem to respect her."

They walked quietly, hand and hand, the wooded hillside on the left and a view of the Mississippi ahead as the creek drained into the mainstream. The trail turned into towering hills on both sides, steep limestone cliffs, the sky blue above in the morning light.

There was a crude wooden bench in an amphitheater-like area where the trail widened. They sat down and Brian put his arms around her shoulders and pulled her close. Both were marveling at the solitude and beauty of what surrounded them, the spring of nature coming out of its deep sleep.

The muffled sound of the phone ringing in Jill's pocket startled them. Jill answered somewhat surprised by what she heard.

"Oh, hello, Sister Margaret." She listened, her eyes getting bigger.

"What?" Brian mouthed.

"We would be happy to, Sister. Two o'clock tomorrow. That would be great. We'll be there." She slipped the phone in her pocket with a cat-like grin on her face.

"You're going to meet my friend Sister Margaret tomorrow, Brian. She wants to talk to us about something that she thinks we might be interested in. She sounded excited but won't tell me why."

•   •   •   •   •

Sister Margaret breathed a contented sigh. Well, she had done it, Almost. She stacked the three folders on her desk. What a lot of meetings and phone calls. She thought she had all the "i's" dotted and the "t's" crossed. One more phone call to make. She waited until 4:45 when it was just about time for the library in Boone Junction to close.

• • • • •

Marilyn picked up the receiver. "Boone Junction Public Library. This is Marilyn Sewell." It was almost closing time and the library was deserted except for a couple of kids using the self-check-out.

"Hello, Marilyn. This is Sister Margaret. Do you remember me, the nun that drove you to Kentucky twenty-nine years ago?"

Marilyn's hand started shaking as did her voice. "How did you find me?"

"Please don't be alarmed, Marilyn. I have met your lovely daughter and hope to meet her family tomorrow. She looks just like you Marilyn. I recognized her. I also called Katie and she told me where I could get ahold of you at the library since you work on Saturdays."

"I have been afraid something like this would happen ever since you brought me here."

"Well, Marilyn. I know you have a secret, but I don't really know what it is. I just know that I played a part in it when you were in trouble, a very small part. When I mentioned to Carolyn that I had connections in Kentucky, a sister and brother-in-law in Mayville, turns out she knew them, Uncle Donald and Aunt Katie. That was quite a coincidence. I was surprised, to say the least." She stopped, and when there was no response, continued on. "When I talked to Katie, she was surprised too. It seems we all are a part of your secret."

For Marilyn, this was the case of the puzzle falling to pieces.

"Marilyn, I called to ask you if I could tell Carolyn and Bob how I know you? I'm seeing them tomorrow. Would that be okay?"

It was then, that Marilyn made the second most important decision in her life. "Yes, and please tell Carolyn to call me when you talk to her. When will that be?"

"Tomorrow afternoon."

Chapter Three

Late April
Changes Go into Effect

Marilyn hung up the phone at the Boone Junction Library. Sister Margaret had tracked her down. She had talked to Aunt Katie who now lived in a retirement community in Mayville with Uncle Donald. Donny had Alzheimer's disease but Katie was still able to care for him. She was going on ninety but didn't look a day over seventy-five. Marilyn tried to visit them on Sundays. They had saved her life. She would go tomorrow to talk with them.

This phone call had really left the aerosol out of her can. She had felt the pressure building up for the past twenty-nine years. It was never far from her thoughts. This was a moment she knew would happen someday. Actually, she had worried it would have been sooner. She knew nothing of the whereabouts of Carolyn's father, but she would try to find out after the story was told. But would it be safe? She couldn't imagine he was up to anything good.

She had been so happy for Carolyn who had met Bob Donovan in Louisville and fallen in love. It didn't even bother her when they got married by a J.P. their sophomore year at the U of Kentucky. What was important to her was that her daughter was so happy and had chosen so well.

Bob's dad was a respected trainer now at a prominent stable near Louisville after years of working on low paying jobs. Bob had grown up working early in life, even following his dad around. Marilyn loved Bob's family and considered them hers too. His mom, Rosa had Mexican heritage, a beautiful smile, and great culinary skills. Bob's four younger sisters were lively and intelligent, all married and living in the area. Marilyn felt close to all of them, but not close enough to reveal her secret. Until now. Now was the time. She had no wish to connect with her parents, but when all was said and done, if Carolyn wished to do so, she could. Marilyn had long ago forgiven their ill-treatment of her, but she had not forgotten.

• • • • •

Brenda was early for her appointment with Sister Margaret. When she had raced through Sunday lunch, for which she had made, butternut squash soup and Rueben sandwiches, Jenny had asked her what the hurry was. She hadn't intended to tell her about yet another possible job because she had had so many rejections this past month. But, it was her way to talk about everything.

"I have a job interview at the St. Francis on the Hill Convent." At least that was what she thought it was.

Eric and Jenny seemed a bit surprised but had wished her luck. Jenny had added, "I don't imagine the nuns can pay too much."

That had hurt. It was almost a foregone conclusion that she would have to get rid of her animals. How could she support them and herself on minimum wage?

Before Brenda had gotten out of her car, Sister Margaret came down the steps, dressed in sturdy black shoes and a fleece lined spring coat.

"Good afternoon, Brenda! Thank you for coming!"

"Thank you for inviting me. I'm anxious to know details. You've certainly peaked my curiosity."

"Well, let's get started then." She led Brenda to the building next door which looked to be new construction. They entered into a large foyer and seating area with a check-in desk at the front door. Straight ahead was a cozy, modern chapel.

"This is Angel Grace, one of our associates." Sister introduced her to the pleasant woman receptionist. "Now isn't that an inspirational name to greet you at the door. Angel helps us out with reception and she's tough. Never try to sneak by or you will be in trouble."

Angel laughed. "Stop teasing, Sister Margaret. I am nothing but kind and patient."

"True. True. This is Brenda Schmidt. I am hoping she will be in and out of here a lot in the future."

"Nice to meet you, Angel." Brenda thought it even felt good saying the name. The woman was about her age and dressed very conservatively and appropriately.

"Look forward to seeing you in and out," Angel smiled. Gosh, she looked angelic. Was she trying to emulate her namesakes? "How about signing in for me?" She asked Brenda.

"Sure."

"Good to get into the habit," Angel said. "I hate to remind people. I would rather visit with them."

Sister Margaret led Brenda down the corridor pointing out the chapel that was simple and plain with a pristine view of an inner courtyard. "This is the new chapel. We have Mass here every day and just use the old one when there are bigger celebrations."

In the computer room further down the hall, an older nun was explaining something to another. Both greeted Sister Margaret and Brenda with enthusiasm. They seemed to know what was going on. She wished she did.

They passed the dining room where 1:00 lunch was in progress and delicious smells were floating right out to the hallway. It looked so inviting and was decorated with summer flowers on each table... artificial.

"This is my apartment." Sister Margaret opened a door near the end of the hallway. It was really small, a living area with a small couch, small table with small chairs, and a small recliner, one bedroom with an attached bath. In the corner by the door, she had her computer set up. There was a crucifix on one wall and a large bulletin board with all kinds of missives that appeared to be works in progress.

"Very nice." The space actually fit the diminutive woman.

"I love it! This building was built in 2000, and I've been here since. Now for the piece de resistance!" Sister Margaret tried out her French accent.

Brenda followed her down the hallway to the end door. Sister Margaret took a key out of her pants pocket and opened the door. It was an empty room just like Sister's.

"Ta-dah! This is yours if you want it!"

"What! What do you mean?"

"Come in. Come in. I would invite you to sit down but you haven't put in any furniture yet. This is yours if you want it Brenda, on the condition that you work for us sisters."

"Well, that's so generous. But what do you want me to do?"

"Okay. Here's the deal. This has all been approved by the board at St. Francis. We're offering you your room and board, full medical benefits, holidays off, and three weeks of vacation. What we want from you is a fifty-hour work week at minimum wage.

"The reason we say a fifty-hour week is that we think you will need it and having everything so handy here, you won't have to drive to work, cook, or do much cleaning. We have a laundry you can use. You'll want the extra time to work."

"I will?"

"You're going to love this Brenda. Remember how you told me you were really a farmer and into organics, back to the earth thinking. Well, so are the sisters. We used to do a lot of farming and have big gardens, but now most of the able hands are getting too old. Last fall, our full-time gardener and maintenance man and his wife retired and moved into our independent apartments across the road. We converted that about forty years ago. It used to be a hospital we ran.

"Anyway, it was time for them. They were such good workers but it was too much for them.

So, here's the deal. We have one hundred and twenty acres of tillable land out back. There's plenty of room for your animals. There is also a barn."

Brenda's head was whirling. "You're—" she almost said "shitting me" but caught herself, "shkidding me. There is really a farm out back?" She'd have to watch her colorful language if she lived here. She had picked up some bad habits in her battles with Kyle.

"Yes indeed. Do you want to see it?"

The next half hour they toured. They drove past an old well-kept farm house where Brenda learned that the former maintenance man and his wife had lived.

An old red barn, which sat further back on the property, was empty and clean. It had a loft for hay that was currently unused. There was plenty of room to shelter the animals in the winter.

The hill to the back would be good grazing for the sheep, cattle, and horses. It was even fenced off. "This barn was built in our *hay day*. Pun intended."

Brenda laughed. "I'm impressed. You know, I have a love of barns and have often thought they would make a good story. If you've ever been in a barn when the snow is piled high and the cattle are contentedly eating, it's almost as if there is a spirit to it…the smells, the sounds. This is a good place."

It was a good thing Brenda had four-wheel drive on her car as she and Sister Margaret drove over some bumpy terrain. She had worn some rather nice shoes with short heels. Hard to walk on. Besides that, Sister was a little old to be negotiating the fields.

"So, Brenda. Here is the deal. We want you to farm this land organically, to provide food for the convent. We're big into sustainability. You don't have to do it alone. There will be a young man to help you, a former farm boy who is an ace with machinery." At least she hoped so. She was counting on her background research and timing. She looked at her watch.

"Oh, it is almost 2:00. I am scheduled to meet Brian and Jill Jacobs. He's the fellow who I hope will be helping you. Why don't we drive around to the front? You can drop me at the Chapel Entrance and take this folder over to the reception area. It contains the employment contract drawn up by our lawyer. Please read it carefully. Everything is spelled out for you. I'll introduce you to Brian and Jill at 3:00 out front. Is that okay? Do you mind staying here for a couple of hours?"

Could she wait around a few hours? You had better believe it! She dropped Sister Margaret off at the Chapel entrance, parked by the new building and went inside to see what she was signing up for. She knew she wanted this!

• • • • •

Sister Margaret should have allowed herself more time for this big afternoon. She was getting old. No, she was old. That Brenda, now she was a find! She asked very intelligent questions and had some really good ideas about making raised gardens for the older sisters who wanted to get out to work in the soil. The way she wanted to involve the sisters in the process of living was refreshing. She had even mentioned carding wool and dying yarn. Exciting. And she loved their barn. Phew, Sister Margaret just had a second to catch her breath when she saw a pickup coming up the driveway.

• • • • •

Jill and Brian Jacobs pulled into the space near where she was standing on the sidewalk. She noticed that Brian was really a handsome young lad. He was wearing a ball cap but removed it before getting out of the truck with Jill. His blond crewcut stood at attention.

"Hi, Jill. This handsome young man must be your husband."

"Good afternoon, Sister Margaret. Yes, and I say that proudly." She smiled at Brian. "We're a little late because my car wouldn't start. Brian says it probably needs new spark plugs so he'll fix it later when he can get to the auto parts store. I don't have to work tonight."

Sister offered her hand and Brian immediately took it. She liked the feel of it, firm but not crushing on her arthritic fingers. He had a shy grin and was looking around the place.

"Have you ever been here?" Sister asked him. "Jill works in this building." She pointed to the chapel entrance in the older building.

He shook his head.

"Brian, if there's time, I'll take you around and introduce you to the sisters I take care of."

"We're really curious about why we're here, Sister Margaret." Brian looked a little uncomfortable. "We aren't Catholics."

"Oh, I have a job for you, Brian. I think you'll like it. And you don't have to be a Catholic. If we can take your truck around the back, I'll show you what I have in mind." This was her nap time and if it weren't for all the excitement, she would be dozing away in her recliner.

"Sister, I have a stick shift. It might be a little crowded for you."

"No worries, Brian," Jill said to her husband. "I'll just go through the building and meet you out back. Sister Margaret, I'm so excited."

Jill and Brian helped Sister into the front seat. When she was securely belted in, Jill headed up the steps of the old building.

"That Jill is a prize, Brian. We love her here. I just got to meet her a few weeks ago but all the sisters and nurses say she is a gem."

"I've known that for a long time, Sister. Just hope I'm good enough for you. I am having quite a hard time right now, missing the farm life."

"Well, you are in luck young man. I think I have that problem solved. Jill told me how you hate to be cooped up inside."

As he turned the curve in the road that led to the back of the three-story brick structure, Brian gave a gasp. "It's beautiful back here. Is that a barn next to the hillside? Well of course, it is a barn." He shook his head and started to laugh as he pulled over to where Jill was standing by the back door.

"Park here, Brian," Sister told him. They helped her out of the truck. She noticed that Brian was scanning the whole horizon, taking in the fields, barn, and wooded hillside. Then he had put his arms around Jill's shoulders and smiled at her. Good sign.

"Okay. Please follow me. She led them on a sidewalk past a three-car detached garage.

"This is one of our garages, the other is in the new building. We have a fleet of six cars in the new garage. Are you handy with cars, Brian?"

"Yes, Sister. Unless it involves computer parts, I am pretty good."

"We keep the riding mower and a scraper blade in here, for the landscaping and snow removal. Just about any tool you need can be found hanging on the walls or in the storage bins.

A cement sidewalk led alongside the garage to the back door of a two story, steel-sided farm house. Before they got to the house, she took a set of keys out of her coat pocket and opened the side garage door. She flipped on the light and they walked in.

"Oh, yeah! This is like a hardware store!" Brian was very impressed and probably would have spent more time looking around but Sister shooed them out and ahead on the sidewalk.

"Here we are." Sister Margaret pulled a key out of her pocket and led them up the steps of an enclosed porch. She opened the screen door which gave a shrill little squeal. Several coat hooks lined the inside wall. There was also a chest size freezer, and an old armoire. She slid one of the keys into the lock of the kitchen door and pushed hard.

"It's a little warped," she said.

"I could fix that for you, Sister," Brian told her. "And that screen needs a little oil."

Sister gave him a big smile. Ah, another good sign. Yes, she had jumped headfirst into this project and so far, so good.

They entered a dated kitchen that spanned the back of the house. There was plenty of light with a large picture window on the west wall in a dining area and a low window above the sink on the opposite end, that looked out on a small wooded area. A large archway led into the wide, bright living room. The original wood paneling had been painted with a neutral off-white shade.

"Oh, Sister. This reminds me so much of Mom and Dad's home!" Jill looked at Brian with a big smile on her face.

"Well, I know young people now would say it needs updating. But it is nice and clean."

"Oh, I always think it isn't the stuff in a kitchen but the person running it."

Jill was excited and more and more animated as the tour continued to the living room filled with light and a gorgeous view of the farmland to the left and straight ahead. Brain just stood transfixed staring out at the open space and the large barn.

He looked at Jill. "That barn has character," he said. "It is waiting for something."

A regular-sized bedroom with the original hardwood floors and a bathroom completed that level. The front door led out on to a railed porch that ran all across the front of the house.

Brian and Jill stood side by side staring over the empty fields now awakening in the moist greens of springtime. It was that time of the year when everything comes alive. She grabbed his hand and squeezed it. Could they hope.

Ah, ha. Just as Sister Margaret had envisioned.

Back in the kitchen, she opened the door that Jill thought was a pantry, but it was an enclosed stairway to the second floor that led to three small bedrooms and a full bath with a shower and tub.

"Sister, this is a lovely home. I didn't know this was back here."

"Yes, it's been here for over seventy years. We had quite a lot of land when the convent was first built in the 1870s, over three hundred acres. That included our hospital, the nursing home, and the independent living facility as well as a boarding school for girls plus our convent and church. Girls were becoming nuns and going all over Iowa to fill our schools and hospitals. This house was used last year by our maintenance man and his wife. They're retired now and living in a condo across the street. I think he's missing the work a bit, but it was just too much for him."

She led them back out to the front porch, determining that this was the place to pitch her offer. "Times have changed. We pretty much have our immediate property of three hundred acres. About seventy of those are buildings. The median age of the Sisters is sixty-one years, and our population is leaking like a sieve.

"But, that is not totally bad news as we're gaining a lot of associates who are working along with our sisters to continue our goals. I'll tell you about that some time. But I want you to know that the sisters want you to have this house if you would like it, with only a couple of conditions." There! She had said it.

Jill opened her mouth to say something and looked at Brian, who also had a surprised look on his face.

"Okay. Let's cut to the chase," Sister Margaret said before they could ask any questions. She handed them a folder containing some documents.

"I'll just kind of summarize this for you now." She pulled a piece of paper out of her pocket and started reading.

"Number one, Jill, we would like you to continue working as a CNA for us. We think you have a calling to help sick people. Besides your minimum wage, we can offer health benefits."

Jill blushed.

"Number two, Brian, we would like you to work with us and with Brenda Schmidt to farm this land and keep some livestock. You will meet Brenda shortly and both of you will be responsible to come up with ways to help us be sustainable, protective of the environment and if possible, proactive in the community.

"You would also be responsible to help with maintenance to the extent that you are able, do the mechanical repairs, carpentry, etc. If there is a problem that is over your head, our former man said he would be happy to help. I talked to him personally. In fact, he wants to spend about two hours a day for the first week, showing you the ropes. He said the tractor is a little touchy. After that, he would be willing to help at your beck n' call. He is also a certified electrician and plumber. If this job works out for you, we would like you to get certified in both of these professions. To help defray the cost, you would work fifty hours a week."

Brian was speechless with a silly grin on his face. *Technology, here I come*, he thought.

"You can read all the details on the contract we will have you sign if you agree. You and Jill will be working minimum wage, but both will have health benefits and a house to live in. All the utilities will be paid as well as the taxes. It will remain the property of the convent.

"Number three, you will both become certified foster parents. I have the papers that you can fill out before you leave today, and I'll let you talk to a case worker before you leave. There is also a small stipend for fostering children."

"Brian, they want us to take care of children. They're giving us a decent house and an opportunity to take care of children. And jobs in a great environment."

"And I won't have to spend an hour on the road every day driving back and forth to work. And we'll have our own family in a safe place."

They put their arms around each other and then impulsively, pulled Sister Margaret into their arms for a group hug. They all had tears in their eyes.

"I don't want you to make any commitments until tomorrow." She turned to Jill. "May I borrow your cell phone, Jill? While Jill dug her phone out of her purse, Sister Margaret reached into a deep pocket in her jacket, pulled out a napkin and made a call to Brenda.

"Hi, Brenda. It's me, Sister Margaret. Can you meet me out in front of the chapel? I have some people I want you to introduce you to… Thanks."

· · · · ·

By the time they had walked through the old building from back to front, a man, two women and two children were standing out on the sidewalk.

"Carolyn. So sorry if we are late."

"No, Sister Margaret. I was so anxious to come that Bob thought he should get me out of the house."

Carolyn turned to Bob. "Bob, this is Sister Margaret. Sister, my husband, Bob Donovan. And these are our children, Conner and Annie."

Sister greeted everyone with handshakes, even the little kids. Everyone started to laugh when Annie grabbed her around the waist and gave her a big hug.

"Have you met, Brenda Schmidt?"

"We introduced ourselves," Brenda said. "It seems like you have a busy afternoon, Sister."

"Whew! You'd better believe it. If I can pull this off, it will be the most people I've helped in a single day. And let me tell you, I've been doing a lot of work on this. God and I have been communing a lot!" *And the slots*, she thought.

Sister Margaret stood up tall.

"First, let me introduce Jill and Brian Jacob."

She turned to Brenda. "Brenda, you and Brian will be sharing the job of farming our land. Brian will also be in charge of the machinery as well as any maintenance issues. Jill assures me he is a jack of all trades."

"Oh, that is for sure!" Jill took his hand. "He's a problem solver."

"Carolyn, Jill and Brian are looking to be foster parents. I have the papers for them to fill out. That will be done by tomorrow if everyone is in agreement."

She looked at the young couple. "Carolyn is a social worker for the county and works with placing foster children."

Carolyn smiled at Jill and Brian. "Wow! That's so good to hear. Foster parents are hard to find. There is a stipend, but it isn't much.

Sister Margaret can tell you this. She's on the review board. You'll need to fill out forms and be interviewed by the county. We are so desperate for good homes."

"Oh, we want children. We both love children and are from big families. I am sure Sister is going to tell you about her great plan."

"Absolutely, I need time with Carolyn and Bob. How about Annie and Connor go to the farmhouse with the rest of you. Brenda hasn't seen it yet. Talk to each other. Make some plans. It's a nice afternoon to sit out on the porch. I am going to take Carolyn and Bob inside to discuss some issues. How about if I send them out in about forty-five minutes."

That being agreeable to everyone, Conner took Brian's hand and Annie took Jill's. With Brenda in the middle hanging onto a hand of each child, the five walked along the road to the back of the building. The kids were laughing because the adults were doing a one-two-three leap, lifting the children into. the air. Giggles drifted back through the breeze.

● ● ● ● ●

"Looks like they are in good hands," Bob noted. "It is easy to tell they're good with children.

"That's what I wanted to talk to you about. Let's go inside to sit if that is okay."

Sister Margaret led the way, her step a lot slower than it had been earlier. After introducing the Donovans to Angel Grace, the three of them found a comfortable couch and chair to conduct business.

"Carolyn, I know you are extremely interested in knowing my part in your life but I have a question to ask you first."

"I waited this long, I guess I can wait a little more." She smiled at Sister Margaret. What a go-getter she was. What was she up to?

"Carolyn, you know that I'm on the Foster Care Review Board for the county and every month I see how difficult it is to place children in homes. Some are overcrowded. So, keeping all this in mind, things are starting to come together here. It looks like this: The convent needed someone to take over the farm which has been sitting pretty much idle for five years now. Brenda is a newly divorced farm woman who loves farming and organics and is just a kind of renaissance woman. But the farm would be too much for her alone. We want to hire Brian to help. He's a whiz with machinery and grew up working side by side with his dad and brother on the farm. He has a lot of useful skills.

"Jill and Brian love children and yearn for kids, but they can't seem to conceive. So, we've made arrangements for them to live in the farmhouse on the property so they have a home to offer children in need. And you have another foster family. I know you have to vet them, but they're great people. And I noticed you were good with your children going off with the Jacobs and Brenda."

Carolyn and Bob were looking at each other with disbelief, a little confounded.

"Sister Margaret, you astound me," Bob said to her. "You actually came up with this idea?"

"It's a complicated story, but it came to me at retreat. It fits my motto of STAND UP! DELIVER. Do you think you can help Jill and Brian with the ins and outs of fostering, Caroline? Jill is a real honey. She is a CNA on the night shift. I just met Brian this afternoon but get really good vibes from him."

"Of course, Sister. I'm thrilled that they are interested."

"Wonderful! Then that accomplished, I guess you want to hear the story of when I first met you."

Chapter Four

Escape

Carolyn moved closer to Bob on the couch. She was filled with conflicting emotions. Finally, she would begin to know who she was, where she came from. Bob knew she was charged with anticipation and nervousness. He put his arm around her and took her hand, smiling his reassurance. Sister Margaret sat back in the wing chair, leaned her head back and closed her eyes.

"Just so you know, Carolyn. I talked with your mom yesterday, for the first, and only time since we met. She gave me permission to tell you this part of your story. Actually, it is the only part I know. And she asked me to tell you that you will hear the rest from her. I have no idea what that is. She said you should call her this afternoon when you get home."

This is the story Sister Margaret told.

• • • • •

In 1975. I was getting ready to take a long overdue vacation. I had decided to visit my younger sister Katie, who lived with her husband of 40 years in Mayville, Kentucky. He was a lawyer, about ready to retire. They are childless. I hadn't seen them more than six or seven times since joining the convent, always at funerals it seemed. Katie is a good correspondent however, and letters went back and forth every month, as they did with the other siblings. In a family of nine, you are always writing or receiving a letter.

And when it got cheaper to phone, we kept in touch every week. Now we have all learned to use group e-mail. Unfortunately, a couple older brothers have died. The siblings are shrinking but their prodigy live on. Katie and I are the only ones without children. And never once did she mention you or your mother.

I was doing double duty on that vacation. I was taking a car to a large convent in Mayville, Kentucky so I had my own transportation and didn't have to take the bus. Someone had donated the car to the convent there. After a short visit with Donnie and Katie, I planned to take the bus back to Dubuque.

At that time, I was just clicking my Samsonite shut, when the phone rang. It was Sister Evangeline from Clinton calling. We were good friends as we had both taught at the same school in Davenport in the 60s. Sister was running a home for unwed mothers in Clinton at the time and was scheduled for retirement in two months. She knew I was driving to Kentucky.

'Margaret,' she sounded a bit panicked on the phone. 'This is Evie. I am glad I caught you before you left. I need you to PLEASE do me a BIG favor. Can you stop here on your way south? I have something important for you. Really important. Let me just emphasize EXTREMELY important.'

Evie sounded so urgent. Usually she was a very calm woman, great with the girls and adoption people. I told her I would be there within the hour. I had already picked up the car. It was a new Chevy Nova, black. Personally, I would have liked a red one, but the donor apparently thought black was more appropriate. Years later I read that the Nova wasn't selling well in Mexico because 'no va' meant it doesn't go in Spanish! But boy did this car go!

Then Evie said, 'Oh, and Margaret, park behind the building, right by the back door. That is very important. Hurry! Don't dilly dally.'

It sounded a little cloak and dagger but I almost forgot about that as I was driving a new car, feeling good that I had read the manual the night before and knew where the wipers and lights were and what kind of gas to use; and thinking about my reunion with my little sister. Since Evie sounded stressed, I fudged on the speed limit on the straight stretches of the highway and made it in less than an hour. What a great feeling, the wind tossing my veil all around. I had to close the window, afraid that it would whip it over my eyes.

When I arrived, I didn't even have a chance to get out of the car before Evie was out the back door with an infant seat filled with an infant!

Sister Margaret stirred in her chair and looked at Carolyn. "It was you Carolyn, looking so cute with a little bonnet and receiving blanket. You were fast asleep".

So, when Sister Evangeline got you secured in the car, she opened the door and this young woman came out looking a bit pale. She was carrying a large diaper bag and a suitcase.

'Marilyn is in trouble and needs to get out of here. Don't stop for anyone.' Sister Evie was actually shaking.

Well you can believe I was upset and tried to get more information from her, but Evie banged on the hood and yelled at me.

'Margaret, get out of here! Remember STAND UP! DELIVER!'

Well, that spurred me on. I backed out of that parking space faster than I had ever done that maneuver before, even laid some rubber with those new tires, and drove back around the building, slowing for the turn to the drive which led back into Clinton and out to the highway. And what do I hear from the floor of the back seat?

'Sister, please take off your wimple for your own safety.' It was Marilyn. I realized she was on the floor when I looked in my rearview mirror and couldn't see her.

I asked her what was happening. She said she couldn't tell me. The sisters would be in danger. If they saw us, she didn't want them to know that I was a nun.

I ripped off my headgear while driving with one hand. I must have looked a fright as I had just gotten a haircut. My hair was almost buzzed. What about Sister Evie, would she be in danger too?

Just then, as I stopped at the corner to turn onto Main Street, a big black Lincoln town car with tinted windows just missed us as they turned into the driveway of the facility.

'Did you see that idiot?' I said to her. I don't usually talk like that but I had a baby on board and a pale woman who was on the run.

She told me that it was probably the thugs who were chasing her, but when I questioned her, she wouldn't tell me more. She pleaded with me to get to the highway as fast as I could because when they found out she was missing; all hell would break loose. She said that, not me. She also said that Sister Evie was going to try to stall them.

So, I got through town, driving at a normal speed, reached the highway and turned south. Then, as the kids say now, I put the pedal to the metal, praying to Saint Margaret for courage to STAND UP! DELIVER.

I was sitting on a cushion because I am so short, I needed one to see over the top of the steering wheel. My goal was Davenport. That was a big enough city to get lost in.

You must realize that the roads back then had a speed limit of 50 and I was going 60! That is probably why it wasn't long before I flew over the top of a hill, only to see a police car waiting on the side of the road. Almost immediately, I heard a siren and saw flashing lights behind me. Evie had said I shouldn't stop for anything, but this might be the exception.

I started to slow down to pull over. It was a two lane in those days and the shoulders weren't all that wide. I was looking out the rear-view mirror, when all of a sudden, behind the police car, this huge black blur shoots over the hill and almost barrels into the cops. It swerves into the oncoming lane to avoid the police car and goes shooting down the road, right past us.

"At this point, you woke up Carolyn, and started crying. Believe me, it was no whimper. I was sweating. If there had been a car in that other lane, it would have been a disaster."

I don't know if the policeman was looking forward to a chase, but he forgot us and was after the bad guys. We noticed he was on the radio talking as he flashed by.

'Marilyn,' I told your mom, 'That little angel is hungry. I am a nervous wreck. Please get off of the floor and take care of the little mite.'

She did as I told her and while you were sucking away with contentment, we went down the road at the normal speed in a group of four cars. The traffic got heavier. About 20 minutes down the road, we spotted two police cars. They had pulled that big black car over. Marilyn ducked down again because they had two guys with their hands on top of the black Lincoln Town Car. I saw them take a gun off the one. They were facing away from the road, so I told Marilyn not to worry.

Well, from then on, it was smooth sailing. We drove when you slept and stopped when you cried so that Marilyn could nurse you and change your nappies. Actually, I even changed your diaper a time or two on the trip. Evie had thought to pack everything that was needed. We stopped in Galesburg that night at the convent of St. Claire. I knew one of the sisters there, a BVM who taught in the Education Department at Clarke when I was working there. She and I had made plans that I would spend the night with the sisters there. I told them your mom was my travel companion and I was giving you a lift to Kentucky to meet your new grandparents. That was one of the few times I ever told a lie. Boy, did those nuns fuss over you.

When you and your mom went off to bed, I called Sister Evie to let her know where we were. She told me that I was to take the two of you to the Adoration Convent in Mayville and then to forget everything that happened. To forget everything that happened?! We got there late the following afternoon.

On the trip, I told Marilyn all about Donny and Katie, how he was a lawyer and she was my little sister. Donny and Katie were expecting me for supper so I invited Marilyn to come too. But she said, no. She and you needed rest. I delivered the two of you to the Dominican Sisters as Evie had directed me. I guess they were in on this too.

And that is the last I saw her. I believe your mom was safe and Sister Evie had instructed me that the Dominican's would take over from there, so I left. And that is ALL I know. Your mom's name was Marilyn, and many years ago, I left her safe in the hands of the Dominican Sisters in Mayville, Kentucky.

• • • • •

The story told, Sister Margaret opened her eyes and looked at Carolyn and stood up. Bob and Carolyn got up and went to her. They all hugged one another.

"Sister," Bob said. "I want to thank you for what you did for my wife. It sounds selfish on my part, but I might not have ever known Carolyn, if not for you.

Carolyn had tears in her eyes. "You are my valiant grandmother, Sister. You will never know how grateful I am to know this much about my life and to also know, Mom will now tell me, for better or for worse, our story."

•　　•　　•　　•　　•

The Donovans drove Sister Margaret around the back of the main building where they met the rest of the group sitting on the front porch of the farm house, talking. Connor and Annie were out in the front yard pretending to be horses, to the delight of the others. When they saw their mom and dad, they ran up to join them.

Everyone was so animated, and it continued as Carolyn asked Jill and Brian if they would be willing to become foster parents.

Jill smiled as Brian put his arms around her shoulders.

"We do want to. Just think of all the aunties I can introduce the kids to. And Sister Margaret, we want you to be the honorary Grandma."

"Well, for heaven's sake. That beats all. I am a grandma and great-grandma in one day!"

"And my Savior, Sister." Brenda put an arm around Sister's shoulders and kissed her on the top of the head.

"Dad, can Sister Margaret be our grandma too?" Connor piped up.

"Well, you have to ask her."

"Sister Margaret, please, do you have room for more grandkids?" Annie was quick to take up the cause.

She laughed and held out her arms to both of them. "I bet I am the only nun with this many grandchildren!"

Chapter Five

Ouija
Early May

Carolyn stood by the kitchen window washing dishes, admiring the back yard sloping down to the left and the five-car garage that Bob had recently remodeled. It included a stall for Palm Reader, who was due to foal any minute, a tack room, and some storage for hay. Connor called it the *barnage* because it served two purposes, garage and barn. The pronounced it with the accent on the last syllable, barnAAHZSH. Behind the *barnage*, Bob had been working on something very special to all of them, a gypsy caravan similar to the one in the picture that they had framed in the living room. He recognized that he was sentimental and lived with it. He had the bottom part of the wagon completed and was well on the way to having the box with the windows and back door as well as the platform for driving it. Pretty soon they would be ready for the finishing touches.

Last fall he had purchased a separate structure he had ordered from Clear Structure, a company in Dyersville. In no time their contractors had the building up, wired, and heated. He had been able to work all winter in his spare time. Connor had been his constant companion. The family was keeping the caravan a secret because they knew of no other in the area and thought it might be fun for a parade or to give friends a ride. Carolyn was in charge of inside decorations and had been working on covering two long cushions for the wide benches on either side. Annie helped her pick out some wild and bold fabric in red, green, and blue.

What a nice weekend they had had at the St. Francis on the Hill Convent. Carolyn had taken some food over for lunch as Jill and Brian were moving into their new home. It was great to see that both of their families were pitching in. She had never met so many people at once. There were enough pickups and strong shoulders and arms to make the transition go like a charm.

She, Brenda, and Jill and Brian's moms helped to wash dishes and organize the kitchen. It appeared to Carolyn that they had also contributed a lot of extras from their own kitchens.

The Jacobs would be a great foster family.

Before supper she had checked on the mare who was about 340 days along in her pregnancy. Carolyn had noticed signs that the foal might come at any time so she had gotten a clean nylon stocking to do up Palm Reader's long thick tail, to keep it out of the way in case she did foal tonight. She and Bob had been doing everything to try to make this a successful first time for the lovely mare.

She was their beautiful piebald Gypsy Vanner horse, the newest member in the family, white with black markings and mane. She had feathery white hair-like boots between the last leg joint and her hooves. Gypsy Vanners were noted for their flowing manes and tails.

Caroline had led the mare up near the barnage and tied her on a lead to graze before she started the supper clean-up. Connor and Annie were running around outside with instructions to tiptoe quietly if they went to check on the horse. Bob had cleaned the stall thoroughly and put a couple bales of fresh straw on the cement floor, when he returned from school. He had also laid out the supplies they would need after the birth, or in case they were needed to assist in the delivery.

It was a momentous occasion for the family. Caroline was confident they could handle it. She and Bob had both been present for foaling at the stables in Kentucky. Bob's dad wanted to make sure that they knew as much as possible. In fact, for a long time, he thought Bob would follow in his footsteps. But Bob had decided to go off to college to learn about history. It was his passion.

Standing here quietly by herself, she was mulling over all that had happened in the past few weeks. She had been helping Jill and Brian with all the paperwork for the foster care. Both were excited to be able to help children. They were such an incredible and selfless couple, especially considering they were barely twenty-three years old. Both she and Bob were becoming really close to them.

But the biggest bombshell was when Sister Margaret had told her the story of her own mom's great escape after Carolyn was born. She and her mom had had a long conversation where she learned a few more things…like the fact that the home for unwed mothers in Clinton closed down in 1984. Sister Evangeline, Sister Margaret's friend, had died in 1993 and would never tell Sister Margaret what had happened. Confidentiality, Sister Margaret had told her. But Carolyn's mom said Sister Evie had made her a promise and probably didn't want to expose anyone else to danger. Sister Margaret agreed.

Too dangerous? That was ominous. Who were those two men that had tried to abduct them. It sounded like they showed up on her grandparents' orders. At any rate, her mom said she would come to Dubuque for a visit in June when she had her two-week vacation planned. Then she would tell all. Once again, Carolyn would wait. She had been waiting a long time.

• • • • •

Bob entered the kitchen, sidled up to her at the sink and slipped his hand around her waist, planting a loving kiss to her upturned lips before grabbing the dishtowel and taking a plate out of the rack to dry the dishes and put them away. It was the nightly routine.

"Are the kids still keeping an eye on Palm Reader."

"Yes, they've been running around and then disappearing for a while. That was good that you told them how they should watch for signs that she was growing restless. I told them that they were NOT to pet her tonight."

"Yeah, there are a lot of little things they can do to be part of this process." He put a plate into the cupboard. "You know, Carrie, we could get a dishwasher. There is money in the budget."

"No, this is fine. I kind of like having you by my side, gazing out of our window of wealth, enjoying the sunset, wrapping up the day, watching our kids tear up the yard." My mom never was blessed with a good man like this, she thought to herself.

Bob peered out the window. There were no kids in sight. "They're gone now."

"They just went into the *barnage* to see Palm Reader I think. I left her right outside the back entry so that the stall will stay clean in case this is the night. It seems we've been waiting forever. But the kids know they have to behave around the horse. I really trust them, Bob. And she is such a calm and patient animal."

"Yeah, well you were calm and patient until you went into labor and then you became rather bitchy." He looked at her with a grin that covered his whole face.

She poked him in the ribs laughing. He grabbed her into a big hug and she placed her wet hand on his neck to pull him closer for the kiss they both were anticipating. God, he was handsome.

"We really need to get out there, Bob. I realize this is her first foal and it's a bit early, but she has all the signs."

"Yeah, I am heading out as soon as we get the dishes done to put her in the stall and start the vigil."

She cleaned out the sink and was reminding him to close the cabinet doors when the back door flew open and Connor ran in, out of breath and already talking.

"Mom, Dad! Palm Reader is acting strange, shuffling around and snorting."

"Stay on the rug, Connor. Your boots are wet from the grass. We're going out now."

At that point, Annie entered more sedately.

"Mom, Dad, Palm Reader says to come because she thinks she's going to have that little baby horsy now and she's nervous. She is wheezing."

Bob and Caroline looked at each other and tried not to laugh. Annie came out with the strangest things sometimes.

"Ouija," Bob tried out the word on his tongue.

"What?"

"Ouija," Bob said. "Wouldn't that be a good name for the foal? I just thought of that when Annie said *wheezing*."

"That is kind of cool, her being a Gypsy Vanner horse. But doesn't that name carry a kind of stigma connected with it? You know, evil or something? Let's hold that thought for a bit."

"Your right. I am going out to check on Palm Reader and then call Harold." Harold was their vet who had just retired. "Everything will probably go okay. but I would hate to have something go wrong and jeopardize either of them. And I don't just mean the money we have invested in this mare and foal. She is like a faithful dog, a real part of the family. I don't want to take any chances. Harold is very interested. In his thirty-year career with large animals, this is the first Gypsy Vanner he will get to see foaling."

Bob grabbed his jacket out of the back closet and pocketed his cell phone from the charger on the counter as he headed out the back door. "It will be good to know he is there, even though he just wants to observe."

"The kids and I'll be out shortly. Tell Palm Reader not to do anything until we get there!" Caroline yelled after him.

She was so excited. The past eight months since Palm Reader had arrived from Florida, they had followed her pregnancy and read everything they could find on the birth of horses. Harold had seen to the vaccinations. They had watched videos on YouTube. Given their previous experiences, they felt well-prepared.

Since names were important to the Donovan family. Bob and Caroline, gave well-thought consideration to what they would name their newborn foal. As yet, they hadn't reached an agreement. Ouija. that might work.

"Okay, kiddos. Would you like to see a little baby horse born? It might take a long time and you have to talk quietly. Remember, we have been telling you about what will happen. And you saw it on the video. Palm reader needs her privacy."

The siblings looked at each other and nodded their heads up and down enthusiastically.

"Mommy, will you blow my nose. It's dripping. I don't want the baby to get infection."

Carrie smiled, pulled a tissue out of her pocket and wiped Annie's nose. Then she went into the adjoining TV room to grab the quilt off the back of the couch.

"This is a really special time for Palm Reader and for us. She'll work hard to give us a new little horse. We can watch but we must be respectful. We can sit next to the stall and talk quietly. I'll bring some books you can look at Annie, if you get restless."

"I want *Annie Oakley, Little Sure Shot*."

"Can I take my cowboys and horses, Mom?" Conner's current favorite toy, when he sat still enough to play with them, was a set of small rubber horses and riders that his grandma Donovan-Dominguez had given him.

"Yes, and I'll bring some bottles of water and a little treat. Just remember, it might take a long time. I'm taking the big quilt. I'll put it on top of some bales of hay where you can sleep if you get tired. Before we go, I need you to use the bathroom. But first wipe your boots on the rug."

"Is this a momentous occasion, Mom?" Connor was into vocabulary.

"Indeed, I think so."

"Oh, yeah," Annie voiced with enthusiasm. "It certainly is!"

•　•　•　•　•

Going outside, Carolyn and the kids hustled quickly down the colorful pavers leading from the patio toward the barnage, Connor and Annie made the distance in gazelle-like leaps from stone to stone, Caroline in long strides, carrying the quilt, the bag of toys, water, and treats swinging at her side. The yard light mounted over the back porch illuminated their way.

What wasn't visible from the pathway was the corral in the back of the barnage. A year ago, when they decided to purchase a pregnant Gypsy Vanner horse, Bob had fenced in a little more than two acres using white PVC. With an open area and running space, it made an excellent place for horses. They had decided to include several of the large trees that grew there, to provide shade in the hot summer months.

Not only did it contain a great running area but a special combination of grasses in the corral area were already sprouting. That had been Carolyn's project last summer, to research and grow nutritious grasses for horse's health. She was very determined to do her part to raise hearty horses.

The end garage door opened to the area of Palm Reader's stall. But, unless Bob was delivering hay or grain, they kept it closed and used the side door to enter. Tonight, they didn't want any artificial light to shine in if their horse decided to give birth.

Connor was the first to arrive and held the door for his sister and mom. His dad had taught him that. The sliding door opposite the garage door, was wide open to the corral, admitting a cool May breeze and the vision of the sky behind still holding on to the dusk.

When Bob remodeled, he had updated the electricity at this end of the barnage and now had good lighting inside. However, he had only turned on the light in the tack room, so that the horse might relax better.

"If you hadn't come soon, I was going to call up to the house to get you. When I got out here she was having a definite contraction so I brought her in. Got in touch with Harold. He is not sure he will come. His wife is having a rough night." Harold had retired to be with his wife who was suffering from cancer and had hospice helping him. So sad to think that she was diagnosed shortly before he retired and now was going downhill rapidly.

Palm Reader was not standing but already lying on her side in the deep straw in the spacious stall. There was sweat on her neck and she was breathing hard. Caroline was glad she had tied up the mare's tail earlier. According to all her reading, the fact that Palm Reader was on her side, meant that she was ready to give birth, although some horses remained standing. Bob was observing from outside the stall. Caroline saw that he had their emergency kit ready in case there were any problems. They were hoping that they wouldn't need any of it, but they wanted to be prepared just in case. It was amazing what the family had learned as a result of their decision to get into the business of raising Gypsy Vanner horses.

Annie and Conner had helped their dad assemble the kit which included about seventeen items that might come in handy.

"How did horses do this in the wild without our help, Bob?" Caroline whispered as she sidled up to him and leaned against his shoulder.

"Isn't that a wonder."

Connor stood on his other side. "Okay, Dad,". "Is this it? What we talked about? This means it's going to happen now, right?"

"Sure looks like it, Connor." He put his hand on his son's shoulder. "Her water broke," Bob said softly to Caroline.

"Hello, Palm Reader." Annie said as her dad lifted her up so she could see over the rails. "I'll sit here on the blanket and be quiet. You're going to have your baby." Annie turned to her mom. "Mom, can we put the blanket very near to the rails so I can peek through the cracks?"

"Sure Annie" Caroline unfolded the quilt while Bob and Connor pushed a couple of bales close to the railed side of the stall. "But remember. Let's be very quiet."

For now, both of the children seemed to take this advice seriously, with heads down, each engrossed in their own activity, looking up only when Palm Rader had a contraction.

Caroline often wondered at the magical life they seemed to live these last four years since inheriting this place from Bob's distant relation, David Donovan, a wealthy Dubuque businessman and third generation owner of a profitable window and door factory. They hadn't even known he existed until they received a letter from his attorney. Bob had spent a year researching and found out that David was a descendent of Connor's oldest son, Sean. David's only brother, James, had been killed in the Viet Nam war. Neither had married. The genealogy on that line stopped with David. This was very interesting for Bob. He was still busy trying to fill in genealogy pieces. Carolyn was awed and sometimes envious that he had such a good grasp about where he came from.

But shortly, Carolyn's attention was back to the present time and place. Their luck continued. as all by herself, with the Donovans looking on, Bob holding Carolyn's hand and Connor and Annie with their eyes glued to the space between the lower rails, Palm Reader gave birth to a new foal, not needing any assistance. She was a gangly little filly. Mother and baby did just what they were supposed to do. The foal was suckling like a pro when Harold arrived.

•　•　•　•　•

The next morning before school, the family returned to the barn. They marveled at Ouija, for that was what they had decided to call her, standing beside her mother, fuzzy-white, with brown markings. She already sported a rather long perky tail that would grow into a longer beautiful swipe of hair as she developed. Her mane stood up bristly, a soft white brush.

"She's skewbald," Bob said. "Like her sire."

"What is that, Dad? Skewbald." Connor asked.

"Well you see her mom is white with black markings?" Connor nodded. "That's called piebald. And brown on white is skewbald."

"Wow, her markings are so distinctive," Carrie admired the foal. "Look at her coffee and cream ears and the way the brown goes across her forehead, kind of like one of your headbands, Annie."

"That section down her neck is so attractive. And look at those long eyelashes and big brown eyes." Bob was like a proud papa.

"She has a brown bib," Annie piped up. "And some brown on her belly and butty, but not by her baby booties. She's a beauty!"

Carrie turned to Bob. "They are working on the 'B' sound in pre-school."

"Those aren't booties, they're hoovies. I mean hooves!" Connor set Annie straight.

"Weegie, you are a cute little horsey." Ouija lifted her head at the sound of her name and stood completely still, staring transfixed into space. She was isolated in her own world.

"She is doing that thing again, Dad." Connor noted. "Like a statue. Look, Mom, she doesn't move!"

"What's wrong with her, Bob?"

"Nothing. She did that before too. Remember? After she was born? But Harold checked her out. She is sound. And he also said Palm Reader has a good milk flow and great mothering instincts."

They all gazed at the little animal fascinated at its stillness and concentration and it wasn't long until she shook her head and sidled up to her mom for another go at eating.

"That is kind of strange, Dad. Don't you think so, Mom?"

"I don't know what to think."

"Don't worry. She was just listening to something far, far, far away." Annie replied with confidence.

"Annie," her big brother said patiently. "There was nothing to hear. It's morning time. It's quiet."

"You don't have to hear only with your ears, Connor. I think she was listening up here, under her headband." Annie pointed to her forehead."

Bob looked at Carrie with some skepticism. She just shrugged.

Chapter Six

White Knight, Ginger, Stang, Pancho

Brenda was settled into her room at the convent and she loved it. She had a large bookcase on one wall that held her cookbooks, organic farming manuals, knitting and crocheting magazines, greenhouse designs, nutrition books and all sorts of natural healing information. Her computer fit right into the corner like Sister Margaret's. She had a couch from Jenny who was wanting a new one anyway, a coffee table from Good Will and a small table with a couple of chairs. Of course, there was her bedroom. She had purchased a sleep number bed and loved it. The closet had built-ins which was very convenient. After almost half a century of sharing space, she cherished her own little nest, and found she could focus and get so much done in the smaller space. She seemed to keep it neater too.

Last Tuesday night, Brian and Bob with little Annie and Conner in tow, picked her up with Bob's truck and horse trailer so she could get her four horses delivered to their new home at St. Francis on the Hill. The trailer was only a double so they had to make two trips.

Bob was so excited to share the news of his new little filly, Ouija. She didn't know him too well yet, but he sure was talkative about the horses. She understood because her own animals were like family to her, and she really felt guilty that she hadn't been able to get out to the farm to groom and ride them as often as she would have liked. They deserved more attention. Of course, Kyle and her son kept them fed, but the soft fuzzies weren't there. Brenda got out two mornings most weeks to groom her horses, and tried to ride each one every week.

She was so excited to have them handy and already had an idea to use them to benefit the community and the sisters. She had to do a lot more research and check into insurance. She also wanted to talk to some organizations in town. Then she would suggest her idea to Sister Margaret. The thing was, now that she had the horses close, she had so much going on that it was difficult to give them any more attention than when she was living with Jenny and Eric. If her idea flew, those horses would be so pampered.

Her horses were all old and rather mellow. She had bought them that way. Once a horse reached an older age, they often got aches and pains, just like people. She liked to call them her rescue horses. There was White Knight who was rather heavy and probably the oldest. Ginger was loving and affectionate with big eyes and a snout that was always nosing around for treats. Stang had some mustang blood and was a bit smaller than the others but probably the most spirited. And Pancho, a bit stiff but a beautiful grey-black and steady to ride. These were her babies and presently, all grazing on the hillside.

The strangest thing happened after White Knight and Ginger arrived in the first transfer. She had backed each one out. Brian held the halters. Bob set Annie on White Knight and Connor on Ginger. Both of the kids sat well bareback. You could tell they had been around horses.

Bob and Brian led the horses out to the pasture. Brenda walked between them talking of this and that. She noticed that Annie spread her arms and laid her head on White Knight's neck, talking to him quietly, ignoring everything else around her. The horses were so well-behaved with the children on them. She felt very proud of them. When they dismounted on the hillside pasture, both kids patted their steed's neck. Annie could hardly reach up to White Knight. Her dad lifted her and Brenda heard her say.

"Now don't you run away, boy. Brenda will take good care of you."

Brenda walked back to the truck hand and hand with Annie while the men and Connor trailed behind deep in conversation. Brenda asked Annie what she had been talking to White Knight about.

Annie replied. "He ran away when he was boy horse in some Misery place. He had a good family, but some wild horses ran loose across the Marymeck River and he joined them. He was gone for a long time. When he found his way back with his halter full of weeds, the rope attached to it, dragging on the ground. He was very tired because he didn't get oats. But his family still loved him. He only ran away once. He is a very kind horse, just like Palm Reader and little Ouija."

Later, always curious, Brenda looked on the computer and found a river named Meramec in central Missouri. Very strange. She had bought White Knight at an auction in St. Louis.

•　　•　　•　　•　　•

On one of the first days out on the land, while Brian was finishing up his two weeks' notice and before they had gotten the horses, Brenda had walked the woods and fields and found treasure galore in the form of plants for healing. She had taken a course at the Community College several years ago, and even had made some salve from comfrey that was surprisingly effective for healing wounds. The timber was filled with that plant and many others. She could teach the sisters a lot of this if they were interested. She had already talked to several who were retired but still busy with other things. However, fourteen of them indicated an interest in raised gardens, canning and drying herbs for tea.

Jill had come up to the wooded pasture with her one afternoon after lunch and before her night shift in skilled care. They had identified several apple trees, which were in bloom as well as a pear tree and three walnut trees. Jill was very interested in getting involved and getting her foster children involved too, that is, whenever the agency placed some with her.

Brenda had her heirloom seeds. She would have to talk to Brian about building the gardens. She had found this really good design where it would be easy to reach to pull weeds and pick produce. They had also found a rototiller in the garage next to an old tractor and a newer John Deere riding mower. Brain said they should get the ground ready as it was warm enough. He was anxious to get his hand on the tractor to see how it performed.

She had noticed some wild blackberries in the timber near the top of the hill. Those would make good jam. It was too late to hunt for morels but that area surely was going to be a treasure trove next spring.

A lot of the retired sisters, having grown up on farms, had some very good ideas. She wanted to organize them according to what they were interested in doing or thought they could handle.

Oh, and she really wanted to see about a greenhouse. They could do so much with that. She needed to check out how feasible that would be in the winter. It might be more expensive to run than it would be worth. What about solar panels?

Damn, she was such a poor organizer. She had all the ideas but didn't seem to have the good organizational skills she needed to implement them. And she was so scattered. There was so much to do. This was the time they should be planting. Sometimes her mind raced like a hamster spinning its wheels and getting nowhere.

Brian was going to help her move the rest of the livestock this weekend as he would be finished with his old job. The previous weekend, he and Jill and their families got them moved and all settled in. All went very well. Even Carolyn and Bob and the kids came over to help. Carolyn brought a large pan of lasagna, salad, and garlic bread.

She had never seen so many kind people. It was fun working beside the women to get the kitchen organized.

Brian was borrowing Bob's horse trailer again. They would get the cattle and sheep. Jill's dad was helping too with his trailer so they should probably make it in one trip. She was bringing twenty chickens too.

Last week one evening, while Jill was working, she and Brian had constructed a movable chicken yard that was 15'x15.' She had seen the diagram in a magazine and was really proud of their finished product. The Sisters thought it was a great idea. She could move it from place to place. They could feed the chickens scraps from the kitchen. Brian felt the barn was big enough for a small coop at the one end, that he could have the nesting boxes and a partition up in a day or two. Things were shaping up. Soon the sisters would have an abundance of fresh eggs and would be able to listen to the rooster crow in the morning. What was a farm without a rooster crowing.

Ah, so much to do. Brenda needed to breath. This was a wonderful opportunity. Sister Margaret had told her not to try to do it all at once. That coming from a lady who engineered this arrangement in about two months' time. What a woman!

Chapter Seven

A Family is Born

Jill and Brian couldn't have been happier the weekend they moved. They realized how great it was to be part of a large family. Things just went so much better. With brothers and sisters and parents, accomplishments seemed like child's play. The grunts and groans of a lot of shared heavy lifting and jockeying of large pieces of furniture were well outweighed by the laughter, joking, and comradery of people helping one another.

They had put a twin bed in each small bedroom in anticipation of their foster children. Jill and Brian thought that since they were working so many hours, perhaps school aged children would be best. There was also a dresser and mirror in each room.

It was a beautiful weekend and many of the sisters had come over to watch the big move. One of them brought a doily she crocheted for under a vase and another brought a beautiful quilt as a gift. The sisters' craft group arrived with three fluffy brown stuffed teddy bears for the kids' beds.

Their house looked so cute. Brian's mom gave them her recliner for the living room. It was very nice but something she didn't use. Jill insisted that Sister Margaret sit there with her feet up to watch them move in. Her mom and Brian's had almost canonized Sister. It was obvious that so had many others. There wasn't a person who walked by her who didn't stop to chat.

"I feel like a queen. Are you sure I can't help?" You could tell she was enjoying herself.

Jill's mom arrived with extra towels, wash clothes, sheets, and blankets, all used but washed, folded, and stacked like new. They smelled like springtime as she had hung them out on a windy day. Everyone who helped her make the beds had to first bury their noses in the sheets to inhale the yearly phenomenon of fresh line-dried laundry. She was eagerly anticipating foster grandkids.

Brenda come over to help get the kitchen organized. Jill admired how she navigated the kitchen without a hitch, cooking and efficiency being two of her fortes.

Carolyn and Bob showed up with food for everyone. Big news at the Donovan house was the birth of a new little "horsey" that they named Ouija. The family was ecstatic about the new little foal and had many pictures to show.

That whole moving experience was wonderful. Not the aches and pains afterward but experiencing the realization that so many people cared for them.

Now Jill was at the old apartment cleaning vigorously for the next renters and hoping to get their deposit back. It was hard for her to comprehend their good fortune. Sister Margaret and the other sisters were just so special. And Brenda and Brian were getting along very well and accomplishing a lot. They even got Brenda's livestock moved and built a portable chicken yard. Brian would be finished at the factory tomorrow and then would be full tilt into the new job.

He had shown Jill the plans he had drawn up for the barn, proudly pointing out where he would install a chicken coop in one corner, with nesting boxes stacked three high. The nests could be accessed from inside the barn but without entering the coop. He had designed these ingenious little doors in the back of each nesting box, that opened downward on a hinge at the bottom and hooked shut at the top. She was so proud of him! The kids could gather eggs for the sisters and not have to worry about the chickens pecking at them. Brian and Jill were visualizing their foster kids like expectant parents.

Summer would be upon them in a couple of weeks. She was hoping that they would have some little ones to foster. With Brian working at home now, he could cover the evenings while she did the days. "Grandma" Margaret had already volunteered to keep the kids occupied between the time when Jill went to work, and Brian finished up. But she and Brian would come up with another solution to fill those few hours, as they had decided that they certainly didn't want to be a burden to Sister.

Jill really hoped she would be a good mother. Many of these kids had HUGE problems. Her mom had warned her that it would take a lot of work. What if Brian and Jill made mistakes? What if the kids didn't like them? They had already talked about this. They wanted to get the kids really involved with the farm and the convent. They even considered that, to set a good example, they should probably start going to church.

She was wringing out her mop when her cell phone rang. It was Carolyn.

"Jill, hi! I have news that I hope you might be ready to help me with."

"Okay," Jill said nervously. Dare she hope.

"We have a seven-year-old boy, Michael Smith, a first grader at Hamilton. That's where my kids go to school. He is in Connor's class, another teacher, another room. He needs a temporary home. His single mom has been jailed for OUI and child endangerment. She was in an accident about 2:00 this morning. Michael was in the car and sustained minor injuries. The hospital has released him. His mom is going into surgery today for a broken arm. It is not something that can be simply set. I know there are still three weeks of school before summer vacation, but do you think you and Brian could take him now? He needs some place to go."

"Oh, yes! But what about our papers? Have they been approved?"

"The judge has waived them, on my recommendation, because there are no foster care homes currently available. It looks like Michael's mother, Joan, will be in jail until she can come up with bail. Tests show she was high on drugs when she crashed. We found out she has parents in Minnesota. The Court will try to contact them to see if they will take, Michael. This could be a very short stay, Jill."

"Okay. What time will you bring him? I'll check about going into work a little later, so I can stay with him until Brian gets back from work at 6:00. Maybe I should call Sister Margaret. She will want to be there as this was all her idea."

Carolyn was smiling. "I'll be over at 2:00 if that is all right? He is with me now at the office. I have him in the other room doing his homework. Got it from the teacher. We will try to keep things as normal as possible for him. His mom has given me permission to go to their house to help him pack some of his clothes to bring along."

"That's a good idea. There is only one more day of school this week. But next week, if you want, we can carpool. I would be happy to pick your kids up in the morning. It is only ten minutes down the street and up your hill."

"Let's talk about it this weekend. I"ll be over in about an hour. Who, knows, perhaps his grandparents will be in contact before then."

Jill secretly hoped not. She had an hour. First, she texted Brian at work. He replied almost immediately. BE HOME, ASAP. WHOOPIE.

She called Sister Margaret. "Sister, this is Jill. We are going to have a boy! He is coming in an hour! I hate to ask, but would you be free to go over to our house and let yourself in with your key? Would you just check that everything is picked up? I am so nervous. I am finishing up at the old apartment."

Sister sounded as excited as Jill and reassured her that she would be happy to do that.

Then she called her mom, and Brian's mom. She dumped her dirty scrub water while talking, satisfied that she had done a good job. She gave the place another inspection and itching to get going, dried her hands and headed home.

When she pulled in, Sister Margaret greeted her at the back door wanting all the information.

"I put some cookies out on a plate. Sister Avita sent them over from the kitchen. Brenda was there with her talking about managing the produce that they hoped to get this summer. She said to tell you good luck and if she can help in any way to let her know."

"That was nice of them." Jill did a little pirouette in the kitchen checking that all was in order. She realized that this little boy was probably traumatized, not excited to meet new people, so she calmed herself down and took a deep breath.

"Now, Jill I am going to leave so that you and Michael have a chance to get to know each other. I'll come over tonight after Brian gets home and connects with Michael too. We don't want to overwhelm him. And listen, take the night off work."

"I think you're right, Sister, about not overwhelming, Michael. Thank you so much for bringing the cookies over. That's a nice touch. But it you don't mind, I'll come into work when Brian gets home. Maybe Brian will bring him over before bed so that he can meet the sisters and see what I do. That will give Brian some time alone with Michael too."

"Okay, Jill. You play it however you want to."

•　•　•　•　•

Michael was quiet sitting in the backseat of Carolyn's car. He had a big bruise on his cheek and looked so small and forlorn.

"Michael, we have a plan in place. Your mom will have to stay at the hospital and then the detention center because she is sick from drugs and needs help. We're trying to contact your grandma and grandpa in Minnesota. I'm going to take you to your house to get some clothes and anything else you might want. We're going to meet a nice couple. Their names are Jill and Brian Jacob. You can stay with them until things get straightened out at home." There was no response from the back seat.

Carolyn pulled up in front of a nice duplex. There was a police car parked outside. She had contacted them earlier to get permission to pick up clothing for Michael and they had agreed to meet her there to escort her inside. They had a warrant to search the place for drugs so would be staying on after Carolyn and Michael left.

The two officers met them in front of the duplex and shook her hand and greeted Michael kindly.

She and Michael followed them up the dark narrow stairway to the upper apartment. She put her arm on Michael's shoulders to reassure him, as the policemen opened the door at the top.

They entered the apartment together, directly into the kitchen. It was a squalor. There was rotting food on the table, the smell of sour milk, garbage overflowing the wastebasket.

"Which way to your bedroom, Michael?" One of the officers asked him? In the kitchen she had stepped on something sticky that was making her left foot squeak every time she set it down. All the while they followed the policewoman, Carolyn was noting the dirt, the beer bottles sitting in the kitchen and living room, the kitchen table full of papers and dirty dishes. Out of the corner of her eye, she saw a mouse dart across the floor. She made a mental note not to forget anything. She had no desire to return. It was so sad to see the way some kids had to live.

"This is my room," Michael said with pride as he opened the door of a small room next to the bathroom. Carolyn couldn't believe it. The room was clean, pristine, and stark. The bed had old faded sheets that looked like they had been through many washings, but they were smoothed so that there wasn't a wrinkle. The floor was spotless, not a stray shoe to be seen. The dresser was dusted and a toothbrush and tube of toothpaste stood tall in a plastic glass. There wasn't a picture on the wall, a favorite toy, or a stuffed animal.

She exchanged glances with the officer.

"Michael, your mom keeps your room looking very nice," Carolyn told him.

"No, I do," he said looking a bit offended. "I won't let her in here."

"You did this? Wow, I'm impressed! Should we get some of your clothes? I brought a big bag. Jill and Brian want you to bring along whatever you need."

Under the supervision of the officer, he opened the top drawer of the three-drawer dresser. There were three pair of grayish underwear, four tee-shirts folded neatly in two piles and a little shoe box with socks that weren't wrapped in a ball but folded carefully in pairs, three pairs. Carolyn was thinking of Connor's dresser and room. How different.

Michael took everything out. When he went to lay them on his bed, Carolyn opened the second drawer. It was empty. As was the third. In his closet was a lonely pair of jeans. No extra shoes, no jacket except the one he was wearing, no hat, no gloves. No toys. Tears came to Carolyn's eyes. She started to pack his clothes carefully in the too-big bag while hiding her tears. For some reason, she knew that he needed to have them packed carefully. The bag dwarfed its contents.

They opened the bathroom door to see if there was anything he needed there but closed it immediately. The toilet appeared to be clogged, the hamper next to it overflowing. The sink was caked in crud.

•   •   •   •   •

Jill was watching from the back porch as Carolyn walked up the back sidewalk with the slim little boy with a serious look on his bruised face. He already knew he was in sad circumstances so she wasn't going to belabor the situation.

"Hi, Carolyn. Welcome, Michael. Come in." She thought she could act the part. He didn't need her tears nor did he need her gushing over him, although she wanted to.

"I'm Jill. My husband, Brian, and I are so happy that you can spend some time with us. Are you hungry?" Michael was looking all around the cheery kitchen. He let out a big sigh as if reassuring himself that this was okay, and then seeing the plate of cookies on the table, nodded.

"Sister Margaret brought these over earlier. She lives in the big building you drove around when you came here. Have a seat. You too, Mrs. Donovan." That felt strange. She and Carolyn had been on a first name basis, since day one. She was easily becoming like another sister.

While Michael happily munched on a peanut butter cookie, Jill poured him a glass of milk. Carolyn told her that she would pick Michael up for school tomorrow at 8:30 and make sure to talk to his teacher. She had to take Connor and Annie there anyway.

"Mrs. Donovan, you have my homework, right?"

"Oh, yes. It's in my purse. Here you go." Carolyn found it in the folder she had put it in to keep it neat. She thought Michael needed to know it wasn't wrinkled. "I'll let you take care of it until tomorrow. I will pick you up for school because my kids go to your school too. Do you know Connor? He's in your grade. Annie is in the preschool program."

"I know Connor. Everyone knows Connor. He is a fast runner and tells funny stories about his sister."

"He does, does he?" Carolyn smiled, picked up her purse and headed for the back door with Jill following her out to the porch.

"I'll call you tomorrow," she told Jill.

"That would be good. Brian won't be able to get him from school as tomorrow is his last day of work. I'll ask Sister if I can take off again."

"No need to do that. Bob is picking up our kids. I'll set it up with the teachers so Michael can ride home with them and stay until Brian gets off work. They'll want to introduce him to Ouija and Palm Reader. Brian can get him at our place."

"Gee, I hate to do that, his second day and all. I wanted to give him stability."

"Don't worry. It will go smoother next week. He'll have the whole weekend with the two of you. Anything you can offer him will be better than what he has now." Carolyn gave Jill a shoulder hug. "Good luck."

Jill returned to the kitchen and sat down at the table.

"Mmmm. These are good," she said to Michael as she took a bite out of a cookie. "Have another if you like, Michael. Brian will get supper when he gets home but that won't be until about 6:00.

The little boy grabbed the last cookie and took a big bite.

"Michael, you're the first visitor to our new house. We're so happy to have you come to stay with us for a while. I work as a helper with the sisters who aren't feeling well. They're ladies who live in that big building on the other side of the garage. I'll ask Brian to bring you over before you go to bed tonight so you can meet some of them."

Michael finished his cookie and nodded his agreement.

"Do you want to see where you will sleep? You can put your clothes away and fix up your room." She looked at the small bag sitting by the upstairs door.

He nodded.

"Come on. Bring your bag." She felt so happy to be able to lead him up the stairs to their clean little bedrooms and bathroom.

"You have this place all to yourself, Michael. I need you to check out all the bedrooms and choose the one you want. Brian and I sleep downstairs. I hope that is okay with you."

He nodded again.

She watched as he went into every room. Each time he picked up the teddy on the bed and gave it a hug and then looked out the window. Every room was the same with a twin bed, a small dresser, a half-closet with a bar for hangers and low hooks. They were waiting for kids who would add their own personal touches. Michael was smiling after his tour. A look into the clean bathroom with a plush rug and towels hung on three towel racks, a high medium and low, made him absolutely beam.

"Can I have the middle towel? I like green."

"Sure, first come, first serve. Do you have a toothbrush? See, we have a holder here where you can hang it up."

Michael ran into the hall, opened the big back plastic bag, found his toothbrush, and hung it up in the holder. He stepped back to admire it.

"Do you know which room you want?"

"The one with the window that looks at the big building." Jill was a little surprised at that answer. "And I like Joey."

"Joey?"

"The bear." His big brown eyes were smiling above his bruised face.

"Oh, of course. Come on, I'll help you put away your clothes."

"I can do it."

"Okay. Go for it. You can call me Jill, Michael. And when you finish, will you come back to the kitchen? We'll set the table so it will be ready for supper and then you can peel some carrots for me. Have you ever done that?"

"No, but I'll be down to learn."

God, she was falling in love with this kid already. She couldn't wait to show him the rest of the house. She would let Brian take him out to see the farm. She hoped he was going to like living with them.

Chapter Eight

Horse Tales

On Friday Bob parked in his usual spot at Hamilton, down the block on the other side of the crosswalks. He got out to stand by the car so the kids could see him. Connor was in charge of picking up Annie at pre-school each day. Bob was so proud that Connor took her by the hand when they crossed the street and then set her loose on the other side so that she could run down the sidewalk and jump into his arms. Today, Annie was between Connor and another little, skinny boy, holding on to both of their hands. He quickly texted Carolyn and Jill, that the kids were all present and accounted for. He was going to take Michael home with him until Brian got off work and picked him up.

"Daddy, Daddy!" Annie dropped both their hands and came running, leaving Michael and Connor behind. They looked at each other, laughed, and ran after her.

"Dad, this is Michael," Connor informed his dad as they came panting up beside him.

Bob extended his hand to the small boy with the big eyes and bruised face. Poor kid! Connor nudged Michael to shake his dad's hand. When Michael didn't respond, Connor said, "Like this," and demonstrated. "Nice to meet you, Dad."

Michael caught on and, shyly shook Bob's hand.

"It's nice to meet you Michael. Brian said to tell you that he will pick you up between 5:30 and 6:00 so you get to do homework with Connor and then you can play and help me with the horses.

"I don't have any homework today," Michael said. "Mrs. Ferguson said it's the weekend and we should have fun."

"Me neither!" echoed Connor. "It's the policy!" Connor was excited to have a friend over to his house after school.

"Yippee! Me neither!" Annie mimicked her brother.

"You never have homework, Annie. Michael is MY friend," Connor told her possessively.

"I don't mind," said Michael. "She can be my friend too. She is nice."

Go, Michael! Bob thought to himself. That little kid has a mind of his own.

Brian and Jill were so excited about being foster parents. Brian had called Carolyn about 9:00 last night to let her know how things were going. He told her everything from what Michael ate for supper until and including the fact that he had fallen right asleep at 8:30 in his new room, without a night light. He insisted on sleeping with the door closed however.

Carrie always called Bob at noon, the time when she knew he had lunch. She had just talked to Jill who was busy preparing a supper that she hoped Michael would like and also feeling guilty that she and Brian were still going in different directions. Jill had had only breakfast time to be with Michael. But that would change this weekend.

Carolyn had told him that Brian had taken Michael over to the convent after supper to see Jill at work and to meet some of the ill sisters. They all had fussed over him. He had also taken him out to the pasture to see Brenda's livestock. Brenda went along too and let him pet her horses, feel the sheep's wool and the rabbits' soft angora fur. Michael had been so intense, not excited exactly, but thoughtful.

●　　●　　●　　●　　●

When they arrived home after school, Bob pulled into the barnage and hustled the kids into the kitchen to change their clothes and have a snack. Connor was all business taking Michael to his room while he changed and showing him his special horses from his Grandma Donovan.

"I met my grandma last night. Brian took me to see her after we saw the sick sisters that Jill takes care of."

"What's her name?"

"Sister Margaret."

"No kidding, she's my grandma too! She is really old. I have three grandmas."

"Yeah, she gave me a hug. It felt funny...really nice."

"I know. She is a hugger. Come on, let's get Dad and Annie and go outside. I'll show you our horses!"

"I have horses too. Well, they're Brenda's. She let me sit on White Knight. But it was too late to go riding."

"Dad won't let us sit on Palm Reader yet 'cause she just had her baby. And Ouija is too little. Maybe next time you come, we can ride."

•　　•　　•　　•　　•

Bob had broken a carrot in three pieces so each could feed a piece to Palm Reader. The kids were now standing on the bottom rail of the fence, watching the horses and talking. Before Bob left to clean out the stall in the barnage, he told them not to go into the pasture until he came back. "Michael will be new to the horses so I want to introduce him properly."

He and Carrie had developed a routine that worked well for them. She came out at 7:00 in the morning during the week and put Palm Reader in the pasture with Ouija while she cleaned the stall and replenished the water and grain. Later, when she and the kids went out to the barnage to head to school, Connor and Annie helped her bring Palm Reader and Ouija back into the barnage. They didn't want them out all day when no one was there. Then, in the afternoon, after Bob picked them up from school, he let the horses out to graze and run while he cleaned the stall. It worked well for them. On the weekends, when the family was home, the horses spent the days outside provided the weather was decent. This summer they would spend most of their time outside.

"I think Palm reader is maybe bigger than Bucephalus," Annie said to Connor and Michael.

"Who is Bucephalus?" was Michael's question.

"He was Alexander the Great's favorite horse." Connor replied. "Do you know who he was?"

"No. Never heard that name. Is he a superhero?"

"Not, really, but kind of. My dad likes him. That's why my parents named me Connor Alexander. Alexander the Great lived a long, long, time ago before there were cars and people had to ride horses or walk. He was King Phillip's son and lived in Macedonia. I can show you on the map in my room."

"Connor tell him the story!" Annie loved her brother's stories.

Palm Reader and Ouija trotted over to the fence as if they were going to listen to the story too.

"Ouija," Annie said crooning as she stuck her hand through the fence and began to pet the little foal. Hearing her name, Ouija lifted her head from under Annie's hands and stared off into space.

"Why is she doing that?" Michael wanted to know.

"Don't worry. She is just thinking," Annie said, continuing to stroke the little animal's neck.

"Annie, you did that on purpose just to show off!" Connor complained.

"Did not. I forgot!"

Connor continued. "So, you see, Alexander the Great was a famous conqueror. He rode Bucephalus in most of his battles because he was a good, strong horse. They think he was big and black and pretty tall, but Dad isn't sure because people in those times were short, shorter than Dad and Brian." Connor began his story.

"Wait, Connor. Ouija says he WAS big and black and wild when Alexander first met him."

"What are you talking about, Annie?"

"Ouija knows the story. I will tell it."

"Annie! It is MY story."

"No, listen Connor. He wasn't wild. He was just afraid."

"That horse wasn't afraid of anything!"

"Yes, he was!"

"No, he wasn't!"

Ouija and Palm Reader both snorted. This stopped the volley between Annie and Connor.

"Tell Ouija's story, Annie," said Michael.

"What? Ouija can't talk." Connor was a little miffed that his new friend wanted to listen to a horse that couldn't talk.

"Connor, yes she can. I'll tell you." And Annie continued to pet Ouija through the rails and told them what she knew.

"One day, a man brought a horse to Alexander's house to sell to his daddy for a lot of money."

"It was a castle, Annie. And the money was called talents. And his dad was the King, King Phillip."

"Right. The horse had a HUGE head with a white star on the top and a mark like an ox head on his," she pointed to her hip.

"That would be a brand on his haunch, Annie."

"Yes. Everybody went outside into the pasture so the owner could show how nice Bucephalus was. But he wasn't nice! He was kicking and squealing. Nobody could get on to ride him."

"Is that true?"

"Ouija says so." Both the mare and the foal now had their heads over the rail, listening to Annie who had stepped down.

"Then what happened?" asked Michael.

"Well, Alexander's dad got mad at the man. 'Go away! Your horse is too wild,'" Annie emphasized. "But then Alexander told his daddy he could ride the horse. His dad thought he was bragging and was angry at Alexander. Remember, Connor, how Daddy and Mommy say we shouldn't brag?"

Connor nodded his head, getting caught up in Annie's story.

"Go, ride him! We'll just see how smart you are!" Annie made her voice sound angry.

"All the other people were laughing and betting on whether Alexander could ride the horse."

"What is 'betting,' Connor?" Annie asked him.

"I know that," Michael interjected. He knew his mother did that. "It's giving money to maybe win more money."

"Yeah, so like some guys say, 'I think he can ride the horse.' And the other guys say, 'No way!'"

"Oh."

"Could he ride Bucephalus, Annie?" Michael and Connor both wanted to know.

"Yes. Alexander went to the horse, took his reins, and turned him into the sun."

"Why did he do that?" Connor wanted to know.

"Because he saw that Bucephalus was afraid of his shadow. He saw it out of the corner of his eye. That was why he was bucking."

"What is a shadow, Connor?"

"See, look here, Annie." He stood in the sun so Annie could see the shadow. She and Michael forgot the story for a while, having fun trying to step on each other's shadows. Then Connor piped up.

"Wait a minute? Is that possible? I am going to ask Dad about that. How do you look out of the corner of your eye?" He and Michael began experimenting trying to see their shadow out of the corner of their eye. Annie was back hanging on the fence.

"Okay, Annie. Finish your story." Connor was interested.

"Well, Alexander talked to him in a quiet voice like Daddy does with horses too. Bucephalus calmed down, Alexander got on and rode fast! His daddy bought the horse and told Alexander he would be a great man. But his dad was still mad at him."

"I know that," said Connor. "And Bucephalus was his best horse for a lot of years. Alexander even named a city for him, after Bucephalus was killed in battle. It's in Pakistan. I can show you that on my map too. Dad helped me find all the places Alexander the Great captured."

"Annie, how did you know that story?" Michael asked her.

"Ouija told me!" The little foal bobbed his head.

The boys laughed at the horse. "Yeah, sure," Connor shook his head.

Chapter Nine

An Enterprise

Brian was up early on Monday. He was a morning person and right in the midst of building the chicken coop in the back corner of the barn. All the while he was watching the time as he didn't want to miss breakfast with Jill and Michael before she took him to school. She was also going to pick up the Donovan kids and Bob would bring Michael home after school. Brian could give him a snack and take him out to help with whatever he was doing. He would plan something that Michael could help with.

The weekend had been so good! They spent the entire time getting to know Michael, shopping at Theisen's for boots to wear on the farm and a couple pair of jeans, a few shirts. and a pair of superhero pajamas. He could wear some of his T-shirts for playing outside. He needed a lot more but they didn't want to spend a lot of time at the store. He clearly wasn't a shopper and not interested, except for the popcorn machine in the middle of the store with free bags of the buttery treat for shoppers. Jill would return while he was at school for socks, underwear, and a better jacket.

They had walked with him on the path they had previously explored in the Mines of Spain. The heron wasn't there but they actually saw a beaver gnawing on a young sapling, and pointed out for Michael, the lodge where the beavers lived. He thought it was a brilliant idea that the entrance was reached from under water.

Jill had packed a picnic lunch which they ate, sitting on the bench in the canyon where they had gotten the call from Sister Margaret. They stopped at the library on the way home and got Michael his own library card. He was thrilled and so surprised that he could actually take books home to read.

Jill had to be to work at 3:00. As it was raining, Michael and Brian spent the evening inside. They made supper, did the dishes, curled up in the recliner and read every single book! Twice!

Brian talked to Carolyn that evening. She called to tell him their fostering papers had flown through and had also shared with him information about the squalid conditions Michael had been living in and how his room was such a contrast. Jill cried when Brian told her about it; he wanted to cry with her.

On Sunday they went to church over in the chapel in the new building. This was a first for Brian. Jill's family went to a Methodist Church. It was interesting and could those sisters sing. Just like angels. He didn't understand a lot that was going on, but it was peaceful. They were invited to Brian's folks for dinner where Michael met some more family. He fit right in. He hadn't mentioned his mom once. Brian thought this was good for him and Jill but worrisome also. They had talked to Carolyn, and she said the grandparents didn't seem too interested in taking over Michael's care. Apparently, there was estrangement between the parents and daughter. Joan Smith, Michael's mom, didn't have any siblings.

His phone dinged a text from Jill that breakfast was on. He was so deep in thought that it caused him to drop his hammer. He left his tools in the barn and headed back up to the house.

• • • • •

Brenda showed up in the barn at 8:30. Brian was on the ladder, tacking a sturdy wire mesh onto the chicken coop for its roof. They thought that since the coop was inside the barn, the mesh would offer more ventilation. It was Brian's idea. He was so clever. The holes he had cut behind each nesting box had little doors on hinges that opened downward and hooked at the top allowing a person to just stick their hand in to remove the egg. He was thinking of Michael helping to collect eggs.

When she noticed his progress on the coop, she squealed with delight. "That is so awesome! I love how we have access to the eggs without having to go inside the coop. My egg-collecting sisters will have no problems! They've already started to save cartons. Sister Margaret stopped in yesterday and gave me a big seven-day calendar so I can keep tabs on who is doing what.

Oh, my goodness! You put a chute for the hens on the east and one on the south. That way we can move the portable pen to either side of the barn."

"Exactly. And there will be a door right here to get in to clean the coop from inside the barn. We can also keep the hens out while we clean in here by closing those small doors that I put in each chute."

"A very smart idea. You think of everything, Brian."

"Thank you. "

She and Brian seemed to be a perfect match for this job. He listened to her ideas and didn't put her down. He talked things out and was open-minded. She wasn't used to that and it was refreshing. She could dream big and he put things in perspective for her.

"Brian, you're going to kill me," Brenda said to him.

"Why am I going to kill you?" Brian never stopped working. He nodded to her to roll the mesh to the other side and hold it tight while he hammered. She was learning to be a helper as well as a planner.

"I have another idea."

"Okay. Give it to me, but I will tell you that I am planning to get the garden boxes up as soon as I finish here. Then we need to line and fill them. They can be planted any time now. It is warm enough. I ordered organic topsoil and have to pick that up from Theisen's this morning."

"Oh, thanks for doing that Brian. If you let me use your truck, I can pick up it up today, and if it's dry enough tomorrow, get our small gardens planted. Last night I met with the Gardening Girls...another list on the board. They planned what they wanted to plant. You can't believe the variety. We'll have beets, rutabaga, carrots, radishes, lettuces, onions, cabbage, kale, chard, Brussel sprouts, broccoli. I am thinking we might have enough for a booth at Market. We also need to get the composting started, and till the big plot for the potatoes, sweet corn, squash, tomatoes. We'll also put in some asparagus. That's a no-brainer. It will come up every year."

"Brenda. Focus. Write it on your board. Check it off when it's done."

"Oh, sorry, Brian. So today, I am going to present this plan to Sister Margaret, if you think it is doable."

"What is it?"

"I think it is a shame that my horses are eating up grass and pooping all over the place and that I don't seem to have the time to give them much attention. They are good animals and very steady. So, this is my idea. Look." She spread her papers over the plywood Brian had sitting atop two saw horses.

"My idea is this. Use my horses as therapy horses. Make it a non-profit business. The sisters can do this for the community. It will involve a lot of volunteers. Sister Margaret inspired this because of what she has done for us. You know. STAND UP! DELIVER?"

"What are therapy horses?"

"Well, picture this. There are veterans who have Post Traumatic Stress Disorder who could benefit from learning to groom and ride my horses. It has been proven that programs like this give people a chance to relax, learn something new, have their mind diverted from their problems. There are teens with depression and other difficulties. There are handicapped children and adults who could exercise their muscles from the motion of the horses. It could help autistic kids that have a hard time communicating with people. Maybe there are people fighting cancer who want to try an experience that will help them focus on something different." She was really getting excited.

"And who will run this program?" Brian sounded a bit skeptical.

"Oh, ye of little faith. I want to become an equine therapist. First of all, I have to take an online course of five days. I can do that at night. I love learning. Then I have to complete a full day of training to be certified. I know horses and have watched some videos on YouTube. AND, before you say anything else, I want to ask Bob to volunteer to help this summer. He'll have the summer off school and knows all about horses. He is good with them. His dad is a trainer in a big stable in Louisville."

"It sounds like a good idea on paper. What's my part in all of this?"

"Your part young man, will be to build a tack room in the barn for all the gear and some special equipment we'll need for people with physical handicaps. I would also like stalls for the horses. If the weather is rainy, the barn is big enough to run the program in here. We need those for winter anyway. And then we'll need an outdoor ring for when the people are learning to saddle and groom and feel comfortable on the horse. A mounting block with a wheel chair ramp and maybe a lift will have to be built.

"You know I'm not a horse person. Just give me the plans and I'll get it built. Do you have a timeline?"

"Well, school is out in two weeks. I'll have to get this approved by the board. I am hoping Sister Margaret will like the idea. I've already contacted the veterans in town and the school for the handicapped children as well as the mental health organizations and all were very responsive."

"Do you have any suggestions on YouTube videos so I can see what other people are doing?"

"Right here on the plans. I wrote down several sites."

"How are you going to have the money for all this. It isn't cheap to make these improvements."

"Oh, we'll charge a small fee, but I checked with all the organizations and they said that they would be willing to donate money for the people who could use it the most as well as solicit donations. Everyone

I contacted think it is a good idea. They were very enthusiastic. Don't burst my bubble here, Brian. It always comes down to money."

"No, it is an excellent idea but we will have to buy materials etc."

"Okay. The material cost can be defrayed by the organizations who are already contacting people they think might be interested. I even got in touch with the United Way. If we are certified as non-profit and give ourselves a name, they can help us out. Of course, I will not be paid anything because I want this to be part of my job. I will try to get volunteers who are horse people and want to get involved. And I'll ask Bob if he might volunteer a couple of days a week. I really trust his judgement. Actually, he is so grounded. He can bring Annie and Connor with him. They are good around animals. And Michael might enjoy it too., although I know he is a little shy around the animals."

"Have you asked Bob yet? Because he told me he was excited because the school district asked him to develop a new elective social studies class for the middle schools, and he was going to work on that this summer."

"Really? I didn't know that." There was a sag in her shoulders.

"And, not to dampen your spirits, because it is an excellent idea, I don't think it would be good to have any little kids around while working with clients, because, no matter how good they are the clients should be getting the complete attention."

"Yeah, now that you mention it, that makes sense." She signed. "Oh, I want this so badly, Brian."

"Well, you have my support. Just point me in the right direction."

"Thanks, Brian."

• • • • •

"Carolyn, this is Mom." Her voice was very excited on the other end.

"Hi, Mom. How are you? We are looking forward to seeing you this summer when you have your vacation." And to hear THE STORY, Carolyn thought.

"That's why I am calling. I have a favor to ask."

"Sure, Mom. What is it?"

"Our branch of the library is closing permanently because of money issues and reorganization. Because it is a rural area, it doesn't generate enough business to warrant the building's upkeep so they are going to service the area with a mobile unit. They would give me the job of driving the bookmobile, but you know how I'm not the best driver."

"Oh, Mom, I'm so sorry to hear that. And you/re so good at what you do."

"Thank you, Carolyn. I appreciate that. The county said they will provide me an excellent reference if I decide to apply for another job. I'm actually seeing this as an opportunity to get on with life, maybe turn some corners and take a different direction.

The favor is this. And you should talk it over with Bob. I won't feel offended if you don't think it is a good idea."

Marilyn went on to tell her daughter that she would like to live with them this summer while she looked for a permanent position in a library in the Dubuque area. She wanted to be near her grandchildren. She was afraid they were growing up so quickly and she was missing so much. Would they have room for her, just for the summer? She knew Bob was starting a new project for the school district. Perhaps they could use help with the kids and housework so they wouldn't need to hire a sitter while she worked and he tried to prepare his program.

"Oh, Mom. I would love it if you came, just to have you here."

"No, Carolyn. If I come I want to feel useful. Please talk to Bob about it. It will only be until I get a feel for some working possibilities in the area."

"I will. I know he'd jump at the chance to have grandma here to entertain the kids. But Mom, we won't take advantage of you. You must promise that you'll let us know if you ever feel we are wearing you out. You know we'll cherish your presence and your help."

• • • • •

Bob pulled around the back of the convent to the sidewalk leading to Brian and Jill's. Brian was waiting to invite them all into the house for a healthy snack that Jill had left out, some pretzels and strawberries. (Now Brenda was talking a strawberry patch in one of the raised beds.) As the kids sat around the table munching the men looked on with amusement at their chatter.

"Brenda is going to ask Sister Margaret about starting a Therapeutic Equine Center for the community."

Bob looked interested. "No kidding? That's a wonderful idea. What horses is she hoping to use?"

"Her own."

"Would you like to go check them out now?" Bob offered. He had seen the horses when they delivered them. They seemed very mellow, like they might be a perfect fit for something like that.

"Yeah. Kids, let's go out to see how the horses are doing. Brenda is off picking up a load of topsoil from Theisen's. I have been working on the boxes for the sisters so we can fill those when she gets back."

He turned to Michael. "I thought you might want to help us Michael. You can put on your new boots and I'll show you how to rake the to level out the dirt in each box."

"Awesome!"

"You are so lucky!" Connor said to his friend. "Dad, can I stay and help? Please!"

"Me too!" Annie chimed in.

"Not today, guys! We're going to take a look at the horses and then head home. Palm Reader and Ouija will want to get outside in this nice weather.

They all headed out to the pasture to check on the horses who were grazing.

"Who's this one?" Bob asked when he reached the fence. A horse was standing there as if waiting for them, his head over the railing.

"His name is Stang." Annie piped up. "He's the lonesome one."

"How do you know that?" Bob questioned his daughter.

"He told me that some helicopters scared him and he got separated from his mom and sister when he was young. He never found them again."

"Annie, are you making up stories?"

"No. That's what he said, right, Stang?" The horse was able to put his head on her shoulder as she had climbed a couple of rails on the fence.

"He worked on a ranch for a while and then got sold in an auction. Brenda bought him at another auction for some kind of factory. He was cheap."

"Hey, Bob. Is this girl some kind of a mind reader? Brenda told me they were all rescue horses."

"Annie, do the other horses talk to you?"

"Yes, they do, Daddy."

"What do they say?"

"Well, Ginger told me that her great-great grandfather horse used to run fast for the Pony Express." She paused. "What is the Pony Express, Dad?"

"Annie, my girl. I think you are your great-grandmother's daughter. Wait until your mom hears about this."

They walked from horse to horse in the field. Connor and Michael chased around the field while Bob looked the horses over. All the horses seemed sound, even though they were old. They were used to being handled and not skittish.

"If Brenda can get her project started, it would be a great boon to the community, Brian. And it would be good for the horses too."

"Yes, Daddy. They want to be helpful." Annie had a handful of grass to feed to Ginger.

Bob looked up to see Brenda walking across the field. He waved.

"Well, she's coming across the field now. You can give her your approval. This project is a leap of faith for her."

Brenda was dusting her hands off and seemed excited to see everyone.

"Hi. What's everyone up to?"

"I was just showing Bob your horses. I told him about your project and he wanted to check them out."

"They look like perfect horses for equine therapy, Brenda. They've already sowed their oats and are comfortable around people. I think it is a wonderful idea you have."

"I am so glad, because I was going to ask you if you could help me out with some volunteering if I can get the Board's approval. But Brian said that you might be too busy with the summer project you have going on. You're writing curriculum?"

"Yes, this is really exciting for me, since it was my suggestion to introduce a new program in the middle school to replace the social studies program that they are so dissatisfied with. I got to thinking that up until the 1900s the horse was the only manner of transportation. People all over the world really depended upon it for thousands of years. This is a great opportunity for me. The object is to help the kids discern the impact the horse had on different people, the economy, history, social status, recreation, movement across the nations. Well the options are limitless, and it has the capability of connecting into the literature, science, and math programs too. It could provide excellent interdisciplinary reinforcement."

"That sounds really challenging and interesting. I suppose you don't have time then this summer to help out."

"Oh, yeah. I will. You see, Carolyn's mom is coming to stay for the summer at least. She lost her job because of financial belt tightening. She said she's going to help with the kids and the house and is interested in looking for a job in this area so she can be closer to all of us. That will free me up some. I'll pour on the steam while you're setting things up if this goes through. I can help with the planning if you want. And I've met some other horse people who might be interested.

One of them is my vet, Harold Oaks, who just recently retired early when his wife was diagnosed with cancer. He wanted to spend time with her. Then she went downhill rapidly and was gone. He lost her two weeks ago. I imagine he is at loose ends. I bet he would be a real asset for finding volunteers as well as helping you out. It would give him something to keep his mind busy. All his kids are on their own."

"What a sad story, Bob. I appreciate your mentioning him. If you think he would gain some peace from helping us out here, that would be wonderful. I know we'd really benefit from his expertise with horses. When you think the time is right, I'd appreciate your telling him about the project. It would be great to have his help if he's interested."

Chapter Ten

Summer Approaches

In the last weeks of May the perennials continued to flower in the convent gardens at St. Francis on the Hill. Brenda and the sisters had planted the raised gardens she and Brian had constructed. Brenda noticed that the sisters were outside often to check if anything was sprouting, watching for those nasty weeds to pluck.

She was so proud of one group who were digging some of the dandelions which had never been sprayed in anyone's recollection. They were digging selectively, trying to get the roots for use in tea and using the leaves in salad mixes. Brenda's dreams were being realized in a way she had never dreamed of.

Brian had gotten the old rototiller cleaned up and running and had worked up a half-acre piece of land which kept her very busy. One day she had enlisted the help of the "kiddies," as she called Michael, Connor, and Annie, to plant potatoes. They were closer to the ground and loved to dig in the dirt. It gave her back a bit of rest. Michael was so precise, doing exactly what she said. They got into a rhythm of Connor digging, Michael planting, and Annie covering. Brenda trailed along supervising, until she noticed their interest waning. That was the key when working with kids; stop before they got tired of the activity. Then she gave them a bucket and asked them if they wanted to pick dandelions. You would have thought she had given them a birthday present. The sisters were talking about making dandelion wine for the alter wine now. That hadn't happened yet but a few of them were researching and looking at some videos on YouTube.

The sisters insisted that it was too late to plant potatoes. The best time was on Good Friday. Well they would see if it was an old wives' tale. So much of growing success involved other factors. She could understand why Sister Margaret, an old farm girl, was a gambler (of sorts). She had taken a risk on her, the Jacobs and the Donovans. It was the best thing that had happened to Brenda in a long time. In fact, she had seen that a class in farm management for women was being offered by the County Extension. She was going to talk to Sister about that.

• • • • •

Coincidentally, as Brenda was thinking of her, Sister Margaret was enjoying her Thursday morning jaunt to the casino, drinking her free soda and watching the reels spin and the bubbles float down the screen of the Mermaids of the Lost Lagoon game. She had hit the bonus. And it didn't want to stop. This was the luckiest spin she had ever made and just at the right time as she was down to her last dollar. It retriggered giving her fifteen more games. The money kept piling up, the dials spinning happily, the bubbles drifting in big batches. It retriggered again! When would it stop? She had to get back to the convent for lunch and her power nap! People would wonder where she was. FIVE BUBBLES ON THREE MERMAIDS! She had bet twenty cents, ten cents above what she usually bet. She must have shocked the machine. It was up to over $3,000! Retrigger! Oh, my goodness, her heart was doing double time. The casino staff with their identifying name tags hanging from lanyards began to stop and gather around her, urging her on as if she had any control over the rogue machine. She accidently touched it and quickly drew her hand away because it was HOT!

And then after a sixth retrigger, more blaring music, flashing lights, and wailing sirens, she followed the floor manager back to his private office where he wrote her a check for $8,473.22 after taxes!

They wanted to take her picture and announce her first name, but she refused. She scurried to the front door hearing the announcement that a lucky patron had just walked off with a jackpot of $8,473.22! She could feel the check burning a hole in her pocket and her cheeks flaming red.

Oh, my. Well, she had prayed at Mass this morning that they would come up with some idea to defer the expense of setting up an Equine Therapy Center for the community, and it looked like her prayers were answered. How would she explain this to Sister Justice, the convent financial guru at St. Francis on the Hill? The convent CEOS didn't know she went to the casino on Tuesday and Thursday for an hour.

She would talk to Bob. Her "retreat" activity was definitely something she didn't want to reveal. He would know what to do. She was in over her head again.

• • • • •

Carolyn was in a bind. The Davis family, an older retired couple who had fostered two children for the past three years, was in trouble. John Davis, a perfectly healthy man, had been diagnosed with early stages of Alzheimer's, and Martha, who suffered from rheumatoid arthritis, was going to be his chief caregiver, along with a son who had never married. They no longer had the strength and stamina for an active eight-year-old boy and ten-year-old girl. Martha, in her love for her husband of fifty years, and needing the help of their children and grandchildren realized that time might be very limited for them. She had begged Carolyn to find a home where Pedro and Silvia could be adopted. She loved those kids like her own grandkids but she didn't think she could handle things by herself. It was stressing her terribly to ask that they be placed in another home.

• • • • •

Jill was feeling so contented. This was the last day of school. For the next three months she would be home in the daytime with Michael. She was really looking forward to it.

Last week she had talked to Carolyn about signing the kids up for the library summer program where they earned credit and prizes for all the books they read. Carolyn was so excited because her mother was coming to live with them. She was a librarian and would be thrilled about that program and would probably want to go along with Jill and the kids to check it out. Jill had offered to take Connor and Annie for books each week. There were also some Rec programs that they had already signed the kids up for. The municipal pool down by the river offered swimming lessons. There was so much to take advantage of.

Jill felt sadness for Carolyn sometimes. She was like a lone tree on the prairie when it came to her history. She had no one but her mother; her genealogy began and ended with Marilyn. This summer, she was hoping her mother would open up and tell her about her family genealogy. It sounded rather ominous to Jill. Perhaps it was better just to leave things the way they were.

Her cell phone beeped in a text. It was Carolyn. PLEASE CALL WHEN YOU HAVE TIME.

"Carolyn, I just got your text."

"Hi, Jill. There's some news I want to share with you and Brian."

She proceeded to tell her the story of the Davises and Pedro and Silvia Hernandez, their foster children who were eligible for adoption. Would she and Brian be interested in fostering them with maybe the prospect of adoption if it worked out for both parties? The children were very connected to the Davises and doing well in school. Although Silvia was dyslexic and struggled with reading, she was a very pleasant girl. It would be a difficult family switch, as both the kids and their foster parents were attached.

"Carolyn, would the Davises be interested in having the kids visit them a couple times a week do you think, if we are able to adopt them?"

"Oh, I know they would. It's just so hard right now. John is the healthy one but getting so forgetful. He no longer has his driver's license. Martha has a sharp mind but in a lot of pain with her arthritis. They just can't handle it all."

"Well, I'll talk to Brian, but I am sure we would like to give it a try with the option that the Davises act as grandparents for the kids when they want to have them over for an hour or two. Do you think that would help in the transition?"

"I think it would be a win-win for the kids and the Davises."

"I'm so excited, Carolyn but it's important we talk it out with Michael. He has only been with us about three weeks. I'll get back to you as soon as the three of us can discuss it. I wouldn't want him to be unsettled by it. I think he'll be okay though because your kids are in and out and he comes and goes to your place too. He seems to be comfortable developing new relationships. Thanks for this opportunity, Carolyn. I'll call you soon."

•　•　•　•　•

Jill picked Michael, Connor, and Annie up at noon. School was officially out for the summer and they were all full of plans, the boys bouncing around in the back seat of the car. Annie was tired as it normally would be lunch and naptime for her at preschool.

Brian came in for lunch. She had made soup and sandwiches with carrot sticks and apples. The kids all dug in, laughing about the funny races they had that morning and how Mr. Nichols, the principal had fallen into the dunk tank. This wasn't the best time to talk but she was so anxious to tell Brian and Michael.

"Brian, Carolyn called today."

"Is it about my mom?" Michael asked with a panicked look on his face.

"No, Michael. I'm sorry. There is no news yet. Things are still tied up in court." Michael looked relieved.

"Then is it about my mom?" Connor wanted to know.

"No, Connor. But she said your dad will be over to pick you up at 3:00."

"What is it Jill?" Brian was carrying his dishes over to the sink.

"Well, there's another little boy and girl who need a home. Their names are Pedro and Silvia. They've been fostered children for three years with an older couple. Now John and Martha are sick and can't take care of them. She wanted to know if they could stay with us."

"Does that mean I have to leave?" Michael was on the verge of panic. Jill stood up and put her arm around him.

"Of course not, Michael! You're here to stay until the court says your mom is well enough to take care of you…even if it is a long, long time!"

He seemed reassured. "Michael, if you're good with it, so am I." Brian gave him a hug. "We have two more beds and two more teddies waiting to cuddle."

"And two more towels and two more places for tooth brushes." Michael added.

"Gosh, you'll have a brother and sister. Now you'll be bigger than our family." Connor seemed a bit worried now.

"And just think, Connor. You and Annie will have two more friends!"

Jill looked at Connor with a smile on her face and then noticed that Annie had fallen asleep in her chair. Her head was nodding toward her soup. She motioned to Brian and he picked her up chuckling as he carried her in to the couch, covering her with a light afghan gifted them by one of Jill's sister friends.

Michael picked up his plate and bowl to take to the sink. "Want to go out to see if we have any eggs, Connor?"

"Sure."

"Take the cartons will you please, Michael. Thanks for carrying your dishes to the sink."

Connor picked up his dishes and followed suit. Then each boy grabbed a carton and ran out the door.

"Jill, how do you feel about two more children? I can manage at night while you work if you can be responsible for all of them during the day. I like to get out to work by 6:00 in the morning anyway. There's a lot I can do, especially if they approve Brenda's plan on Monday night."

"Let's try it, Brian." She told him all about the Davises. "I was worried that Michael might not be in favor of it. I think he just needed our reassurance. We're good with kids, don't you think?"

"Are we ever!" He gave her a kiss that said 'more later' and headed back out to the barn to check on the boys.

•　　•　　•　　•　　•

Bob was on his way home from school when his phone dinged. The traffic was heavy so he let it go into voice mail and pulled into the Hardee's to answer it.

"Bob, this is Sister Margaret. I need to talk to you ASAP. I've gotten myself into a bit of a predicament. Please don't say anything to anyone."

Sister Margaret in a predicament? He was filled with curiosity as he called her back.

"Sister Margaret, this is Bob. I just finished with classes and am heading over to pick up the kids. They're with Jill this afternoon. Are you okay? You sounded a little stressed out."

"Believe me, I am stressed. Can you stop in to see me for a bit? I'd really appreciate it."

"Well, I'll ask Brian if he can watch the kids for a bit longer. Where do you want to meet?"

"How about the chapel. I'll need His help too."

•　　•　　•　　•　　•

Carolyn was so happy for Silvia and Pedro. They would have a good home to go to and still be able to see the Davises. In fact, when Jill called after lunch to say they were eager to take Silvia and Pedro, she had asked Carolyn to invite the Davises to stay for lunch when they all came on Monday. Carolyn had conveyed that message to John and Martha and they were relieved. She just hoped the children would adjust.

• • • • •

Before he left Hardees, Bob had called to ask **Brian** if he might be able to watch the kids a little longer. Sister Margaret wanted to talk with him about something and he needed to come a little later than planned. Brian took all the kids to help him out in the barn. He was cleaning and had brooms for all of them to push around. They were having fun gathering the dirt in a pile, admiring how much they were accumulating. He had found some old paint and planned to spruce things up a bit as he got time.

• • • • •

Jill had checked in with the head nurse on the second shift and was making a run with the cart to the storage room for more diapers when she happened to look in through the glass doors of the chapel as she passed and saw Sister Margaret and Bob sitting side by side near the middle aisle talking. Sister looked a little distressed. Bob was listening to her. What was going on?

• • • • •

Sister Margaret wrung her hands. "You see, Bob. I won over $8,000.00 at the casino. I have NEVER won much money. I only go for an hour twice a week. It quiets my brain. I almost always play ten cents a spin. I almost always go home with empty pockets. But today I bet twenty cents and this machine went nuts. I am so embarrassed. I don't want anyone to know. Well, I told my confessor, but he said as long as I was responsible and didn't take more than $10.00 it was okay. I am ninety-two. Should I have to be telling people about these things, Bob? What will Mother Superior say?"

"What do you think you should do, Sister?"

"Well, I was thinking that I would like to give that money to The Equine Therapy Center. It's a very good idea and would help other people. STAND UP! DELIVER, Bob. That's my motto. We could say it is an anonymous donation. But the thing is, I have to get to the bank and set up an account for the center. Then when we present to the board on Monday, I can show them the account. Do you think you can help me?"

"Yes, I can help, Sister. I'll pick you up tomorrow morning at 9:00 and we'll go to the bank."

"Thank you, Bob. One more thing. Would you take this blasted check? It makes me nervous."

• • • • •

Saturday morning at 9:00, Sister Margaret was waiting for Bob at the steps outside the chapel, dressed up wearing a tailored business suit and sturdy shoes.

"You look very professional, Sister Margaret."

"Thank you, Bob. That was the look I was going for. You know, I've decided to give up gambling. All this has given me such a headache and stomach ache. But, I think I have this figured out. I'm going to have to explain about the account and the money to Sister Justice, the accountant here. I'm not going to tell her that I won it at the casino. I'll just tell her it was a gift from an anonymous donor. Of course, she will want to write a thank you note. She's so clever. She sniffs everything out. And she is so righteous. I hate to tell lies! She makes me nervous. It is a lie of omission. Things can sure get tangled."

"Okay, Sister. Now calm down. Sister Justice sounds like a formidable woman, but I know what to do."

They went to the bank. Sister Margaret cashed the check and handed it to Bob. Bob thanked her profusely and said that he would like to contribute "his" money to the Equine Therapy Center development fund. She thanked him profusely and told the teller that she wanted to set up an account for St. Francis on the Hill Equine Therapy Center. The teller said certainly and proceeded to do that. Bob handed the teller $8,473.22, which she entered into the account with the stipulation that all checks written for the project would be through the office of Sister Justice. He would like to remain an anonymous donor.

"You have my eternal gratitude, Bob. I feel light enough to float. This will be my last lie! I told Him that in Mass this morning. I am going to miss the casino. That will be my penance."

Bob laughed. She was such a character. In a good way.

Chapter Eleven

A Mother's Story

At 4:30 on Saturday afternoon Marilyn pulled into the drive in her Chevy compact. Before she could open the car door, Annie and Connor ran around the barnage.

"Grandma Marilyn! Grandma Marilyn!" They shouted their greeting. By the time the children were in her arms, Carolyn and Bob were headed over the pavers to greet her. She set the children down with big kisses and went into her daughter's arms with tears. And then she pulled Bob into the hug too.

"Oh, it's so good to see everyone and to get here finally!"

"We were so glad you called along the way so we knew you were safe. I know you aren't keen on driving in the traffic. The kids were following your progress on the map."

"Yeah, Grandma," Connor said. "I'll show you where you have been."

"It's a good thing I did it in two days. I know one day would have been too much."

"Grandma, come see our new horse. Her name is Ouija. And her mom is Palm Reader."

The whole family went out to the pasture. Marilyn was so surprised when both kids crawled through the fence and waited for the animals to come to them. She watched with pleasure as they laid their heads up against the animals and crooned to them. How beautiful and well-groomed they were. She climbed the fence as Carolyn and Bob looked on. She stood watching. Connor and Annie led the horses over. Marilyn had always wanted a pet but was never permitted one. She knew that Bob and Carolyn were going to start raising Gypsy Vanner horses. She had never seen one before.

"How beautiful! Hi, little Ouija." The foal jerked her head up and stared off into the distance.

"What did I do?"

"Nothing, Grandma. You just said her name. O-u-i-j-a. We can never use it around her because it makes her listen to something she hears." Connor tried to explain.

"Grandma, she's getting news under her headband." Annie thought she said it better.

"Annie's right. When she does that, it seems she hears horse stories. In fact, a week ago," Connor said, "she told Annie about Alexander the Great's horse."

"How did Annie know?" Marilyn looked a little baffled.

"It seems our daughter has a super power." Bob helped Annie over the fence.

"Yeah, I know what horses are thinking." Palm Reader and Ouija wandered off to graze.

"Mom, it's no big deal. Bob's great grandmother was rumored to be able to see into the future. Annie sees into the past through the eyes of horses."

"In fact, Annie and Connor are going to help me this summer. And so are the horses. I'm writing a new curriculum for the middle school social studies. It will be called Hoofprints in History. We're going to see where this goes, what Annie learns from Palm Reader and Ouija.

"Daddy, remember I told you about White Knight and Stang too? I'll be happy to listen to Brigitte's horses."

"Thank you, Annie."

"We probably should change Ouija's name, Mom, but we weren't aware of this quirk when we registered her and now it is a big rigmarole to change it. "

"Let me tell you, I know about name changing. In fact, I am going to tell you about that later tonight."

"Good, now let's go in and have some ice tea. Come on kids, lets help Daddy and Grandma get her things into her bedroom in the house."

Marilyn shook her head. Listening to horses? Was this healthy? Well, what was wrong with it? It was going to be an interesting summer.

Carolyn was feeling so happy. Bob and the kids loved her mom. Marilyn loved all of them. After a nice evening dinner and good general conversation Carolyn and her mom got the kids ready for bed while Bob went out to check on the horses. Both children had their favorite bedtime stories and were tucked in without too much fuss.

Carolyn was nervous with anticipation. Her mom was going to come clean about her background. She had been waiting for this for most of her life.

• • • • •

"You know, Carolyn, I knew this time would have to come someday. It doesn't make it any easier to tell you your story, and mine. I'm glad you have Bob here and the children. You're doing wonderful things helping less fortunate children and parents in your job. You're a super mother and a caring person. So, no matter what I tell you, and it will be the truth, don't EVER forget that who you are today, is due to your own accomplishments. Nothing that went before has any bearing on what is now, unless you start to have doubts or anger or regrets. Promise me you will try to look at it objectively."

Marilyn sat in the chair facing the loveseat in the living room. She pulled the afghan off the back and wrapped it around herself. The night wasn't that cool but it gave her comfort.

"I'll try, Mom. If I fail, I am counting on you and Bob to set me on the right path."

Bob and Carolyn sat hand in hand on the love seat. "I'll tell you the first part of my story, about your grandparents, my parents. When I tell you the second part, I would like Sister Margaret to be present if that is okay. Uncle Donny and Aunt Katie are involved in it."

"Mom, are you going to be okay with this?"

"Yes. I've told this story twice, thirty years ago, once to Sister Evangeline and once to Uncle Donny. Both were told in confidentiality. I hope you'll keep it confidential too. Your grandparents are still alive. I have forgiven them. I have accepted that they are my parents and that I don't like them. But I did okay despite them. Here goes."

•　　•　　•　　•　　•

Adele and Jasper Wallace are your grandparents. They lived, live on an estate in North Chicago along Lake Michigan in a beautiful mansion. Your grandmother is a totally self-centered person whose goal in life is to dress to the nines, always doing anything she could to boost your grandfather into powerful circles. Your grandfather found her to be the perfect wife for his ambition. Their focus then was in themselves, each other, and their fortune to the exclusion of anyone else, including their only daughter. There is no reason to think that has changed.

I spent my first twenty years as an invisible child and young woman, cared for by a series of nannies, driven to school and back by chauffeurs until the time my parents could send me off to a private girls' boarding school in Wisconsin. Summers were spent in camps and then to Switzerland my first two years in college. If it weren't for the books I read constantly, I wouldn't have known what a normal childhood was. It was a very lonely life.

When I was about twelve, the housekeeper, who saw to my needs, was very angry with my parents' treatment or lack of connection to me. She told me she heard that when I was two weeks old, Adele took off to San Mauritz with Jasper where she spent a month in a spa trying to regain her pre-pregnancy beauty while he traveled around making business agreements with clients who had connections with the financial company he worked for. They told everyone that one child was enough. My mom had her tubes tied within the year. The only reason the housekeeper told me was because she was handing in her resignation. She was ashamed to work for parents who was so unkind to their own child. I can't say her revelations made me feel any better. There must have been a lot of talk among the household help.

I tried to do the things I was taught in school. It was pathetic how hard I tried to please my mother when I did see her. It was like I was forgotten to both of them, wandering the halls of that big house on rainy days.

Once, when I was six and the teacher in my first-grade class told us that we should make a card to give our moms for Mother's Day, I worked so hard. All the other children were telling me how pretty my card was.

On that Sunday morning, I took her breakfast in bed. I had fixed it myself with toast and juice. Cook gave me coffee. I placed my card. which I had worked so hard on, next to a bud vase with a rose from a bigger bouquet on the dining room table. The house was always full of fresh flowers. I was so proud but frightened at the same time. In books I read, this was the proper way to help a mom celebrate. But my mother barely acknowledged me.

When I got to my parents' room, I set the tray down carefully on the floor, knocked on the door, something that I had never done before…and would never do again. When I opened the door, she was curled up next to Jasper.

I remember her sitting up with her hair all wild and no make-up. When she saw me standing all dressed ready for the day, holding a folding breakfast tray, she groaned out loud and told me to go away, it was too early in the morning.

I did…with the tray, with my card, with the flower and the coffee I had worked so hard not to spill, the toast covered with a little top to keep it warm, and the fresh squeezed juice that I had labored to squeeze under the watchful eye of cook. I was six, confused and tearful. She didn't fit the descriptions of any mothers I would ever read about."

· · · · ·

Carolyn was sobbing into Bob's shoulder. She dealt with all kinds of dysfunction and hurt in her job. She had trained herself to meet it with compassion and detachment, with a purpose toward solutions for the better. But this was her mother.

She looked at Bob who had tears in his eyes. Detaching her hand which was gripping his tightly, she knelt down in front of her mom, putting her arms around her waist and laying her head in her mother's lap.

"Oh, Mom. I am so, so sorry. Just so sorry."

Marilyn stroked her daughter's hair. "Ah, honey. That is just the beginning. Just the beginning. Enough for one night."

"Mom, I am going to give you the same advice you gave me. This is now, you are here with the people who love you. You are here with the daughter you guided. You love her and she loves you."

"As does this whole family," Bob added.

•　　•　　•　　•　　•

It was a busy Sunday morning. Despite having dark circles under their eyes, mother and daughter were not people to stew over things that couldn't be changed. Carolyn and Bob wanted her mom to feel welcome so they had invited the Jacobs, Brenda, and Sister Margaret over for dinner. These were such good people and Carolyn wanted them to meet her mom.

She had prepared a big lasagna the day before as they awaited Marilyn's arrival. It was Carrie's specialty with variations. This time it was with butternut squash and spiced pork sausage. Marilyn prepared a vegetable salad with the ingredients in the fridge. They washed some strawberries and prepared a couple large loaves of garlic bread. Bob added a couple of extra sections to the table and Annie and Connor helped to set the table in the big kitchen. Carolyn and Bob had converted the dining room into an office for both of them.

It was a lovely time. The kids went out to play after dinner. Brenda and Marilyn and the men went out to look at the acreage. Sister Margaret took a little snooze on the couch. She said she had been missing some sleep lately, she winked at Bob and told Brenda that she thought her plan for the Equine Therapy Center would go through at the board meeting the following evening.

Jill and Carolyn insisted on doing the dishes and clean up as they wanted to discuss Pedro and Silvia, who would be coming on Monday morning. Brian was going to stay too but Jill told him she would relay all the information. She knew he and Bob were becoming fast friends.

Marilyn was really interested in the Equine Therapy Center, and Brenda explained her idea as they wandered around outside. Marilyn marveled over the perfect view of the Mississippi, the wonderful trees and again, the beautiful horses. The children were playing Hide 'n' Seek, squealing and running with abandon. Annie didn't seem to mind when she was "it" and couldn't catch anyone.

Marilyn and Brenda realized they were the same age and had a lot in common. Both were avid readers and interested in gardening. They loved music and Marilyn was so excited when she heard that every Thursday night they had live concerts at Eagle Point park which was walking distance from their house.

"I wonder if Connor and Annie would like that?"

"Well, if they would rather run around, the play area is close enough to hear the music. Very casual. I like to go to the Arboretum on Sunday nights. You take a blanket or lawn chairs. They have groups from all over. If you want to go some Sunday, I would be happy to pick you up. My mom and sisters often come too. We bring snacks and wine."

"Oh, Brenda. I know I would enjoy that."

"AND they also have free music in midtown by the art gallery every Friday night. You will never be without music this summer."

•　　•　　•　　•　　•

Brenda and the Jacobs left about 4:30 taking Connor and Annie along to play at the farm for a while at Marilyn's request. She asked Sister Margaret if she would mind staying. They would give her a ride home and retrieve the kids after Marilyn finished her story.

"You bet. I've been wondering what happened in your life, Marilyn. Remember, I have lived a long life and there isn't too much that surprises me. My motto is STAND UP! DELIVER."

"Which you did for me and are still doing, I hear!"

The adults all sat around the kitchen table. Carolyn had poured ice tea.

"Sister, this is really emotional for Mom and me. Even Bob feels it. Hope you are ready for some tears."

"Well, let's hope that they are the tears that will wash away grief. It's not good to carry that kind of baggage around."

"Sister, last night I told Carolyn and Bob about my childhood of wealth with no love or caring. My parents ignored me. The house staff raised me. I was sent off to Switzerland for college when I was eighteen. Tonight, I want to tell what happened after you took us on our hair-raising trip to Kentucky."

"Now, wasn't that something, Marilyn? How we eluded those thugs and got you safely there?"

"It was one of the most terrifying times of my life, Sister. A terrifying time, until we slipped out of their slimy hands. This is what happened after you left me with the nuns."

You dropped me off at the convent assuring me you wouldn't say anything about Carolyn and me to anyone. I had to have you make that promise for your own safety. You gave me all the money you had except enough for your bus back to Dubuque. You had told me that Donny was an incorruptible lawyer. I filed that in my mind. I knew that I had to disappear to keep Carolyn and myself safe. Apparently, I was good at disappearing.

"As a child, I had no trouble being invisible. I had already been thinking about this when I was pregnant and on Carolyn's birth certificate I had put the name Sewell as the father. This of course wasn't true. The first book that I read repeatedly as a child was *Black Beauty*. Most parents, but my own, would have made a connection if they ever came across the name. They never paid any attention to what I did or read."

"Mom, who was the father? What happened?"

"Carolyn. I need you to be patient with me. I'll answer all the questions but I want to do it this way so Sister Margaret understands too. She was a big part in my plan to protect you. You know, she really does live up to her motto."

"Oh, she certainly does. I'll just listen and learn."

"Those first few days, the sisters at the convent were really good to me but I knew I had to get out of there. I couldn't stay forever. I didn't want to get the nuns in trouble. So, I found Donald Bergfeld in the phone book in Mayville and called his office making an appointment for the next day. I didn't tell the sisters, just wrote a thank you note and called a cab when they were all at Mass. I headed to Donny's office. I was way too early but the receptionist was there and got us settled in and started to fuss over you, Carolyn."

"I bet Donny did too, when he got there. He and Katie could never have children. They helped in a lot of programs for kids in the city. They love children."

"He did indeed, Sister. At any rate. Donny knows my story. Or he knew it up until the time he got Alzheimer's. I told him that I wanted to change my name so I couldn't be traced. He helped me make it happen. I already had it on your birth certificate, Carolyn. Sister Evie helped me with that as soon as you were born and I had already applied for your social security under that name. Donny was a whiz."

"Do I know that! Why he has helped the Sisters at St. Francis on the Hill a couple of times."

"Well, it was rather easy as it turns out. There were not a lot of bases to cover. I had never had a driver's license nor applied for a social security card as I never worked and my parents had never applied for one. I can't imagine. They must not have claimed me on their taxes as a dependent! Donny took care of all the legal documents I might have ever had. He never told, Katie.

You had left to take the bus back to Dubuque the day before, Sister. He took Carolyn and me to his house, introduced us to Katie who proceeded to sit us right down for a beautiful lunch. When he told her that he was going to find us an apartment because I wanted to finish school, she would have nothing of it.

'Donny, that is nonsense,' she said. 'We have our basement set up as a little apartment with the kitchenette and bedroom. The Sewells can live down there. Marilyn can help me with the housekeeping and I can take care of this precious little Carolyn bundle.'

I will never forget that. They were so good to me. I stayed with them that first year and attended classes. Sister Margaret, Katie and Donny were my salvation. You led me there."

"I never knew that. Why, can you believe that? I talked to Katie at least every month. And we wrote letters. She never mentioned you."

"I guess maybe Donny did confide in her. Their friends only knew that they were helping out a young mother.

Sister Evangeline also took a huge risk. But, I'll tell you about that later. Why don't I give you a ride home, Sister Margaret, and you can show me where the Jacobs live? I'll bring the kids home, Carolyn, if that is okay."

"Well, sure it's fine, Mom. While you're gone, I am going to write a note to Katie.

"Do that please, Carolyn, but please don't mention anything about the story. I told her before I left, that I would be talking to you. The part hardest for me to tell is what comes next. Give me a little more time please, Carolyn."

"I will, Mom. When you are ready. Thank you.

Chapter Twelve

Memorable Monday

Brian had gone out early to set up a hose and shearing tool for Brenda. She talked about shearing her sheep this afternoon. They certainly needed it, each looking like bilious clouds. While he did that, he pondered on the remodeling of the barn. He had plans to construct four stalls for Brigitte's horses at the side opposite the chicken coop. The horses, cattle, and sheep would need a winter shelter. He was also thinking that in another week or so, he would be able to cut and bale hay. They had a tractor but no baler. Maybe he could borrow his dad's, but that would be too much trouble. Perhaps he would trade some help on the farm on a weekend so his brother could get away. Maybe they would reciprocate in bales. He would have to think about that.

Michael was fast asleep after the big day with his friends Connor and Annie. He had had so many questions to ask before bed last night, wondering about his new brother and sister who were coming today. Would they yell at him? Would they like him? Would they help with the chores? Pick up eggs? Help the sisters pull weeds? Would Brian and Jill have enough arms to hold all of them when they read books? Would they go to the same school? Would they join the reading program at the library? Take swimming lessons?

Yesterday, Jill had taken him upstairs and they had looked at the rooms to see which one he thought Silvia would choose and which one

Pedro would take. Michael thought maybe he should put his towel on the bottom rack since he was the youngest. So, they did that.

"Do you think Silvia will want a pink towel? We don't have a pink towel."

"Actually, I do Michael. Come look in the linen closet. And I have a couple of pairs of different sheets that they can choose from. Remember how you wanted the ones that matched your towel?"

"That's good. Let's show them and let them decide."

"Michael, I noticed that your bulletin board is bare. Do you want to draw some pictures to hang up there? Kind of to decorate your room?"

"No, I like it neat."

"That's okay. Did I ever tell you that I appreciate that you pick up and put your clothes in the hamper when they're dirty, and keep things looking so good?

"Do you think Silvia and Pedro will be neat like me?"

"Well, I don't know. But we'll take good care of them just the way they are. Things will be different for them. It might take them a while to feel comfortable. Remember when you came?"

"This is a good place to come to, Jill."

"Aw. Thanks, Michael." She lifted him up for a quick bear hug. He wasn't able to be too demonstrative yet, but they would work on that.

Last night Brian had stayed late in Michael's room. They had chosen a "chapter" book at the library, and Brian was reading it to him. Jill thought he was enjoying it as much as Michael was. In fact, she peeked her head in to see what was taking so long. Brian was reading while Michael was fast asleep! Did she ever tease him about that?

• • • • •

At 9:30 Monday morning, Brian closed his paint can and put the brush in a container of water. Then he went to get cleaned up before the Davises arrived with Pedro and Silvia. Michael had dressed himself in his school clothes and had combed his own hair. He was helping Jill make some deviled eggs from the eggs he had collected earlier. The hens were laying well, supplying the convent with at least four dozen a day. Jill and Brian kept the leftovers.

Michael was having fun cracking the hardboiled eggs and putting them in ice water so that the shells came off easier. Jill loved to have the opportunity to teach him some useful skills around the kitchen. She sure hoped Pedro and Silvia would have an easy time getting used to all of them.

"Hurry up, Dad. they'll be coming soon, when the big hand gets to twelve."

Brian looked at Jill through moist eyes. She thought he was going to cry. That was the first time he had ever been called Dad.

At 10:05 Michael came running into the kitchen. He had gone out to the back porch to await the arrival of his new brother and sister.

"They're here! They're here!" He stuck his head into the kitchen.

"Great, let's go meet them." Brian's hair was still wet from the shower. By the time they got to the back-porch door, Carolyn was coming up the walk with the Davises and Silvia and Pedro.

The two children were hanging close to the older couple. The man was smiling and helping his wife who was obviously in some pain. She was quite crippled. Jill could already see that the knuckles on her hands were swollen.

"Come in, everyone," Jill opened the door for them. Everyone smiled, shook hands, and greeted each other. Pedro, wearing an Iowa Hawkeye cap and T-shirt looked all around, checking out the porch and his surroundings.

"Pedro," Martha said in a loud whisper. "No hats in the house."

Silvia, her tight black curls hugging her head, was dressed in jeans and a white T-Shirt. She looked a bit overwhelmed, like she was about to cry.

Michael took her by the hand. "I'll show you our kitchen," he said to her as he led her off the porch into the bright, airy kitchen. "I put cookies on the table. You can sit wherever you want."

Silvia sat down with her hands folded in her lap, while Pedro prowled around the kitchen looking out of the windows, then into the living room to look out the front window. Jill watched him, seeing that he was curious. That was a good sign. At least he wasn't completely devastated about having to change homes. She had asked Carolyn to assure the Davises that they would still welcome them into the children's lives.

"Is this a farm?" Pedro asked Michael as he returned to the kitchen and sat in the chair next to him.

"Kind of. This part is a farm and those big buildings you passed coming in are a convent for sisters."

"I have a sister," Pedro said to Michael. "How many do you have?"

"Oh, about a hundred, I think," Michael responded.

"You're not telling the truth," Pedro told Michael. "Nobody has a hundred sisters."

Michael looked to Jill who had come into the back door, for some help. "Pedro, there are almost a hundred women who live in those buildings. They call themselves the Sisters of St. Francis on the Hill. They all live together and are not married."

"Yes, and one of them, Sister Margaret, is my great-grandmother," Michael announced proudly.

"That's right. And she told me personally that if you and Silvia need a great-grandmother, she is available," Jill told the boy.

"Okay. I'll take one. And you can share Silvia with me too. Silvia, do you want a great-grandmother?"

She nodded. She looked miserable. Then she said quietly. "John and Martha are my grandma and grandpa."

"And they will always be," Jill told the girl. "We'll visit their house every week and they'll visit us. You'll see them a lot."

John sat down next to Silvia and rubbed her back and smiled at her. "Be happy, little girl."

Martha sat next to Pedro. Jill passed out cookies, glasses of milk for the children, and coffee for the adults. They visited together for a while and then Brian said, "Michael, why don't you take Silvia and Pedro upstairs to check out their rooms. See which ones they want. Let them pick out some towels and show them where to hang them."

"Yes, and you can show them where the sheets are so they can pick the ones they want. I can come up later to help make the beds," Jill added.

"I can do that," Silvia said in a timid voice. "Martha taught me how. She has a hard time with her arthritis."

"Yes. Silvia is very competent. She has helped me a lot."

"That's wonderful. I can use your help too, Silvia. While you're getting organized, Martha can tell me about what you know how to do and what you like to eat."

"Cheese burgers!" Pedro shouted and pumped his fist in the air. Michael laughed, opened the door to the stairway and led his new brother and sister up the stairs, the pounding of feet sounding like a stampede.

It wasn't long before Pedro was clopping down the stairs.

"I took the room where I can see the barn," he told them. "Martha, if you can get up the stairs you can come see it. Silvia is going to make the beds with Michael. I am supposed to bring up our clothes."

"Carolyn, I can go out to help Pedro bring things in if you want to give me your keys." She dug in her purse and handed the keys to Brian thinking how fortunate these children were.

"Everything is in the trunk," she told him.

"Thanks, Carolyn. Come on Pedro. John, will you help carry the bags in?"

"Sure." John was smiling and eating his third cookie. He followed them out the door.

"Pedro is restless," Martha told Jill. "He has so much energy it's hard for us to keep up with him."

"Thanks for telling me that. Do they like to swim? Read? Ride horses?"

"Well, Silvia is very obedient and will do anything you ask, but she isn't very interested in life. I worry about her sometimes. She is very private. Pedro isn't a very good student. He doesn't like to read. He likes to be busy, can't sit still for long."

"I'm so glad you told me that, Martha."

"They are good kids. Not perfect, but good."

"Well, I would say that we're very lucky then."

At that point, Brian, John, and Pedro trooped in muscling two big suitcases. two backpacks and a net bag filled with balls...footballs, rubber balls, tennis balls, baseballs, whiffle balls, nerf balls.

"He enjoys throwing balls," Martha told Jill and Carolyn.

"Pedro, do you want to hang your ball bag on the back porch?" Jill asked him. "It'll be handy when you want to go out to play. There's a row of hooks on the wall."

"Good idea." He went back out to the porch dragging the bag behind him.

When he returned, the men lugged the big suitcases up the narrow stairway while Pedro followed, one backpack on his shoulder and another against his chest.

When the men came back down, Brian was chuckling. "Jill, you should see them. Silvia has the beds all made and now Michael is showing them where to put their clothes. The towels are hung up and Pedro wants Michael to come help him decorate his room. They want another chair, so they can reach up higher on the board. I think everything is going to work out fine.

•   •   •   •   •

Brenda had been working all morning at the computer. She had made a list of all the equipment she would need to open the Equine Therapy Center which she would now refer to as the ETC. She had the master plans which Sister Joyce, a former secretary had typed up for her so that she could hand out copies at the board meeting this evening. Brenda was rather proud of the handout. Sister Joyce was a skilled lady and had offered her help to construct a website. She told Brenda that all the sisters thought this would be a good idea provided they could come up with the funding

Brenda had also priced some equipment so she had a better idea of the start-up cost.

Then she had called Bob to ask if he would present her ideas to the board. She got sweaty hands and extreme anxiety if she had to speak in front of groups. She would be happy to answer questions. He had kindly agreed. Having stood before classes of high school juniors teaching world history, had made him a confident presenter. Sister Margaret said she wanted to make an announcement too. Brenda had no idea what that was about.

Whew! She was going to go out to work in the big garden. And she had to see about getting the sheep sheared before it got too hot. In fact, she had decided to do that in the afternoon to keep her mind off the meeting tonight. Maybe she would meet Jill and Brian's new kids and see if they wanted to see how it was done. She would go over after lunch. Brenda found that doing farm work provided an environment where she was able to step back and untangle the myriad of things to do and new ideas overcrowding her mind—much like Sister Margaret's weekly retreats to the casino.

· · · · ·

At 1:30, after a lunch of deviled eggs, tomato soup, and toasted cheese sandwiches, Carolyn left with the Davises. Jill and Brian took Michael, Silvia, and Pedro up to the pasture where the sheep were grazing with the two Highland cows and the horses.

It had been a bit of a teary goodbye for the Davises. They were going to miss the kids so much. The kids would miss them too, but Jill had suggested that they call the Davises tonight to tell them what they did during the day. She explained to them that she worked at night taking care of the sisters that needed help but that Brian would be home to fix them supper and tuck them into bed.

She also arranged to pick John and Martha up to go on a picnic at the Arboretum on Sunday evening, her night off work. There was a local band playing and Brenda had told her about the nice lawn where they could spread a blanket for the kids. The adults could sit in lawn chairs. John and Martha knew all about that and were happy to have someone take them.

Jill noticed that Martha had to hold onto John and Carolyn when she went down the porch step. She could see in Martha's face the pain it caused her. She also could feel her visible relief to know that the children would be well-cared for.

Brenda was up on the hillside when they arrived. She introduced them all to Lano and Lyn. She had halters for the wooly animals, that were about as wide as they were long.

"Do you kids know why I called my sheep Lano and Lyn?"

"No" came from three little mouths and their foster mom.

"Well, when Brian and I shear these sheep you will feel that the wool is greasy. That's because it has an oil in it called lanolin which they use to make lotions. Since I have two sheep, I call this one Lano and that one Lyn."

"Clever." Pedro said, petting Lano.

"Did you say I was shearing?" Brian asked her. "I have never sheared a sheep in my life. My dad has a dairy farm. All milk cows."

"You mean you have NEVER had sheep?"

"Never, but I did get your electric shears attached to that sliding rod. I looked that up on YouTube last night. I attached the hose in the barn, so you know, you can clean their bottoms?"

Pedro jerked his head up to look at Brian.

"That will work really well, Brian. I only kept these two sheep because I like to make sweaters and mittens with the wool. It's a hobby for me. I can show you how to do that, Jill. Some of the sisters want to help card and spin the wool."

"Can I help too? That sounds like fun." Silvia asked shyly, a hopeful look on her face.

"Of course. And you boys too."

Brenda took hold of the ropes attached to the halters and led her pets through the pasture gate and down the hillside to the barn. Brian had her electric shears set out, all ready to go. On a row of folding chairs sat six elderly ladies expectantly waiting. Earlier, Brenda had called Angel Grace and asked her to send a message over the intercom to invite the sisters to watch the shearing.

"Hi, sisters," Jill greeted them and did the introductions and got the kids sitting on the barn floor in front of them, while Brenda tied Lyn to a barn pole.

"Okay. Now I have to tell you that this is hard and dirty work. There are some professional shearers that can do a sheep in about four minutes, but I do this only once a year and, as you can see, these sheep are really wooly. It will probably take me a lot more time. I want to do a good job. If I do it right, the wool will come out in one big piece, not a bunch of little ones."

As it was, it took her forty minutes, but Lano and Lynn were very patient. Brenda showed her appreciative audience how to turn them on their backs and start by cleaning off their bottom end first for better hygiene. This caused a lot of giggles from the younger crowd and some pink cheeks among the sisters. But in the end, she was pretty pleased with her job and the reaction of the kids and the sisters on seeing the skinny, bald animals that were underneath the wool.

"They're naked!" Pedro laughed.

"Shush, Pedro," Silvia admonished him.

While Brian and Pedro led the animals back up to the pasture, Brenda let everyone feel the lanolin before she rolled up the wool which was mostly in one continuous piece. Shearing was hard on the back. She felt muscles she didn't know she had beginning to tighten and ache.

Jill gave Brian a call and told him she was sending Silvia and Michael back up to the pasture because she had to get ready for work.

She was grinning with delight as she watched Silvia grab Michael's hand and race up the hill to where Pedro and Brian were waving. She was feeling relieved that things were off to a good start.

• • • • •

The Board of Directors of St. Francis on the Hill consisted of a local banker, a retired teacher, Mother Superior, a financial consultant, a representative of the archbishop, the representative of the Associates, and Sister Justice. They all assembled at 7:00 P.M. in the large room off the dining room in the new building.

Brenda had dressed in her only skirt, a lightweight, loose flowered piece she had had for at least twenty years. The elastic waist was a bit tight but she wore a flowing blouse over the top and her favorite piece of Navajo jewelry. She had opted for low-heeled black shoes and was feeling more confident. She had looked in the mirror and was surprised to see a tanned and toned woman staring back at her. The work was doing her body good.

The chairs were starting to fill up with interested sisters. Brenda took a seat in the middle of the front row right next to Sister Margaret. Bob arrived dressed in a suit and tie, looking very well-groomed and professional.

"Carolyn sends good luck wishes," he whispered to Brenda as he sat in the chair next to Sister Margaret. He wrapped an arm around Sister Margaret's shoulders and gave her a little squeeze. "Good to see you, Sister."

Brenda noticed that Sister Margaret winked at him. What was that all about?

When everyone was assembled, Father Kane led a prayer for wisdom. Mother Superior opened the meeting with the reading of the minutes. They were approved. Old business was reviewed in quick order, and then it was time for the presentation. Brenda's hands were sweating.

"Now it is time for new business," Mother Superior said to the Board. "This is Brenda Schmidt. We have hired her and Brian Jacob to revive our farm to make us more self-sustainable. Brian couldn't be here because his wife Jill is working and so he is in charge of their three foster children.

"Already Brenda and Brian have built sixteen raised gardens that our sisters are tending this summer to provide food for the convent. Everything is organic. No pesticides or herbicides are being used. Brenda has also planted a very large garden that supports all kind of vegetables that can be preserved for the winter months and perhaps given away to the less fortunate. She has only been with us a month!"

There was applause and smiles from the Board. Brenda blushed.

"Now our friend and neighbor, Bob Donovan, is going to present a proposal for a new project that originated with Brenda, an Equine Therapy Center. Bob?"

"Thank you, Mother Superior. Brenda is passing around a sheet of paper that explains the project." He paused while the papers were passed out and then proceeded to go down the list one by one, letting Brenda answer questions as they went along.

> **What**: St. Francis on the Hill Equine Therapy Center
> Equine therapy is experiential in nature. This means that the participant will learn about themselves and others by participating in activities with the horses, and then processing (or discussing) feelings, behaviors, and patterns.
>
> **Why**: To offer a service to the community for persons with mental, physical, and emotional disabilities. Equine Therapy has been shown to help veterans overcome PTSD
>
> **Where**: St. Francis on the Hill Farm
>
> **The Plan:**
> - Paint barn inside and build stalls in the present barn for four horses.
> - Construct a tack room in the present barn to hold equipment needed for the horses and riders.

- Construct an outdoor corral/riding area with a mounting block that is wheel chair accessible.
- Build a website to describe the program and provide answers to frequently asked questions.
- Develop a plan for a non-profit that will make the ETC eligible for tax breaks and grants for its continued operation.
- Enlist the service of Brenda Schmidt, to complete the course required by PATH International, The Professional Association of Therapeutic Horsemanship, to attain the required certification to run the program.
- Enlist the help of qualified people of the community who are knowledgeable about horses or therapy, willing to be trained to help on a volunteer capacity with individual horses and riders.
- Assignment to the Financial Department of the Sisters of St. Francis to handle monetary expenditures and assets.
- Arrange for a person to handle appointments for clients and volunteers.

Then Sister Justice stood and spoke up. "Definitely, this is a wonderful service that we can offer to the community, and once it gets started, it will probably be self-sufficient with grants and donations. I am just wondering where the initial money will come from to purchase the equipment and to prepare the property." She sat down.

Bob offered Sister Margaret his hand. She took it and stood up.

"Well, this is very amazing," Sister Margaret said. "Just a few days ago, I received notice from an anonymous donor who has already deposited more than $8,000.00 into an account at the Premier Bank. The account is in the name of the convent for the express purpose of the Equine Therapy Center. Can you believe that?" *I hope*, she thought.

Sister Justice's expression of amazement was something to behold.

The Board was very impressed. That and the fact that Brenda had already talked to three non-profits in town who said they would be willing to contribute, made quick work of granting permission to organize. Brenda suggested that the opening date be scheduled for July 1. They asked Brenda to report on the program at the July 8 meeting.

Brenda smiled her thanks and hugged Sister Margaret and Bob her thanks. She was so surprised. Who did that money come from?

"Sister Margaret, who?" she whispered.

"No clue," Margaret lied.

Chapter Thirteen

Another Day

When Jill returned home from work the house was quiet. She tiptoed up the stairs to check on the kids. Both Michael and Pedro were sound asleep but Silvia was still awake, so she dared a kiss on her forehead. It was received without fuss.

"Did you call John and Martha?"

"Yes. Martha was really happy that I am going to make yarn and mittens."

"And how about you? Are you happy?"

Silvia nodded, a smile on her face.

"Tomorrow we are going to pick up Mrs. Donovan's mother and her children to go to the library to sign up for the summer reading program. You'll get to meet Connor and Annie. Annie will be so glad to have another girl in her life."

"I don't have a library card."

"We'll get you one."

"I can't read too good."

"Then Brian and I will read to you and help you. Now I'm going to shower and go to bed. See you in the morning.

"Okay." Silvia rolled over on her side. Jill gave her another peck on the cheek and headed downstairs to the shower.

At midnight, she slid into bed, snuggling up next to Brian. He rolled over and wrapped her in his arms.

"Hello, Jilly." He kissed her slowly, sleepily. "How was work? I'm glad you're home."

"Me too. Work was fine. The good news about the Equine Therapy Center was all over the place. Seems Sister Margaret was involved in that too. She sure gets around."

"I know, Brenda texted me. She was so excited. We can really get started now. Apparently, they were endowed with some kind of big anonymous donation. That was really unexpected."

"How were the kids? Do you think Pedro and Silvia will be happy with us as their foster parents? Is Michael included in their lives yet?"

"Jill, we had such a nice evening. I got them all working to clean up after supper, and then I took the kids out to play ball. That little Pedro is really talented. He can throw and kick. I think he could go for hours and hours. We played soccer, three against one. I was on the team with Michael and Silvia."

Jill started laughing. "Well, I knew you weren't an accomplished ball player. Remember you didn't make the cut for basketball junior year?"

"Do I ever. I cried on your shoulder."

"You did not! It wasn't that you were not a good player. You just weren't competitive. That's one of the things I like about you."

"Oh, yeah? This is getting interesting. Are there any other nice things you want to say?"

"Of course. You are a great dad. You don't get frazzled or impatient. For you, time is like forever. You are mindful of opportunity. Everyone likes to be around you because you don't brag or try to steal the lime-light. You listen and make things happen in quiet ways."

"Well, Jill. I'm speechless."

"Now a lover? We haven't had much practice lately with this big change in our lives. We've had triplets this past week! Let's not become tired parents, Brian."

"Do you know that I was lying here thinking the same thing while

I waited for you to come home. I see this as one of those opportunities. Am I right?"

"ABSOLUTELY!"

•　•　•　•　•

A tour of the town began Tuesday morning when a sleepy Jill loaded the three kids in her old battered Lumina van, picked up Marilyn, Annie, and Connor. That required that Annie's car seat go along too. First stop was the Andrew Carnegie Library downtown, only a ten-minute drive. Dubuque wasn't all that big.

They looked an impressive group as they lined up to get the kids enrolled in the reading program. Marilyn was in her element, helping Connor and Annie load up on books and gave Jill a lot of suggestions that were popular with the kids right now.

When Michael came to live with them, Jill and Brian began to take turns reading to him. He liked anything. Pedro, on the other hand, didn't seem too interested until Marilyn started to question him, found out he liked sports and led him immediately to that section. He was so excited that he had his quota of books for the visit, proudly stashing them in the tote bag the library provided for its summer readers.

Jill determined that they would all take turns at night reading. They could learn a lot from each other with these children's books. The stories had to be darn good to be interesting enough to grab the attention of a child. Silvia took two cookbooks and some age appropriate books that Marilyn recommended.

Since they didn't have a TV, Jill envisioned that maybe they could read to each other at night or in the afternoon and discuss the books. The whole family would be learning. And she was anxious for the kids to check out the recipes in Silvia's cook books. They could share the adventures of cooking.

•　•　•　•　•

Marilyn was enjoying herself tremendously. It was fun to see what other libraries did. She had worked in Boone Junction for twenty-five years and was proud of the programs she had set up. The library was in a rural setting in the hills outside Mayville near the Ohio border in northern Kentucky, but they shared an exchange each month and rotated books through all the satellites in the rural counties. She asked the woman at the reference desk if the head librarian was there. It was impressive how helpful and pleasant all the staff were. And when she met Mrs. Vogel, her day was made.

"Hi, I'm Marilyn Sewell. Your library is awesome, and the staff is so friendly."

"Well, thank you. We try hard because we want these books, movies and audios flying off the shelves and being used."

"I am a librarian also."

It only took that statement and Mrs. Vogel took her in tow, with Jill and the five kids, for a tour of the entire facility. The biggest hit for the kids was the glass floor above the main level of the old part of the library. Annie, afraid of falling through, insisted on taking Silvia's hand. Of course, the railed opening in the middle of the foyer on the third floor was a draw. They could see all the way to the first floor of the main entry.

"Marilyn, we don't have any jobs right now, but if there is an opening, would you be willing to fill in? It is summer, and sometimes we are short with help during vacations. You would be a shoe in for a substitute. And we are always looking for volunteers too."

"Oh, please do keep me in mind, Mrs. Vogel."

"Call me Kate." After they exchanged information, Marilyn and Jill returned to the car for the remainder of the tour.

The rest of the morning was spent with a trip to the lovely river walk where the children marveled at the sailboats, ski boats and fishing boats trolling along. Experiencing the cable car ride to the top of the Fourth Street hill above downtown Dubuque was a real hit with the boys trying to scare each other with "what if" stories about the cable breaking.

Annie had climbed unto Silvia's lap and wrapped her arms around her new friend's neck, which sent Pedro and Connor into hearty laughter. Marilyn and Jill were just about to admonish them for frightening a small child when Michael piped up.

"That's bullying to try to scare someone." At the same time as Michael said this, Annie remembered her role model, Annie Oakley. She lifted her chin and released her stranglehold on Silvia's neck. "Just kidding!" she said.

"Sorry, Annie," Pedro and Connor said. The kids had taken care of it themselves. Marilyn and Jill looked at each other. It was pretty impressive.

Jill drove them to their house where the kids played outdoors in the yard with the balls. She and Marilyn fixed soup and sandwiches. Brian came in for lunch with news of materials ordered and progress on the set-up in the barn for the ETC, radishes and lettuce sprouting, hens laying well. On hearing that, the kids took two cardboard cartons and Michael led them to the barn while Jill and Marilyn cleaned up and sat out on the porch awaiting their return.

• • • • •

Meanwhile, Bob was sitting in his office enjoying the quiet morning while Marilyn was off with the kids to "do the town" with Jill and their gang. Carolyn said the vibes were really good with the new foster kids and that both the Jacobs and the Davises were handling it well. Plans were in place for a picnic and concert at the Arboretum next Sunday night. The whole gang was going. Carolyn told Bob she was going to ask Sister Margaret too. They could pick her up. Or Brenda could bring her. Sister Margaret seemed to be the hub on all their wheels.

Bob knew Carolyn was really torn about the story of her mother. She had gone online last night after they had tucked the kids in and Marilyn had turned in, still tired from her long drive from Kentucky and all the activity. In her search, Carrie found a picture of a youngish couple at a gala fund raiser. She put in their address and saw a picture of a gate that led into the estate, but no pictures from inside. She told Bob she had no feelings for them. The picture made them seem quite untouchable. She was determined to get the rest of the story.

Bob had the computer humming. He was working on the Hoof-prints in History curriculum for the seventh grade next year. He was brainstorming ideas for teaching the history of horses, beginning from the time they served as meat for people right up to modern day and work and recreational use of the beautiful animals.

The Amish. He would need to contact them to learn firsthand about the use of horses in their lives. It might include the dangers of driving on busy roads that, in turn might lead to safety issues. He hoped the kids would come away with an idea of how life must have been in former times and the value of the animals to the improvement of people's lives. There was an Amish community not far away in Wisconsin. They were often at the Farmer's Market. Maybe they would be interested in talking to the kids about their lifestyle. The Saturday Market would be a good place to meet and talk to them.

Marilyn had already surprised him with a list of 'must-read' horse stories for seventh and eighth graders. He was going to get that to the English Department to see if they could fit anything like that into their already packed programs. At any rate, he would read them.

There were so many things he could cover…the history of the horse, the number of breeds. He went to Wikipedia and found the Gypsy Vanner. Good, Wikipedia was up to date with that. He added that link to his growing list. Kids always went to Wikipedia first, but he was going to be sure to have other links listed for each topic.

There was the pony express in the U.S., but also other mail routes from the time of the ancient Mongolians and Genghis Khan. What about horses in the economy and business? Who owned the first horses? What about horse races? Chariot races? Famous horses, wars, literature, science, anatomy, mythology? That's when he thought of Annie and Ouija.

Something was going on there. Annie had this uncanny ability to tell stories that horses communicated to her. He should think that was odd, but she was a normal little girl in all ways. Maybe it was his great-grandma's gypsy genes.

And Ouija. Ouija also acted like your regular horse, except that every time she heard her name, she spaced out for a minute. Annie said she was learning information. He had seen Ouija do it when he worked with her and Palm Reader. They were the friendliest animals. Connor didn't like it when the little foal stared into the distance. He never said her name but always spelled it.

Bob thought that maybe he and Annie would become horse listeners while he did this project. He could listen to Annie who would tell what the horses told her. Mmmm. Now *HE* didn't sound too normal. Sometimes his gypsy blood helped him to fantasize.

His phone rang. It was Marilyn asking if he would mind picking them up so Jill could have some quiet time with the kids before going to work. He collected the keys and his phone, his mind still full of ideas.

• • • • •

Brenda caught Sister Margaret before she headed off to tutor with her "man from Iran."

"Sister, I'm so excited that we're able to go ahead with the ETC. I think you probably know the anonymous donor since he or she contacted you. I've written a thank you note. I hope you'll get it to the donor. This could really make a difference in the lives of many people. I already talked to one of my friends, a retired physical therapist who has a horse. She would be thrilled to volunteer and she understands how riding a horse could help strengthen a lot of muscles for people struggling with physical problems."

"That's really good news. Our first volunteer."

"Well, actually we have two. Bob has a friend. He's a retired large animal vet and would be happy to help out two days a week. And, of course Bob volunteered his time too. That makes three."

"It just keeps getting better! I'll see that our donor gets your note, Brenda."

"Thank you, Sister. You're a gem."

•   •   •   •   •

Later that morning, after reviewing the citizenship questions with her student and having a good discussion on whether Jesus was a prophet like Mohammed or the son of God, she dropped into the office of Mr. Boden, who ran the casino. She handed him Brenda's envelope and another given to her earlier. Then she high-tailed it out of there as fast as she could, the cushy carpeting bouncing her along, the dinging and singing machines trying to lure her in. She was safe, however. She had left her $10.00 at home. She was done.

When the manager opened the cards from Margaret Sorenson, he read:

> *Dear Anonymous Donor,*
>
> *Your generosity in donating over $8000.00 to the St. Francis on the Hill Equine Therapy Center is greatly appreciated. Please know that you are helping disabled people dealing with mental illness, physical illness, or other problems to heal and become whole again. Your donation has enabled us to purchase the equipment and prepare the facility to open on July 1st.*
>
> *Please know that it is because of people like you that the world is a better place.*
>
> > *Gratefully yours,*
> > *Benda Schmidt, Director ETC*
> > *For the Sisters of St. Francis*
> > *On the Hill*

And:

Dear Generous Donor,

The Sisters of St. Francis on the Hill are very grateful for your generosity in donating a large sum of money to help us establish our Equine Therapy Center. In helping us, you are helping Veterans, disabled people, people suffering from anxiety and depression as well as children with social problems. May God bless you and keep you.

With all respect,
Sister Joan Daily, Mother Superior

Mr. Boden, felt a bit embarrassed by his generosity, which must have been Margaret Sorenson's, and decided right then and there that he would contact Margaret Sorenson, whose address he had and send her a form to sign up for a community grant. They came out every September and she would be sure to get a substantial grant. She could give it to this Brenden Schmidt. Wouldn't she be surprised.

Also, his wife worked for a mental health organization and he knew she would be happy to volunteer to help with people suffering from mental distress. And he knew all about taxes; perhaps their financial department at the convent would be happy for his help in filing as a non-profit. Sister Margaret would be so glad he was involved.

•   •   •   •   •

Carolyn felt so good about placing Pedro and Silvia with the Jacobs. Boy, Sister Margaret had started something. Not only did she have a connection to Carolyn's own mother, but she was also providing homes to needy children. With any luck, Brian and Jill would want to adopt Pedro and Silvia. She knew that they would take Michael too if the opportunity arrived. He didn't even ask about his mother when Carolyn visited him. She was in rehab and not doing well. Both Jill and Brian were so young, only twenty-two years old. But they were perfect for this job. They had the energy that was needed.

After hearing from her mom on Saturday night, Carolyn was processing everything she learned. Her grandparents' treatment of her mother was atrocious. The picture of them on the internet was taken three years ago. They looked like they were fifty years old instead of in their seventies. Her grandmother didn't appear to have a wrinkle in her face. She was wearing a slinky, low cut gown and her grandfather was dressed in a black tux. He had a full head of hair.

Now she had to find out about her biological father. That was really scary. Her mother was gearing up her courage. There had been so much going on the past few days, that they hadn't had the privacy to sit down and talk.

And she wanted Bob to be with her when she learned of her origins. Maybe tonight would be the right time.

•　　•　　•　　•　　•

It was almost 10:00 when Marilyn came into the den wrapped in her summer robe and wearing slippers. Bob was reading a book on horses and Carolyn was sitting at the computer, searching for anything on her grandparents.

"Mom, everything okay?"

"Yes and no, honey. I want to talk. I want to tell you about your father and what happened. No, actually, I don't want to tell you, but you need to know."

Carolyn got up from the computer and sat on the couch next to Bob who put down his book.

"Sit down, please, Marilyn. Are you sure you're up to this? We don't want you to be hurt."

"Oh, I was already hurt. I'm just worried about you Carolyn. The worst has already been done to me. You are not going to like what you hear, but like I have said before, you are you. You are a good woman and a good wife and mother. You made your choices and chose well. Nothing that happened to me before determines anything about who you are."

"Mom, you just keep reminding me of that until I get it, okay?"

Marilyn sat in the chair across from them and began.

"I came back to the States the summer I was twenty years old. Two years in Switzerland was enough. I had applied to the University of Illinois in the Library Science program and been accepted with actually only one more year of college to go. I had enough credits to transfer as I had opted to stay in Switzerland for the summer semester the previous year. I notified my parents in January of my plans and that I would be home on June 15 but when I arrived, I found out that they had taken a six-week business trip to China. They never told me they would be gone. I made it a point to write to them every week. They never responded but did call me once in May to tell me that if I was going to the U of Illinois, I had to pay for it myself and couldn't live at home.

The day I returned, I was raped in my parents' home. By the time they returned from China, I knew I was pregnant. I told my parents and their solution was that I shouldn't embarrass the family. They sent me to Clinton, Iowa, to a home for unwed mothers. It turned out to be my salvation."

"Mom, my goodness! What happened?"

"Your grandfather has a younger step-brother. His name is Dale Scarlone. He was in his forties and was staying at the house. He had always creeped me out, a very aggressive person. As a child, whenever he visited, I would disappear. And the few times I was home when he was there, he reminded me of mafia." She shivered. "He met me at the door when I put the key in the lock.

When I found out my parents weren't there and he was, I decided to call a cab and get a hotel. Before I could do that, he grabbed me by the arm and hauled me into one of the guest rooms. Believe me, I was making a lot of noise, screaming at him to leave me alone. No one responded as with my parents gone, the staff was on vacation. Well, he raped me and left. It was my first and my last time with a man."

"That was my father? A rapist."

"Now, before we go any farther, Carolyn, I want you to know that at NO time did I ever regret your presence in my life, before or after you were born."

Bob put his arm around Carolyn. He knew she was not taking this well. Jeez, who would? Her mom raped.

"Did you press charges?" Carolyn wanted to know.

"Unfortunately, no. I was a devastated and traumatized. I had no one to talk to. I could have called the police, I guess, but...well, Carolyn. I was so dumb, so naive. I wasn't sure what had happened.

"And in the back of my head, I heard Scarlone warning me not to tell anyone about this.

"The first thing I did was call a locksmith to come and change the locks. And then I allowed no one in except the housekeeper. I didn't give the keys to anyone until my folks came back from China.

"By the time I realized I was pregnant and had gotten up the nerve to tell my mother, Scarlone had disappeared, gone off somewhere. She didn't believe me, said I had probably gotten pregnant in Switzerland and planned it to shame them. Their solution was to send me away to a home for unwed mothers. And they told me in no uncertain terms that I was to put the baby up for adoption.

"You might wonder why I just didn't go off on my own and get help. Well, I wasn't raised to be self-sufficient. I had never had a job, never driven a car, never had an allowance. Add that to the fact that I was as timid as a mouse. I was a total wreck.

"While I was pregnant with you in Clinton, I received one letter from my parents reminding me that I should give the baby up for adoption and let them know when I delivered the baby. Actually, this demand was probably the best thing that happened to me as I was capable of anger and confided in Sister Evangeline my plan to keep you, to disappear, and to start a new life. She and Sister Margaret helped me do that.

"Sister Evie and I devised a plan. I wanted so much to keep you, Carolyn. You were the only thing in my life that was ever mine. You were precious to me. We didn't tell anyone. I opted to have a midwife. I was in labor for ten hours and all went well. As soon as you were born, Sister filled out the birth certificate and entered your name as Carolyn Sewell with Marilyn Sewell as mother. The midwife and Sister Evie signed it. She had planned that after giving us a couple of days to recuperate, she would buy us a bus ticket to a destination somewhere yet to be determined. However, the same day you were born, she received a call telling her that Dale Scarlone would be coming to pick me up to bring me back to Chicago immediately after the baby was born."

"Jeez! The stinkin' skunk who raped you!" Bob growled as he pulled Carolyn closer.

"Yes, needless to say, I was panicked. Sister knew we had to hurry. That's when she conceived me of the idea that I could go with her friend, Sister Margaret, who knew nothing about any of this. I had just delivered and was rather weak and bleeding quite a bit, but knew I had to do it. You already heard that part of the story.

"So, I guess that is it."

"But where is that scum today?"

"I don't know. I am afraid to know."

"Wait, Mom. The cops pulled them over. One had a gun. We could check the records."

"Carolyn, I hope you can understand. Right now, I want to leave sleeping dogs lie. You're right. We'll do that, but please. Not now. Let me get my feet firmly under me. Please?"

"Okay. Tell me when you are ready."

Chapter Fourteen

Growth and Prosperity
Uncertainty and Anxiety

Silvia was anxious to learn to prepare wool so she could make mittens, but that had to be put aside until later in the year as Brenda was swamped with gardens and preparations for the Equine Therapy Center. Silvia was happy living with Brian and Jill. There was always something to do. There were a lot of laughs. Jill was funny. She couldn't tell a story without acting it out. Silvia even enjoyed being with her "brothers." She considered Michael to be her brother too.

In the morning it was swimming lessons, going to the library, or staying home to bake and cook. Sometimes they met in the park with their friends Connor and Annie.

Jill liked to make things by watching it on YouTube. They tried slime. That was a lot of fun. She liked to work alongside Jill because they talked. She taught them how to fold T-shirts in a special way. They laughed because Michael did it even better than Jill. And Jill had read somewhere that you could get a lot of clothes in dressers if you folded them in rectangles, even the underwear! Embarrassing!

In the evenings they all read books, played card games, or ballgames with Brian. Pedro insisted they keep a chart on the upstairs door to record wins. That was a lot of fun. Jill bought little stickers to put on the chart and said it wasn't fair because she had to work nights and missed out on many games. In the afternoons, they always tried to get some games in. Silvia's favorite was Go Fish.

Michael and Pedro were outside much of the time, checking out the progress of barn remodeling, collecting eggs, helping the elderly sisters pull weeds in their gardens, and helping to hold posts for the new arena being constructed for the ETC, as the new center was now being referred to.

Sylvia helped make a discovery in June that she was very proud of. Michael could draw. Really well. No one knew that until one rainy afternoon when Jill gave them all some cool sketching paper, crayons and markers asking them to make something to hang on the boards in their rooms. She and Pedro chose all the bright colors and made pretty pictures not paying any attention to Michael, who used only a pencil. He drew a picture of all of them, even Brian in his cap which he hardly ever took off, and Jill in her CNA smock. They were all standing on the front porch. The drawing contained such detail, even shadowing. It was almost like a photograph. When Silvia finished her picture, she noticed that Michael had turned his paper over.

"Michael, what did you draw?"

"Nothing. It isn't pretty and colored like yours."

"Turn it over, Michael."

He did. "Jill, come look at this. Michael is an artist. This is genius!"

"You should get a star on the chart, Michael. That's a winner!" Pedro told him with awe.

Jill was astounded. "Michael, this is so wonderful! You are blessed with talent. Let's go hang this in your room."

• • • • •

But **Michael** didn't want to. He liked everything neat and didn't like extra stuff. He was anxious, afraid that his mother would get better and he would have to go back to his dirty apartment. Already, he was making a remembrance. He put the picture in one of his empty drawers but was asked to bring it out so many times that he said Jill could have it until he had to leave. She framed it.

Carolyn had taken Michael to see his mother once, on special permission from the court. It had been a disaster. They met in the park. While he played by himself on the equipment. His mother just sat on the bench and watched, or rather stared straight ahead. She didn't say anything. Carolyn had already put her on the list for the therapy rides. She almost felt like a traitor doing this because she knew Michael wanted to remain with Jill and Brian.

Brenda saw Michael's picture one day when she stopped in to eat lunch with them and discuss the ETC. Immediately she had an idea. The next day she returned with a picture from the internet of a child wearing a helmet on a horse.

"Michael, I would like this picture on our brochure. Would you like to try drawing this for me?"

"Sure."

"Wonderful! When can you have it finished."

"I'll do it right now."

"Thank you, Michael."

"And kids, I have a surprise for you. I want a mural on the wall in the barn. It's all painted white and looks very nice, but I was thinking that we could divide it into sections and have you and your friends, plus the sisters and their associates at the convent, each paint a section. Even Annie. Would you like to do that?"

"I guess so," came from Michael.

"Yeah, sure," Silvia and Pedro chimed in.

Brenda said everyone could have their own section to paint. The mural painting would take place on the last Sunday in June. It would be a big surprise to see how it turned out.

"You can start thinking what you would like to paint. It can be something to do with horses helping people, or it can be something bright and happy, like sunshine and rainbows. Actually, do whatever you like that you think will make people happy when they look at it."

• • • • •

Pedro was loving summer. It was such a busy time and there was so much to do. He was an excellent swimmer. At lessons they put him in the shark group. He even got to dive off the boards into the deep water.

Brian had shown him a YouTube video on juggling. First, they started with scarfs and now he could do three tennis balls. Brian was also teaching him how to put up fencing. It took some planning, not just digging holes, but measuring the height of the land and the distance between poles. It was mathematical. They wanted to move the cattle, all two of them, down below the hillside, and were enclosing an area just for them. He liked the cows. They were shaggy and could stay outside in the winter, Brenda said. They liked the cold weather.

This was the best and busiest place he had ever been. When he went to visit John and Martha, he was never sad. John couldn't remember him and Martha was so worried. He was glad to be with Jill and Brian.

• • • • •

Annie felt very special because, for an hour every day, her dad needed her to listen to Ouija to discover more stories about horses that he might be able to use for his work. She also listened to Brenda's horse Pancho, who told her about how his great-great grandfather was the prized horse of the Arapaho, Little Raven. Her daddy liked this story a lot, especially how he led the "white men" to Colorado to help them find gold. Poncho's great ancestor traveled all over the plains with Little Raven on his back. Her dad thought if they got enough stories, teachers at his school could ask the kids to write the stories from the horse's perspective...whatever that means. She would have to tell him about Target, Annie Oakley's horse. Now, Annie and Target were travelers. And Target had to be a good horse for Annie to always hit her targets.

• • • • •

Connor also spent time with his dad every day. They were building a caravan and Connor was very excited. His dad ordered the big wheels and the wagon bed but was building the house on the top by himself with Connor's help. It was going to be so cool. It was a secret. They kept it hidden in the new storage facility behind the barnage and covered it up at night. Only their family knew. They were hoping to have it ready in time for the Fourth of July parade downtown. His mom was making little curtains for the windows and Grandma Marilyn was sewing covers for the cushions on the benches they had inside. Palm Reader was practicing to pull it in the parade. They would be advertising the Equine Therapy Center as well as displaying their heritage, his dad said. He told Connor that the Romany people dated back a long, long time, originating in India. Connor marked it on the map.

Annie and Conner spent a lot of time with Grandma Marilyn during the day. She took Connor to swimming lessons and to the library with Annie. Sometimes they invited the Jacobs over to play. Everybody liked to ride on Palm Reader. She always came near the fence so they could climb on her back. She was very careful with them. Ouija like to trot along behind.

Annie and Connor were both a little worried about their mom. She sometimes looked sad. They tried to do things to make her happy. Their dad took her hand one night when she came home from work and told her she needed to ride Palm Reader because she needed the exercise. He climbed up behind her. He and Annie wanted to watch but Grandma came out to get them and told them to set the table and wash up. Their mom seemed much happier when they got back.

• • • • •

Marilyn really liked Dubuque. The freedom she now had gave her the opportunity to take advantage of the many venues the city had to offer.

She had substituted at the library three days and loved it. There was something about libraries that always attracted her, the smell of the books, and just the idea of having so many items of interest and entertainment, surrounding her. From her childhood, it had been her oasis. But she also liked helping Carolyn and Bob with the kids. And Brenda with the ETC project. Things happened all the time. She was enjoying being with her family in Dubuque.

She knew Carolyn was worried about Dale Scarlone. Was he alive or dead? Where was he? Most likely he had been arrested the day that Sister Margaret had taken her from the Clinton Home for Unwed Mothers. Maybe they could look at the police records like Carolyn and Bob had suggested. Maybe later.

• • • • •

"**Brenda**, you're spinning your wheels," Brian told her one day when she stood there talking as he dug a post hole.

"But there is SO much to DO!"

"Okay. I'll tell you what to do. Take a notebook and pen with you out to the garden. Start hoeing or whatever. If you think of something, write it down. When you finish in the garden, go inside. Make a list of all your ideas and jobs. Then think of people you can ask to help out. Write those names next to the job and contact those people."

She did. It worked. Everyone wanted to help.

Carolyn said she would contact foster parents who presently housed troubled kids to see if they would be interested in reserving an hour slot each week.

Mrs. Boden, a mental health volunteer that Sister Margaret told her about, was going to research patient records to see who might benefit from spending time at the ETC.

A staffer from the Community Mental Health Association, that Carolyn knew, was happy to make suggestions to clients he felt might benefit from the program.

Sister Margaret had given Brenda the information to apply for a $4000.00 grant from the casino. However, Brenda just couldn't get focused enough to follow through. Bob volunteered to take on the task. He had been keeping in such close contact with what was going on that it was done in one day and mailed in.

Jill, took the brochures that Brenda and Sister Joy had designed, to the printer, picked them up and took the kids to distribute them in the hospitals, clinics, nursing homes, and to the local veterans' group. They dropped them off at all the school counselors' offices even though, school was basically out for the summer. The picture on the cover was the one Michael had drawn for Brenda. She knew he felt special behind that serious facade.

Marilyn volunteered to be listed in the brochure as a contact for questions. She answered phone calls, set up schedules for riders and maintained the list of volunteers that had grown substantially.

Brenda did all the online work and attended the sessions necessary to get accredited in Iowa. She loved to learn and found out that they contained little she didn't already know. Her plans were coming together.

Brian had the kids fill the new tack room, putting helmets and grooming equipment on the shelves, hanging the bridles and harnesses, laying blankets over sawhorses where he could rest the saddles for White Knight, Pancho, Ginger, and Stang. But he changed that when Brenda explained to him and the kids that the horses would be sweaty after working, so it would be best to put the blankets on top of the saddles, dirty side up, so they would dry out between sessions. She told him that she would be giving the volunteers a talk on caring for the tack and he should come too. If she forgot to mention anything, he could add his two cents worth. They would be expecting the clients to do these things if able, as part of their experience.

Mother Superior, Sister Margaret, and many of the other sisters stopped in the barn regularly to see the progress. They were all excited about the mural painting day coming up the last Sunday in the month and had suggestions for how the long wall could be divided.

Brian could see that in the future, they might need a bit more parking, especially if they had four horses working at one time. But, for now they would make due. That would take more money. Maybe they would get a grant from the casino that could be slotted for parking or for a sidewalk to push wheel chairs out to the barn. All in time. It would happen.

·   ·   ·   ·   ·

Sunday, June 27 was a big day. The Donovans and Marilyn attended 9:30 church with the Jacobs, Brenda and all the sisters. Two of Brenda's boys were there. They were going to help paint the mural. They were also going to volunteer this summer.

After Mass, they went to the barn where Brian had laid tarps on the floor. Brenda had divided the wall into sections. Each contained a post-it note naming its "artists."

When everyone was assembled and seated on the tarp or folding chairs, Brenda addressed them all.

"Thank you so much for coming to our painting party today. First of all, I want to tell you not to be afraid that you will make a mistake painting. There are no mistakes. Whatever we paint is good. It is a part of the whole effort to do something good for the community.

Many of you have already been hard at work. We have two-on-one volunteers who will be training this week. We already have the first day booked solid and many slots filled throughout the remainder of the month. I am very encouraged and very grateful to all of you and the many others that have helped.

Now, I know you are ready to paint, but first, I have a few instructions. There is a post-it note in the section I would like each of you to do. Please remove it when you are ready to paint. On that long table, the sisters have assembled the paints, brushes of all sizes, and plenty of rags. Paint should be put in the smaller containers. Just ask for the colors you like, and the volunteers there will get you set up. Please try not to take more than you need. When you finish or want to change colors, you can clean your brushes at the other end of the table. Volunteers can assist you.

Finally, and most importantly, walk carefully on the tarps. Why? First, because I know they could cause someone to trip and fall. We don't want anyone to get hurt. We also want to avoid spills because I have volunteered to clean them up!"

There was a lot of good-natured laughter.

While everyone else rushed to the table to get paint, Michael went to the wall to look for his name. He found it smack dab in the middle. Brenda came over to him.

"Brenda, mine is too high. I can't reach it."

"Don't worry, Michael. I have this sturdy stepstool with a handle for you to hold onto. Do you think you can do that?"

"Yes, thank you."

Michael walked over to the table where some of the sisters were pouring paint.

"Can I please have some black and some white?"

"Don't you want some other colors too?"

"No, thank you." Michael had never painted, but he thought he would need some rags. He was trying to envision how to sketch with a paintbrush. This was new to him, but Brenda said there were no mistakes—it was all good.

In the hour that followed something, beautiful happened. It wasn't only in the result of the efforts of the painters, but in the good-natured comradery, the joking, the kind helping of human beings cooperating. For some reason, the combination of the bold and bright lines of some of the paintings, and the tentative strokes of others, as well as the primitive and the accomplished, the abstract and the weird, it came out right. And in the middle, one of the littlest painters had managed a large horse head in blacks and grays and whites. It was the focal point of the whole mural. The horse was smiling. The success of the project was in the painters' pride. Every section was someone's work of heart.

Chapter Fifteen

Opening Day

At 11:00 A.M. on July 1, a hot and overcast Friday, the Sisters of St. Francis on the Hill were gathered out by the barn and new exercise area for the ribbon cutting ceremony of the Equine Therapy Center. Cars were parked in the pasture and all the way down Church Hill Street. The Telegraph-Herald had sent a photographer and reporters. KWWL News and KCRG TV had cameramen in place.

White Knight, Ginger, Pancho, and Stang were positioned at separate stations along the perimeter of the riding area next to mounting blocks. The horses, in their halters and flanked on either side by two volunteers, waited patiently. They hadn't been saddled, because the first clients wouldn't be arriving until 2:00. Also, it was part of the program that the clients who were able, would help with the saddling and grooming.

Brian was finishing hooking up the speaker system the convent used in the church. He had spent time last night watching YouTube videos on how to do that with all the kids hanging over his shoulder. He had brought the equipment inside the house and had followed directions exactly as shown. Everyone was so excited when it actually worked. The kids had a blast using the microphone and Brian was happy to have learned something new. The speaker system was working fine.

Sister Margaret, sitting in one of the chairs in front, had found a new summer skirt and top in the hand-me-down store at the convent.

It had been left behind by Sister Vi when she passed—the white skirt with big, bright red poppies and a red leather belt, topped by a red blouse, light-weight and long-sleeved, its white collar covered in small red poppies. She was hoping that she hadn't overdone it. The outfit had originally belonged to Sister Vi's niece. She had been a catalog model.

Bob, Carolyn, and the kids were all present with Marilyn at their side, having put in a lot of time helping to get the project going. Carolyn had taken off work. They were standing next to Jill, Silvia, and Michael. Pedro was wandering around checking everything out.

Promptly at 11:00, Brenda stepped up to the microphone, looking a little nervous. This was her first time talking in front of an audience. She was dressed in jeans, her usual attire, but had forgone the T-shirt for an attractive green blouse with sparkles on the front. All her kids and her two grandkids were there.

"Good morning everyone. Thank you so much for coming to the ribbon cutting ceremony for the St. Francis on the Hill Equine Therapy Center. And thank you for helping me turn a dream into reality. I would like to introduce Sister Margaret Sorenson, who just five months ago, hired me to work here on the Sisters of St. Francis on the Hill farm. It has changed my life! Sister Margaret."

The applause went on for a long time, the heartiest of all seeming to come from Mr. Boden, the casino manager. He was grinning from ear to ear.

"Oh, for heaven's sake. Thank you. That is enough. I want to say that Brenda Schmidt's idea to use her own horses to help others, was not only brilliant, but also was realized only through the help of MANY people, including my honorary little great-grandkids, Michael, Silvia, Pedro, Annie, and Connor. Come up here kids." She motioned to the kids whose parents encouraged them to move forward to stand beside her. Silvia, the last, took her place beside Annie.

"Also, thank you to Mother Superior, Sister Joan Daily, who was totally on board. People have made and delivered brochures, searched out clients who would benefit from the program, and offered to serve as volunteers. Others helped to set up the financial part of the business. Well, what you have accomplished is amazing. And on behalf of the Sisters of St. Francis on the Hill, I thank all of you!

I would now like to introduce our illustrious mayor, Mr. John Hemper, who promised he will only say a few words. It is pretty hot out here. I think he also wanted to ask Brenda if he could volunteer to shovel manure to help keep the place clean."

Everyone laughed, including the elected official. Sister Margaret ushered the kids to sit on the grass in front of her chair.

"Thank you, Sister, for that rather unorthodox introduction, and you can count on me Tuesday mornings for doing my share. Be sure to have the wheelbarrow and shovel ready.

"I would like to thank Brenda Schmidt for conceiving of this idea, Sister Margaret for supporting it, and Brian Jacob,who did most of the physical work to ready the area for the project, and, who Brenda says keeps her from derailing whenever she overextends herself. Their efforts and those of their friends and families, as well as volunteers. will help people from all walks of life come to terms with issues that are causing them pain, be it physical, mental, or social. This is a not-for-profit endeavor aided by start-up money from an anonymous donor, I am told. So, I encourage anyone who has the time and expertise, to volunteer your services. I would like also to remind the companies in our area that pay their employees to volunteer for designated charitable causes, that this is one they should consider. Any money you wish to donate to support this endeavor, can go to St. Francis on the Hill ETC. Now let's cut this ribbon and start helping!"

With that, Brenda rounded up over half the crowd who had been helping. Carolyn stood between her mother and Bob, who had hoisted Annie hoisted onto his shoulders and Connor had slipped in front of Carolyn. Jill stood between Brian and Sister Margaret with the three kids tucked in front of them. Jill whispered into Sister's ear. "You look flash in Sister Vi's skirt and red top. Good thing we only have cows!"

Sister Margaret laughed heartily in response, just as the ribbon was being cut, with cameras rolling and photos snapping.

No one expected the publicity that would be generated by the picture that would appear in the July 2 Telegraph-Herald, and on the local TV stations, National News and, especially, on all the Chicago networks.

•　•　•　•　•

That afternoon marked the beginning of Brenda's summer schedule. The ETC would be open every day from 8:00 to 11:00 in the morning, as well as 2:00 to 6:00 in the afternoon, with the exception of Sunday morning and Mondays. That would give the horses a break between the hour-long sessions and in the hottest part of the day. It wasn't that the horses would be ridden too much. That hour also included bonding with the horse by brushing it, learning how to saddle and bridle, actual riding with a volunteer on each side. Learning how to talk to the horse, how to pet it and the safety issues involved with being around the animal, were a part of the training. There was also walking the horse to cool it, giving their animal a horsey treat, and putting the helmets and tack in the proper place. The horses were going to be treated as royalty. There were only five daily sessions. Brian had suggested to Brenda that they allow a little extra time in between so that people didn't feel rushed and to move traffic as there was limited parking space.

After the ceremony, Brenda left for lunch. Someone, probably from the newspaper, was taking pictures of the mural. Brian, Jill, and the kids remained at the ETC keep an eye on things. Brenda hoped that a photo of the mural would be posted in the newspaper. It really was a synthesis of the whole operation. She was so excited to get started. A quick lunch and then she would be back.

•　•　•　•　•

Marilyn was taking charge of the appointments and was finding that her life was fulfilling and a lot of fun. Bob had had their house phone hooked up to an answering machine that just took messages for the ETC since he and Carolyn had their cell phones. Now Marilyn could take care of business at night if she was helping with the kids or subbing at the library during the day. It worked well.

For some reason, she was very curious to meet the man she had talked to several times on the phone. He was one of their volunteers. His name was Harold Oaks, Bob's friend, the vet. He had a soft, low voice that seemed to hum. She hadn't been around when the volunteers trained as she had been subbing at the library. He was on the docket to be here in the afternoon. Maybe he had been there this morning, but there was such a crowd. She hadn't known half the people.

She didn't know exactly why, but since moving to Dubuque, she was taking a greater interest in life. Things were different now that she had exposed her story. She felt free. She was thinking that she might even be able to go out with men and have some kind of social companionship of her own.

Since the kids and grandkids had planned to go to the museum this afternoon, Marilyn decided to take the copy of the schedule for next week with her back to the ETC to hang on the tack room door next to today's schedule. She would stay around to meet people so she could get to know them personally. Especially Harold Oaks. This was kind of gutsy of her. She wasn't one to take the initiative with a guy.

When she arrived at the barn, Marilyn saw Brenda was walking around with a tall grey-haired man, who had a bit of a pot belly. He was wearing nice slacks, a long-sleeved white shirt, and a black Stetson. They were stopping at each stall so he could examine each horse's hooves, legs and back. He had big hands and the animals stood quietly as he checked them out. When they finished, Brenda brought him over to the tack room where Marilyn had hung the new schedule.

"Marilyn, hi. I'd like you to meet Dr. Harold Oaks. He's a retired vet and will be helping as a volunteer here a couple of afternoons and mornings a week. Harold, this is Marilyn Sewell."

So, this was the man. "I am sure Brenda is happy to have you. Me too." What had she said? Me too? Where did that come from? She was acting like a stuttering teen. Then she tried to recoup her losses, "I mean, we have talked on the phone several times. It's nice to finally meet you."

He stuck out that big hand to shake hers. It was warm and encompassing. She felt a big rush of friendship, nothing else. "It's good to meet you too, Marilyn. Before I retired, I helped Bob and Carolyn with Palm Reader. Saw little Ouija right after she was born. Beautiful animals."

Oh, that voice. Even better up close and in person. He could be a broadcaster. She loved that voice, but she felt nothing special toward the man.

"Harold," Brenda said to him. "Marilyn will post the schedule here. We want to keep her up on things as she has the job of organizing the volunteers and clients. She is going to do her best to make sure that if there are cancellations, the concerned parties can be notified before they make the trip. I'll be working all the shifts, except for Saturday. Of course, there won't be any on Mondays. And only Sunday afternoons to provide more opportunities for working people to participate."

Harold nodded his head.

"Marilyn, Harold is going to be my stand-in to oversee the place if anything should come up that I have to attend to. We're hoping, that if things go well and we can get enough good help, it will work for just one of us is to be here in charge."

"Like I told you on the phone, Marilyn. My wife has died rather suddenly, and right now I am somewhat at loose ends."

"Yes, that has to be difficult. It's good of you, using your expertise as a vet to help Brenda."

Then as an afterthought, she turned to Brenda. "Brenda, if you don't mind. I think I'll hang around this afternoon. The phone company has the answering machine set up here in the tack room as well, so I might make a few calls and just see what happens at this end. It will be good to meet some of the volunteers. There were a couple of high school kids that called this morning and asked if they could help. They're only fourteen. I talked to both sets of parents and they're comfortable with it. The kids have been around horses quite a bit."

"That might really be good for them, Marilyn. Kids that age are too young for employment and often find the summers long and unproductive. I think we could have them shadow a pair of volunteers and maybe help with clean-up."

"Exactly what I was thinking. We used to do that in the library in Boone Junction. They would shelve books, dust, and check in items. They were very helpful."

"You worked in a library?" Harold was surprised.

"Marilyn *is* the library. No, she is a librarian. This summer she is subbing downtown at the library as well as helping Bob and Carolyn with the kids and us with this project. She's a busy woman." She looked at Marilyn and winked.

"I guess *so*." He smiled a beautiful wide smile and a little dimple peeked from the corner of it. Marilyn returned the smile. He would make an awesome friend.

•　　•　　•　　•　　•

Brenda was so pleased with the way things were shaping up. That afternoon they had twelve clients and ten volunteers. Harold hung around. He was calm and reassuring, really got along well with people.

Two veterans who were buddies and wanted to come on the same day, suffered from PTSD and one was an amputee. One had ridden before and the other one, never. Each had a counselor from the mental health organization and one, a psychiatrist from the local hospital. Two of Brenda's sons worked with them. She was so proud of her boys.

A five-year-old girl with Cerebral Palsy wore leg braces, which gave the ETC staff a chance to try out some specialized equipment just for this situation. After they removed her leg braces, they lifted her onto Stang, who had the narrowest back. They strapped her legs into special holsters that hung on either side. Her volunteer climbed up behind her to add support. The little girl had such a good time. She couldn't stop laughing. Her mother felt so comfortable that she went over to Marilyn to ask if she could volunteer at the same time her daughter came. Marilyn signed her up to shadow. She would be learning right along, or maybe behind her daughter.

There was one boy and two girls with Down Syndrome, a woman suffering from depression, two teens with anger issues, two recovering drug addicts, and a middle-aged woman with mobility issues.

Marilyn was glad she had come over, pleased that she had done a good job of matching volunteers and clients. They would try to have two for each person, one for the counseling aspect and one to help the client learn to interact properly with the horse.

• • • • •

It still amazed Brenda that she had come up with this idea. She had never realized how involved it would get. She was genuinely relieved that Harold was willing to devote so much time. as it was already apparent that the sisters' gardens were yielding bumper crops and her own was growing like gangbusters too, even though planted later. She had talked to the sisters and it looked like they might have to set up a booth at the weekly market. Or perhaps, now this was another idea, they could sell their produce with all the people coming and going to ride or volunteer at the ETC. They would also have a market with the people at the assisted living across the street and the big care facility. They employed 300 people. Forget the Saturday Market. She would get the sisters on that. She would ask Brian if he would build a produce stand. Maybe they could put it by the road leading up to the convent.

Get some of the sisters out with the people. Jill would probably let the kids help, one at a time if there was a sister present. Maybe they should ask for donations instead of charging. She wondered if there were any laws about that. Ah, so much to do! Brian would tell her to put on the brakes and make a list. Tonight!

• • • • •

Sister Margaret's afternoon power nap turned into two hours! She was never this worn out last winter before she came up with her ideas to hire Brenda and the Jacobs and to help Carolyn find homes for foster kids. Whew! She barely had time to read e-mails any more. Just this morning, she had to cut short her story rounds with the sisters so that she could attend the opening of the ETC. Just look where meeting Brenda in the casino had taken her. And now Carolyn had confided the latest of her mom's revelations about being raped by Dale Scarlone. They had no idea of where that scoundrel might be now.

"Yes," Sister Margaret thought, "I am getting to old for all this excitement and drama."

Chapter Sixteen

Notoriety

Sister Margaret was in her usual spot in the chapel waiting for early Mass to begin when Mother Superior slipped in beside her, made the sign of the cross and handed her a paper with an out of town phone number.

"Angel took the message," she whispered. "I think you should take care of it. It's from NBC. Good work!" Margaret had no idea what Mother was talking about.

Yesterday afternoon she was so exhausted after all the hubbub. She had done her visiting with the ill sisters and had to cut it short to make the ribbon cutting ceremony. It was quite the production! Afterwards, she stood around until 1:00 visiting with the volunteers and a news reporter. She made the late lunch, just. Then she went to her room to take a power nap but woke up at 4:00!

Wanting to see how things were going at the ETC. she took a long walk out to the barn-about three or four blocks from her room. It was beautiful seeing all the horses carrying people around on their backs with everyone talking quietly and looking happy. Even the horses looked like they were enjoying it!

She spied Marilyn, who was sitting on a hay bale talking to a volunteer and eyeing a cowboy in a white shirt.

Brain came in to check things out. The kids were with him, observing quietly. He had just finished cutting and raking the hay into windrows with equipment borrowed from a neighbor on the next hill. He told Sister Margaret that the farmer, Pete Dolter, said he would also lend him the baler if he could get it going. Seems there was some tangle up with the baling twine. Brian said that was like offering him candy. He loved a puzzle.

"Nice guy, I'm glad I met him. I think we could be a big help to each other."

By 5:00, Sister Margaret was hot and tired again. She stopped in the cafeteria for a sandwich and ice cream and then went back to her room, thinking she would sit down for just a minute. When she awoke, it was getting dark and she barely had the energy to head off to bed. Today, however, she felt totally refreshed—ready to take on the world.

• • • • •

When she left the chapel to make the phone call, all her sisters gathered round, laughing, and congratulating her. "You've put the convent on the map, Margaret!"

"We're all going to have to get our hair done!"

"I think the ceremony went viral. I saw it on Facebook this morning."

"I saw it mentioned on Twitter."

What were they talking about? When she got back to her room, she sat down by her phone and contacted Angel for an outside long-distance line.

"Oh, Sister Margaret. You were so good on the news last night. I laughed so hard about your joke for the mayor. And you looked marvelous in your new outfit, even with your tennis shoes."

"Well, let me tell you, Angel. I know that is not fashionable, but an old lady has the right to be comfortable."

"I absolutely agree! Should I put this number through for you, Sister?"

"Please do, dear girl. Thank you."

• • • • •

"Al Roker."

"Hello, this is Sister Margaret Sorenson. Sister Joan Daily asked me to call."

"Oh, Sister. I am Al Roker, one of the hosts of the *Today Show*."

"Congratulations."

"Well, thank you, but I called to tell you that we saw the clip from the opening of the Equine Therapy Center in Dubuque. We would like to come there to do a story on the center and how the sisters got it up and going. It would make a wonderful segment on the show, the community pitching in financially and with volunteering so that it can be a non-profit. It's good seeing people taking initiative and not counting on the government. We would like to interview you. You are so camera perfect."

"Hold on a minute. *Who* are you?"

"Al Roker. Do you watch the *Today Show*?"

"I'm afraid not. When is it on?"

"Eight o'clock A.M., your time in Dubuque."

"Sorry, sir. We only have one TV, and besides, I am having breakfast after Mass, because the mornings I don't do storytelling with the older nuns, I go to tutor my man from Iran. I am preparing him for his citizenship. We are also trying to solve all world problems."

"Wow! You're ambitious. Good luck with that. But Sister, what we would like to do, is bring our crew to Dubuque to produce a segment on the convent and this project. The Fourth of July is Monday, so we would travel on the fifth and film on Wednesday, the sixth. Live. Would that work?"

"Wednesday? Live? Holy cow! I don't know. I am just an old nun. Let me get back to you Mr. Roku."

"That's Roker."

"Oh, I'm so sorry. One of the sisters was telling me that we just got Roku for the TV but I never watch TV That's not you, right?"

He laughed. "No, not me. Please get back to me as soon as you can. I need to know by 4:00 today, that would be 3:00 your time."

• • • • •

Margaret wished she had a pair of roller skates. She talked to Mother Superior, who said to talk to Brenda. Mother had shown her the Saturday morning T.H. newspaper. There, on the front page, it had a beautiful picture of everyone lined up to cut the ribbon. Inside there was a full-page article including pictures, one of Brenda next to one of the children on a horse, and another of all the children gathered by the mural.

Since Margaret didn't have a cell phone, she set out on foot to see if Brenda was interested in doing the *Today Show*. She found her in her garden. Brenda said she wasn't sure. It made her kind of nervous. Brenda had trouble making decisions sometimes. She always had a dozen things going on in her mind. But she did tell Sister, that they all looked really good on TV, and that both stations had taken great shots at the afternoon therapy session.

"You know, Sister Margaret, I was thinking that now might be a good time to get the green house, that is if we are going to get one. Think of all the people we could feed. And maybe I should get some dairy cows instead of keeping the two head of beef. We could butcher them for this winter's meat at the convent. Red meat is kind of out of favor now. Still, I am so sentimental about those shaggy Highland cattle. They are such hearty girls."

Brian arrived as Brenda was going through her new wish list. He had been in the field checking to see if the hay was dry enough to bale. He had gone over to the neighbor's and fixed the baler. Piece of cake. Pete told him he could use it today if the hay was ready.

He looked patiently at his co-worker. "Brenda, you need to put those ideas on hold for at LEAST another month. They will last. Put them up on the board in your room. For the time being, it's very important to let this ETC take hold and concentrate on getting it running as best you can. Very important."

"Yeah, you are right. I don't know why I always think I have to be marching off in all different directions."

"You have awesome ideas. Let's just deal with them well, and not haphazardly. The ETC has been dedicated, but not proven. We want to handle that right."

"Brian, I hope I have told you that you are extremely important to my mental health." Brenda smiled at him. "When you rein me in a bit, I am encouraged to keep thinking and planning. The ball and chain you have attached to my ankle is just what I need!"

He laughed.

Sister Margaret asked Brian what he thought about being on the *Today Show*. Brian expressed that it would probably be good publicity for the convent and the ETC. More people in Dubuque might see it and want to get involved. It might help their produce sales. Free advertising.

They could put a stand out the same day the crew planned to arrive in town, if they came. He told Brenda that he and Jill didn't have a TV but the neighbor had nothing but congratulations for all of them. Brian was hoping that Jill could bring home a copy of the newspaper after work tonight so that they could show it to the kids.

His enthusiasm made the decision for Margaret. She stopped by Angel's desk to have her buzz Mother to see if she was in. And lucked out! She reported her findings, and Mother gave her the go ahead to call Mr. Roku back. And so, on Saturday at 11:00 in the morning, she gave the *Today Show* permission to film on Wednesday morning, July 6. Who would have thought she would be working with TV stars?

• • • • •

Lunch was always soup, sandwich and fruit for Jill. It made it so much easier when she had to be at work by 3:00. She had the Forman grill set out for Brian to grill the chicken she was marinating for tonight. The kids had helped her make some no-bake cookies for an after-supper treat. Also, Pedro had brought home some salad greens, radishes, and green onions from the sisters. He liked to help them weed. Michael liked things neat but didn't like to weed because it was hard to get the dirt out from under his fingernails. None of the kids were very keen on salad but Brian was working on them, experimenting with different dressings and having the kids rate them. Sometimes, he would challenge them to see who could take the biggest bite out of a radish and chew it up. Of course, when told they would get cookies if they ate salad, that helped it go down easier.

When Brian came in for lunch, all the talk was about the *Today Show* coming to Dubuque the following Wednesday to film at the ETC.

"They could see our mural," Silvia said.

"Maybe Pedro could juggle," Michael offered.

"Yeah, Dad. And you could set up the sound system and we could all sing!" That was Pedro's idea.

"And I could act," Jill said. She began talking in her Donald Duck voice, setting the kids off into a fit of giggles.

"Well, I am not too sure that's what they're looking for. I think they want to talk to Brenda, Sister Margaret, the clients who use the horses and some of the volunteers. Jill, maybe you can take the kids over to watch."

"Maybe? Of course, I will!" Jill said dramatically. "This will be my opportunity to become a star."

"Well, this old farmer is going to bale hay this afternoon. Pete next door said I could borrow his baler since I fixed it. I should be done by 3:00, Jill. It's a small field. Can the kids stay by themselves for fifteen minutes when you go to work?"

"What do you think, kids? What would you do by yourselves in the house for fifteen minutes, while Brian is finishing his work?"

"I'll practice juggling. I am up to four balls now." Jill looked askance at him. "I know, Mom. I'll do it on the porch, so I don't break anything." He had said "Mom". Jill wanted to cry with joy.

"I'll read. I got a Laura Ingalls Wilder book at the library on Thursday. It's really good."

Michael considered for a while. "If I can use the good paper, I'll draw pictures of Silvia reading and Pedro juggling. They can give it to Martha and John next time we go to visit."

"All great ideas. Well Brian, it sounds like you are good to work till 3:00. These kids have their own plans. And both our cell numbers are by the phone. We can give it a try."

•   •   •   •   •

The Donovans had spent all day Saturday out working on their caravan for the parade on Monday, the Fourth of July. Bob had gotten permission from the city to enter, as long as they were at the end, because of the horses. They also had to pick up after them if they didn't have rump bags.

Bob had conceived of the idea last winter and he and Carolyn had perused as many pictures as they could find for the model they wanted to do. Bob had kept his eyes open and got a solid wagon flatbed and had been purchasing the materials he needed as the winter went on. He and Connor had spent the month of June putting on the finishing touches.

They were able to build a part of it in the barnage where Bob kept his tools but had to move it to the new storage building they had purchased when it was evident it would be too tall for the barnage.

The adults had carefully painted it by 8:00 that night. It was a clean white background, with the carving enhancements in yellow, red and brown with a blue door. They had declared it a masterpiece.

The wheels were red with steel rims and hard rubber tires. The curtains were airy white. Annie even took a short nap on the cushioned bench inside. It was covered with an assortment of decorative pillows the ladies and Annie had been working on

The answering machine was blinking steadily when Marilyn walked into the house. After washing her hands, she pressed the button.

"You have ten new messages. Hello and congratulations. This is Calvin Daykins. I am a police officer and would like to volunteer at the ETC. My number is 884-2765. Thank you…Good morning, this is Jane Mills. Congratulations, you are doing something wonderful…

Hello, I am a parent with a child with debilitating anxiety issues. I would like to talk to someone about getting her into the program. My number is 848-4329…Yes, this is Mrs. J.F. Wallace. Marilyn, call me now!"

The tape continued, but Marilyn froze. That was her mother's voice, as demanding as ever, even after twenty-nine years. She stayed sitting on the chair by the phone, her pencil still in hand. Ten minutes later, when Carolyn and the kids walked in to tell her goodnight, she was still sitting there thinking.

"Mom, what's the matter?"

Marilyn went back to the beginning, skipped the first few messages, and played the fourth. YES, THIS IS MRS. J.F. WALLACE. MARILYN, CALL ME NOW!

"Oh, Mom. Let me put the kids to bed. I'll be back." She turned to Connor and Annie. "Tell Grandma goodnight. I think she deserves an extra good hug for all her help today, don't you?"

"Here are two squeezes, Grandma," Connor said. "Good night. Sleep tight. Don't let the bed bugs bite. Who was that crabby voice on the phone?"

"I'll tell you tomorrow, hon." Marilyn hugged him again.

"Grandma Marilyn, don't worry. We love you." Annie climbed into her lap. She laid her head on Marilyn's chest. "We take care of people in this home. We protect and help like Great-Grandma Sister Margaret."

"Thank you, Annie. Good night, baby." Annie hopped off her lap and started for the stairs. Carolyn looked over her shoulder and said, "I'll be right back."

Before Carrie could come back downstairs, Bob showed up. Carrie had sent him down when he came out of the shower. They played the whole tape through. Messages eight, nine, and ten were her mother. "Marilyn, I said pick up. I know you are working there…Marilyn, I saw you in the video with a woman who looks just like you…Marilyn, enough of this. Give me a call!"

Bob was shaking his head when Carolyn returned. They played the tape again. This time Marilyn recorded the messages she needed to respond to.

"My grandmother sounds like a witch if her voice is any indication of her personality," Carolyn told her mom.

"What a lousy ending to a perfect day with the family here." Marilyn shook her head. "I haven't heard her voice in twenty-nine years and it still sounds the same."

"What will you do?" Bob asked her.

"Any suggestions? This is your call too, Carolyn."

"Well, Mom. I think she has us pinned down by city anyway. We can't very well ignore her. She knows we are in Dubuque."

"Carolyn is right, Marilyn. She has found you. Why don't you sleep on it? It is almost 10:00."

"I don't think I'll be able to sleep. Let's do it now. I'll put her on speaker phone, so you can listen. Except I don't know her number."

"Here," Bob took the phone and went to the menu for missed calls. "Do you want to write this down? It's 1-605-472-9965."

Marilyn laid down her pencil and punched in the number. The first ring had barely finished ringing when a voice said, "It's about time. I'll call you right back. We are entertaining, and I want to go into another room."

Carolyn and Bob looked at each other in disbelief.

The phone rang and Marilyn answered it. She hadn't even finished saying "Hello?" when the angry tirade started.

"How dare you! We paid for you to have that baby and get rid of it. You tricked us!"

Carolyn turned white. Bob scooted closer and slipped his hand in hers. Marilyn held the phone out as her mother kept ranting. "I had things all set up so that when you got back from your trip around 'Europe,' I would introduce you to a nice young banker and then you go and disappear. I have spent the best part of my life looking for you! You ungrateful girl! We sent Dale to pick you up early to keep you from sneaking out. Where did you go?!"

Bob took the phone from Marilyn and pressed the END button.

Carolyn went to her mother and drew her into her arms. "She sent my rapist father to pick you up. I'm so sorry. She's despicable. Sick."

"Where is your father in all of this, Marilyn?"

"I have no idea, he never talked to me. Never held me. Never asked me a question."

"Mom, maybe he isn't your father?"

"I never thought of that. I just assumed. I don't know? Who are these people? I wish they were no relation."

"Marilyn, what if they aren't? We could have DNA tests, blood tests? We should get to the bottom of this. We'll help you. It needs to be resolved."

"But, Bob. I have my birth certificate."

"So do I, Mom," Carolyn said. "I won't accept those people as my grandparents."

The phone rang again. Bob unplugged it.

Chapter Seventeen

Sunday, July 3

Sister Margaret genuflected and sat next to the Jacobs at 9:30 Sunday Mass. Little Michael crawled over his dad's lap to sit next to her. They were surprised when Carolyn, Bob, Marilyn, and the kids showed up and knelt down behind them. There was a lot of excitement among them, smiles and quiet greetings. Marilyn whispered into Sister Margaret's ear, "Pray for us." Something was afoot.

The Donovans had never been to church at the convent. They weren't Catholics but felt they needed to be with their friends. It wasn't long before they scooted over for Brenda. They had called her. as well as Jill, at 8:00 this morning about meeting after Mass. They felt they needed to tell them about the vitriol Marilyn's mother was spewing from Chicago. They didn't want any of it to spill over on their friends and children, nor to dampen the good vibes emanating from the convent.

When Mass was over, Bob invited them for breakfast at the Outlook restaurant, at the bottom of the hill near the river. He had never eaten there before but had noticed it many times and heard people say that the prices were very reasonable. Everyone took him up on the offer, as they could see that the family was upset and likely had some news to share.

It was during the morning lull, that slow time midway between lunch and breakfast, when they arrived at the restaurant, so there was a lot of available seating. The five kids slid into a vinyl-upholstered booth. Connor was holding court with tales of their "surprise" and how they were going to drive it in the parade.

Brian and Bob pushed together two smaller tables for the seven adults. They had Marilyn sit at the head with her back to the children. After everyone's orders were settled and before the food was delivered, Marilyn told them that she had asked Bob and Carolyn if she could speak to all of them.

"Last night I got a phone call, actually many were on the answering machine, from my mother, whom I haven't heard from in twenty-nine years. Sister Margaret can tell you the story sometime if she wants to share it." Sister Margaret nodded her head.

"The thing is, my mother and father were horrible parents. At least to me they were very distant when I was a child, and now very hateful. Well, my mother anyway. I have no idea about my dad. You see, when Carolyn was born, I decided to get out of that life, and with the help of two lovely nuns, we 'disappeared.' Again, Sister knows the story. I asked Bob if we could all meet so that I could warn all of you that my mother may show up at the convent looking for me. Her name is Adele Wallace. You would NEVER want her around the kids! She saw the clip from the opening of the ETC. and might show up and start making a fuss. She is at least seventy years old but looks about fifty because of her fanatical interest in her appearance. Since she doesn't know where I live, I would like you to please give her Bob's cell phone number if she shows up pestering you, and we'll handle things. So that is the long and short of it. Carolyn has never met her; in fact, she didn't know anything about either of them until just recently.

The two waitresses arrived just then and began dispensing food to the kids.

"You know, I don't want to discuss any more of this for now. Please enjoy your food. If any of you are free after we eat, you are invited to our place, or I guess I should say to Carolyn and Bob's. We have a very nice surprise we want to show you. The kids will love it, Jill, but I think Connor has told them all about it by now."

"Mom, you know our house is your house." Carolyn smiled at her mom, who returned the smile.

"I'm very sorry to hear about your problem, Marilyn." Brenda responded. Then looking to the Donovans, "I would love to stop by to see your surprise, but I need to be back by 1:00 because the gardening sisters want to have a meeting about the produce booth that we are setting up when the TV crew comes on Wednesday. The loving care they are giving their gardens is shown by the abundance. We want to get the kids helping too."

Sister Margaret looked intrigued. "I'm riding with Brenda, so it's a go for me."

"We are invited to Jill's folks this afternoon, but we'll just leave from your house," added Brian. "I'm rather curious. The kids haven't said anything to us about a surprise."

"Well, good! That means that Connor and Annie took it to heart when we told them it was a secret." Bob said proudly.

• • • • •

Sister Margaret rode in the car with Brenda, who was always interesting as she was full of ideas. That woman's mind worked like a spinning top. She certainly was an asset to the convent. She was always coming up with ideas and giving the sisters useful things to do. They all loved her. And everyone was excited by all the energy these new people were bringing to the community. Why, already in June, they had had six associates sign up to help with the gardens and the ETC.

Mother had told her just the other day that they had had inquiries from a college girl looking into becoming a postulant! Now that was a rarity these days! And there was also a forty-something widow and mother of three grown children who was interested in being an associate with the option of perhaps becoming a nun herself. She and her aging sisters had been sitting on the heavy end of the scale for so long, and now it was starting to balance out a bit. That felt good. And it felt good that she had a taken a little responsibility to get the ball rolling. Brenda would keep it going if she kept coming up with many more ideas; that is, if Brian could keep her on track!

•   •   •   •   •

At Bob and Carolyn's, they all piled out of the cars. Connor was almost bursting his buttons. "Can I show them, Dad? Can I!"

"Yes, but wait until we get around back, okay?" The kids took off running the length of the barnage and around the corner.

"We'll take the shorter route. Bob opened the last door on the end. The adults cut through the building and out the rear sliding door to the pasture. He closed the door after him."

"I noticed you had this other building, Bob, when I was here last time," Brian said to him. "Kind of unique."

"Yes, I had to get it especially for our project. It is one of those new frame structures. It has worked well and went up slick as can be. It's sold by a company out of Dyersville, and they seem to have a team that has its setup down to a science."

"I'm taking note, Brenda," Brian teased her. "With all the ideas you come up with, we might need another building!"

Brenda smiled and turned to Bob. "Do they make greenhouses too?"

"They certainly might."

Bob slid open a wide door on rails, and they all went inside.

There stood an intricately painted and beautifully designed gypsy caravan.

"So cool!" Pedro was the first to express his admiration. It was followed by more ooh's and ah's.

Bob whistled. Palm Reader and Ouija came running from the other end of the pasture.

"Can I ride Palm Reader, Dad?" Pedro asked Brian.

"We need her just now, Pedro," Carolyn interjected, "so we can hitch her up and take you for a ride in our new caravan."

Before they hitched up Palm Reader, Bob, and Brian, with all the kids pushing from behind, rolled the caravan out into the pasture. Everyone walked around to check it out. They were extremely surprised and admiring of the work that had been done. Brian was down on the ground looking at the wheels and undercarriage, Pedro right beside him with Brain pointing and explaining something. Silvia was running her fingers over the tastefully painted designs, her other hand holding Annie's. The little girl was talking with all the animation she possessed. Michael had taken out a sketch pad, which was becoming his constant companion. He was sitting against a fence post across the way, his pencil flying across the paper, with Ouija's nose in his hair.

Bob let down a board attached to the back of the wagon and magically three-step stairs unfolded neatly and locked tightly in place as they reached the ground. Above the stairs was the freshly painted blue door. He offered Sister Margaret a hand, reaching up to open the door with his free one so she could enter.

"Oh, Bob. This is like a fairy castle!"

"Thanks to Carolyn and her mom. They decorated the inside and helped paint the outside. They sewed the curtains and covered the cushions and pillows on the benches."

Everyone, climbed the steps to sit inside. There was room for all. There was even a little stove in the center with a venting pipe going out the roof, only for more authenticity, Bob told them. Michael was the last to squeeze inside. He sat on Brian's lap holding his sketch book.

"Let's see what you have there, Michael," Brian gave him a hug. Michael opened to a page with a scene of many people admiring the caravan. Brian whispered in his ear. Michael went over to Bob, who was standing in the doorway, and handed him the paper that he had carefully torn out of his book."

"For you."

Bob looked up incredulous. He handed the paper to Carolyn, who smiled somewhat stunned. She passed it on for everyone else to see. In very little time, Michael had replicated the scene he had witnessed, including all the characters: Brian and Pedro on the ground; Connor bent over them trying to see; Annie, holding Silvia's hand; the women standing shoulder to shoulder; Sister Margaret, holding Bob's hand and lifting a foot to the first step; Bob, his hand on the door, ready to open it. It was like a photo had been snapped. It was genius. The only one missing was Michael.

"It's for the Donovans," Michael told Jill.

"The next time you come, Michael, this will be framed and hanging in our living room. Thank you." Carolyn held it carefully and slipped it on a shelf above her head for safe keeping.

Sister Margaret was thinking her life had sure become more interesting since she introduced these people to each other. All of a sudden, her thoughts were interrupted by the beeping of a car horn in the driveway. Everyone made their way out of the caravan, through the pasture gate and around the barnage.

There, parked in the driveway, were Bob's parents, his dad standing behind the open car door, honking. When he saw Connor and Annie charging toward him, he slammed the door shut and held out his hands "I thought someone had to be here! It's like a parking lot."

Bob's mom was standing on her side of the car waving and grinning. When Annie saw her, she ran to the passenger side and jumped into Rosa's outstretched arms for a big hug.

When the rest of the family caught up with the kids, there were *abrazos* all around.

"Roberto mio!" Rosa was so happy to see her only son. "Y Carolina! Y Marilyn."

There was a period of hand shaking and hugging while friends were introduced.

• • • • •

"That is some caravan the family built and decorated," Jill said. "We all came over to see it. Bob says he's driving it in the parade tomorrow and Palm Reader will pull it."

"And Connor and I get to take Ouija on a halter up by her mama, so she doesn't get lonesome," Annie told her grandparents.

"We came to see it. I am dropping Rosa off for the night if you don't mind. For some reason she prefers to see all of you! We were in Arlington for a race yesterday; I have to be there again tomorrow. As long as we were so close, we decided to make a quick trip here."

Marilyn and Carolyn hugged Rosa between them. "We insist she stay! I even took off work for the week thinking that you might stop in," Carolyn told her mother-in-law.

It was obvious there was a lot of affection between all of them. Kevin was very interested in the ETC. "We saw all of you on television! Sister Margaret, it sure is good to finally meet you. I keep hearing glorious things about you, and you looked pretty darn cute in that snazzy dress. No one would know you are fifty years old."

"Sounds like a bunch of blarney there, Kevin." Sister Margaret laughed. Bob wasn't anything like his dad, who was very gregarious.

"Carolyn, what are you doing for the ETC? I know your mom is scheduling."

"Well, I am providing some clients for one thing, Kevin. And I guess, in a pinch, I could shovel manure. I've had a lot of practice. I didn't tell you that Brenda," she said to her friend.

"Ah, this is Brenda. I'd like to see your horses and operation."

"Well, you're welcome to. The horses aren't anything like you're used to working with, but they are good for this. The *Today Show* will be filming there on Wednesday. If you get back in time, come over and see us."

"They are! That's impressive. Thank you. That would be great."

"Dad," Pedro said. "Bob said we could have a ride in the caravan."

"They have company now, Pedro," his dad told him.

"No, no. Stay. I can have Palm Reader hitched up in no time. Come on everyone. Let's go back and climb aboard. We'll give the kids a test ride."

True to his word, Palm Reader was pulling the caravan within fifteen minutes for a ride across the back pasture, around the trees and back. Bob let all the kids ride inside and insisted Sister Margaret sit in the seat beside him. Kevin lifted her up like she was a kid.

"Oh, for heaven's sake!" was all that she could say. She looked like she might giggle.

It was a rather noisy caravan, but the mare was calm and strong. The adults watched on the sideline, grinning at the twinkling smile on Sister Margaret's face. They didn't know that she was having a day-dream of being on the road—a gypsy queen in a little fairy castle.

After the ride, Bob unhitched Palm reader and turned her loose. Everyone returned to their cars to head to their afternoon destinations.

"Thanks again for breakfast, Bob and Carolyn."

"We'll see you at the parade tomorrow, Connor," Michael and Pedro yelled out the car window.

When the dust settled, the Donovans and Marilyn walked back to the caravan to show it off again. Rosa and Kevin were so impressed.

"It looks like Grandpa Connor's caravan in the picture," his dad said to them.

While Rosa stayed behind to look over the interior with the women, Bob walked Kevin and the kids into the field and gave a whistle. Palm Reader appeared from behind a tree where she was standing in the shade, and trotted toward them, her thick tail waving in the wind. She was followed by a frolicking little filly. They came right up to the men and children.

Kevin walked over to the mare and ran his hands appreciatively over her back, neck, and legs, checking her out.

"Quality. These are really sound animals, Bob," his dad complimented him.

"Their disposition is really calm. I trust them around the kids," Bob told him. "Not high-strung like your big boys and girls, Dad. Cold-blooded."

"And this little girl is Ouija." Kevin walked over to her just as she jerked her head up like a fist and stared off into space.

"Oh, oh, Grandpa," Connor said. "She's okay. We forgot to tell you that any time she hears her name, she spaces off."

"What?"

Annie started to stroke Ouija's neck. "It's okay, Grandpa. She'll be back with us soon. She's hearing information."

"What?" Kevin turned to Bob, who just smiled.

"Yeah, and Annie listens to the horses; they tell her things." Connor was now very proud of Annie's super power as he called it. It had taken him a while to get over his jealousy.

"Remember what we heard about Great-Grandpa Connor's wife, Agata?" Bob asked him. "She was a mind reader. Well, Annie is a reader of horse's minds."

"That's right, Grandpa. And I am telling Daddy the stories for his 'riculum."

"That's curriculum, Annie." Then turning to his dad, "I am working on a project for the middle school this summer, Dad. Annie has been helping me."

By this time, Ouija was standing quietly next to her mother. Annie laid her head on Ouija's back.

"Dad, she said she just talked to a horse named Chetak from India. Do you have a horse from India yet? Didn't the gypsies come from India? He has a monument. Maybe you want to check that on the internet. I guess there are songs too. Oh, and listen to this. He was bluish. Would that be a horse of a different color?"

Kevin looked at his son. "Yep, an Agata." He didn't seem surprised.

"Hey, Dad," Connor added. "Do you remember about the horse of a different color from *The Wizard of Oz*? Maybe you can use that in your curriculum."

• • • • •

At about 2:00, Carolyn and her mom pulled some leftover lasagna out of the fridge, made a salad, and toasted some bread to slather with garlic and butter. After the casual meal, Kevin went out with his son to hook the caravan up to Bob's truck, so it would be ready to go in the morning. Kevin planned to drive to Arlington when they finished. He would return sometime Tuesday after he got the race horses trailered up and sent on their way to Louisville.

Brian had offered to drive the two horses. He was going to borrow his dad's livestock trailer that afternoon to take Palm Reader and Ouija downtown in the morning. Bob would tow the caravan with his pickup. He didn't want Palm Reader pulling it on the busy streets, so decided to hitch her up at the beginning of the parade route. The police were going to cordon off a section for him to park the trailer and the truck. It was quite a process to get everything coordinated. Of course, it was made easier by all the people who had offered to help.

Meanwhile, Annie and Connor were practicing leading Ouija in a halter with a rope attached on each side. The funny thing was that Ouija would have followed them without a halter.

Rosa and Carolyn were visiting while doing the dishes and cleaning up the kitchen. Carolyn had shown Rosa the incredible sketch that Michael had drawn, and they had exclaimed over his talent.

Marilyn was checking the messages; two people wanted to volunteer and three wanted to become clients. One suffered from severe epilepsy when excited. His mother said she was willing to be there with him in case he had an episode. Marilyn had this whole week booked. No more calls from her mom. She was a bit nervous about that.

Everyone's activity was interrupted by the loud slam of a car door. Rosa and Carolyn looked out the kitchen window to see a black stretch limo with dark tinted windows parked by the barnage. Marilyn looked out the window of the den where she was working and saw a bald-headed, thick-necked, muscular man open the back door. First came a pointed foot with stylish stilettos, a stockinged leg, and then… her mother.

Bob and Kevin came through the barnage and walked over to the car. Connor and Annie peeked around the corner, saw it, and encouraged by some unbidden instinct, took off running for the house, banging to a screeching halt in the kitchen, out of breath.

Their mom looked nervous. Grandma Rosa looked concerned. Grandma Marilyn was angry.

"Connor and Annie, will you please go upstairs until we are finished here?" They ran up the steps.

Rosa and Carolyn walked on either side of Marilyn out to the back yard. Mrs. Wallace was screaming at Bob. "I insist on seeing her immediately!"

"You are seeing her, Mother. What do you want?" Marilyn walked forward with the determination that said she had had enough and was no longer going to kowtow to the belligerent woman, who was her mother.

"Get in this car, Marilyn. You are coming back to Chicago with me immediately. I have plenty of clothing for you there, which I am sure is much nicer than anything that you have. We are going to get things straightened out."

What in the world? "How did you find me?" Marilyn was cool.

"I saw you on that show that was broadcasted on national news on Friday. Young lady, you have made my life hell!"

"Really? I am not so young, Mother. I am forty-eight years old. See the wrinkles. Notice the extra weight? Twenty-nine years have passed."

"You don't take care of yourself. We are going to put an end to that. I am setting you up with a trainer, and you can see my plastic surgeon. Then we will be able to present you to the public."

Marilyn started to laugh. "Mother, I'm not ten years old. Why would you even want me back in your home? You never wanted me there when I was a girl. And how will you make that happen?" Did her mother have dementia?

"I have Bruce here to help me get you home. I will not take *no* for an answer." It was then that Bob noticed the black holster clipped to the man's belt. His hand had slid over the top and, he was grinning. Bob stepped over in front of the women.

Back in the house, Connor and Annie had returned to the den to look out the back window. Connor grabbed the phone and dialed 911. He felt suspicious.

"Nine-one-one. What is your emergency?"

"There is a black man with muscles and a fancy lady with high heels. The lady is screaming, and I am afraid she wants to hurt my Grandma Marilyn."

"Connor! I think he has a gun!" Annie hid behind Connor.

"He might have a gun. A REAL gun," Connor told the dispatcher.

"We have your address and are sending the officer from the park over since you are so close. Are you in a safe place?"

"Well, my sister and I are in the house."

"Do you know how to lock the door?"

"Yes."

"Good, then I want you to do that now. Tell me when you have it locked."

They followed her directions and then ran back into the den and knelt on the floor so they could peek out the window to see what was going on, all the while talking with the dispatcher.

● ● ● ● ●

"Marilyn," her mother was growling at her. "You have cost me a fortune! Not only, nannies and private schools, but also by getting pregnant and disappearing before I could set you up with a rich husband. And for the past twenty-eight years, I have had private investigators trying to find your whereabouts! Do you know how much that costs! And now my husband is divorcing me because I am draining our accounts with this nonsense! You have ruined me! This is all your fault! You aren't even my daughter!"

"What do you mean? Not your daughter." That sounded like music to Marilyn's ears. Was that hope in her own voice that she heard?

• • • • •

"Connor," the dispatcher said. "The police officer is there. He knows the man is armed so he is going to block off the park road and wait for help."

"Connor, I am trying to talk to Palm Reader in my head. Please tell the lady to be quiet for a while."

"Excuse me," Connor said into the phone. "Can you be quiet for a minute?"

Annie crawled behind the couch which sat against the wall on the side facing the window. She squeezed her eyes shut and thought: *Palm Reader, help. Help Daddy and Grandpa and Mommy and the grand-mothers.*

Connor was whispering to the dispatcher when he glanced out the window and saw Palm Reader sticking her head around the *barnage.* How did she get out of the pasture?

"Annie, Palm Reader got out? How did she get out?"

"Excuse me," the dispatcher said. "Is there another person there?"

"No, it's just our horse."

"Oh." She didn't have anything else to say.

Annie scooted up next to the window to watch.

• • • • •

Bruce took a long step over to Bob and pushed him aside with one swipe of his arm. While brandishing his gun, he grabbed Marilyn's arm, jerked her off her feet, and shoved her head first into the back of the limo and slammed the door shut. His gun trained on the others, he opened the front door for Mrs. Wallace.

Bob got back on his feet. "Don't make a move!" the man shouted, "or she is dead." He waved the gun at the startled Donovans. And then in a fluid movement, ran around the car, jumped into the driver's seat, and started the engine.

He was looking over his shoulder to back the car up when there was a cataclysmic thump on the front of the limo. The vehicle shook like an earthquake. Again, and again! Adele screamed and hit her head on the window.

Bruce aimed his gun on instinct and shot at the beast outside through the tinted glass. He had forgotten it was bulletproof. It ricocheted back and put the bullet through his shoulder, causing him to lose the gun, which flew from his hand into the back of the vehicle.

At that point, Marilyn's "mother" threw open the car door and tried to run. Palm Reader, who had been pummeling the hood of the car for all she was worth, turned and chased after the woman, running around her in circles. Adele couldn't escape in any direction. She stumbled in her stilettos in the gravel of the driveway.

It was then that the police arrived, followed by the park ranger. Bob tried to open the back door of the limo but it wouldn't budge.

The policeman pulled Bob away and told him to take the ladies up to the porch.

"Oh, Bob. Is Mom okay, do you think? I am so worried."

"I think she is okay, Carolyn." Bob put his arm around Carolyn's and squeezed her shoulder. They walked up the pavers to the back porch, Carolyn looking over her shoulder. Kevin gave Rosa a hand up the porch steps.

"She'll be okay. The police are here," Kevin told her, although he didn't really know, as it was impossible to see through the tinted windows. Just then the porch door flew open, the screen banging against the siding. Connor and Annie ran out into their arms.

"We called the police, Mommy. Don't worry. The lady said we could come out by you now."

"Oh, you are so smart, you two!" The children found themselves wrapped into three pairs of arms.

"Hey!" One of the policeman yelled. "Will you get that horse out of here!"

"Annie, can you tell Palm Reader to take care of Ouija?" her dad asked her.

Annie closed her eyes. Palm Reader made one more circle, stopped and looked at them and then trotted off around the barnage with her head held high.

"How did she get out here anyway?" Bob wondered aloud.

"Sorry, Dad. I forgot to fasten the gate when I ran out," Connor told him.

"Lucky for us," his mom said.

Finally, the officers cuffed Adele Wallace and her driver. They helped an unhurt Marilyn out of the car and led her up to the porch. Everyone breathed a collective sigh of relief, and then started to laugh nervously. They hugged each other, relieved that what could have happened, didn't.

Everyone was so wonderful. Marilyn still couldn't get over what had happened. When the big brute shoved her into the back of the limo, she had crawled over to the other side and tried to get out, but that door was locked. Then she heard the loud bangs of collapsing metal. The limo was bouncing with each bang. Her "mother" was screaming! That was followed by a shot and a yelp when the thug fired at Palm Reader and sent the bullet into the protective windshield which flung it right back into his shoulder. She hadn't seen it happen as she was huddled on the floor with her head down, thank goodness.

Then there were more sirens and the ambulance came for Bruce, the bodyguard—big, bald-headed, now crying in pain. Her mother, who Marilyn would refer to her as Adele from now on, had been cuffed, dirty with torn nylon's and bleeding knees, stuffed unceremoniously into the back of the police cruiser, whining all the while to the officers. that it was just one big mistake. The ambulance and the police car left. Then a tow truck showed up, taking the limo away for evidence.

Later they all walked out to the pasture with treats for Palm Reader. Bob was surprised that the gate was wide open. After everyone thanked the horse profusely with pets and praise, she left them, prancing like nobody's business, her head held high, Ouija right beside her. Annie had told them later that, Ouija was going nuts because Palm Reader had forbidden her to leave the corral.

● ● ● ● ●

It was dark when Kevin left. He had a three-and-a-half-hour drive back to Arlington but said he would return early Tuesday morning. He needed to be there for the Fourth of July races. He told Rosa not to worry that he was too tired to drive. It would take him a long time to wind down after all the excitement.

The family had been asked to show up at the police station sometime tomorrow afternoon to be interviewed. Bob and Carolyn had told the sergeant that they were going to be in the Fourth of July parade. Since most of the officers would be supervising the traffic and parade route, they told Marilyn that Adele could sit and stew in jail and talk to her lawyer. The police had a guard posted at Bruce's hospital door. He wasn't in serious condition, having only a clean wound to the shoulder. He could have killed himself. There was prison in his future.

The family stayed up unusually late that night recounting the day's events, and because of their frightening experience, none of them slept very well. Marilyn was puzzled. How did she end up in the Wallace's household in the first place? Was there a woman and man out there somewhere who were her real parents?

Chapter Eighteen

Independence Day

Marilyn woke up with an ugly bruise on her arm but otherwise felt the best she had felt in forty-eight years! Adele and Jasper Wallace were not her parents. The police were filing attempted kidnapping charges on the woman she had called her mother for her entire life. What a scare yesterday. But thanks to the kids and Palm Reader, the police were able to come to her rescue.

• • • • •

Rows of people, sitting in lawn chairs or standing, lined the sidewalks of the one-mile parade route stretching from Taylor Park to downtown Dubuque's main square. With Brian's help, the caravan was lined up with Palm Reader hitched in front, waiting patiently. Early that morning Carolyn, Rosa and Marilyn had groomed her from head and tail. She stood proudly holding her head high, looking like a beauty queen.

The five kids were now inside the caravan, its windows open so they could stick their heads out and wave to people. Rosa and Carolyn were going to walk Ouija so that the kids could enjoy the parade together. Marilyn would sit up front next to Bob and share the driving. They all thought she shouldn't be walking after her scare the day before. The truth was, she was so relieved to know she wasn't related to the Wallaces, that she felt like she should be leading the parade, or floating high above it.

Down the street, on the steps in front of the Methodist Church, Brian and Jill sat behind Sister Margaret, who had a folding lawn chair. She had come with Jill and the kids. They were sitting with Brenda and her clan. Sister Margaret had brought everyone small flags to wave as the different groups came along. Brenda's grandkids were having a ball climbing up and down the church steps, until they saw a police car approaching, its lights flashing and sirens sounding in short, intermittent bursts. The parade had begun.

There was quite a contingent of antique cars, marching bands from the high schools and middle schools, a color guard from the Veterans Association, and a group of veterans dressed in uniform. Pete, one of their PTSD clients, was marching with them, grinning and carrying a homemade sign that read *EQUINE THERAPY IS HELPING ME*. Two of Brenda's college-age boys, who were volunteers, started to yell his name and when he spotted them, he saluted.

Everyone was surprised to see a float from the Sisters of St. Francis on the Hill. It was decked out in red, white, and blue, with a big sign proclaiming *People Make Freedom and Democracy Work*. Sister Margaret stood up, waving her small flag, and cheered. They waved back. Mother Superior was driving the truck.

At last, at the end of the parade, behind a group of equestrians with their horses all festooned in red, white, and blue, came Palm Reader with Ouija walking beside her, led by Carolyn and Rosa. Bob and Marilyn had big grins on their faces as they sat in the driver's seat of the caravan, holding a large flag between them. The kids were waving wildly out the windows on either side. At first sight of the caravan pulled by the striking horse, and the enthusiastic kids inside, applause broke out and continued throughout the parade route. People even marched along the sidewalks with them. By the time they reached the end of the parade route, there were crowds of people waiting to see them, the spectacular mare, her foal, and the lovely gypsy caravan.

Jill and Brian accepted a ride in a police car to the beginning of the route to pick up the truck and trailer. Bob stood by the caravan with Carolyn at his side, greeting people, including many of his students who wanted to know all about Palm Reader and Ouija. When they asked what the filly's name was, he said Gypsy. No need to set her off into one of her trances and have to answer questions about her name. The people around the caravan could look inside because Brian had lowered the steps and opened the door. He told the kids to stay inside until they brought the vehicles back.

Connor stood by the door and started to tell the bystanders about his gypsy great-great-grandpa, who had a caravan like this, but had to sell it when he came to the United States from Ireland. And he had a great-great-grandma who was a fortune teller. It was evident the Donovans, their horses and caravan, were a big hit. They could have stayed longer talking to people, but everyone had plans.

Brian helped trailer the horses. Jill and the kids followed in their car. They were going to Brian's folks to celebrate the holiday.

Sister Margaret hitched a ride with her sisters and waved her flag all the way back to St. Francis on the Hill.

Brenda took off with her daughter, son-in-law, and grandkids. They were going to the fireworks by the river and wanted to get a good spot.

•   •   •   •   •

It was 2:00 by the time the Donovans showed up at the police station. They had to take Connor and Annie along too as they had played a big role in apprehending Adele Wallace.

They sat in a tight group in the interview room, Connor on Bob's lap and Annie, fast asleep in ten minutes, on Carolyn's lap. They met a Detective Byrne, who was going to handle the case. He was a short man with curly, brown hair. His calm demeaner gave Marilyn good vibes. Marilyn knew that his investigation meant she would have to tell her whole life story again. She emphasized the fact Adele had said she wasn't her daughter. Early on, the detective realized this was going to be lengthier than his little notebook could accommodate. When he got the gist of things, he asked her one final question.

"Ms. Sewell, where were you born?"

"I have no idea. I'd always thought it was Chicago."

"Well, we will get to the bottom of this. I am going to be interviewing Mrs. Wallace. Her lawyer arrived in town at noon and has been with her since then. Be assured, I am going to be doing a lot of digging."

•   •   •   •   •

On the way home, Marilyn's mind was churning, bouncing back and forth. How had all this happened? Who were her real parents? (Was the detective married? She didn't see a ring.) If she wasn't born in Chicago, where was she born? (Why did she have such an attraction to Detective Byrnes? Who had turned her hormones loose?) How did Jasper Wallace fit into this? How could they pull this off all her life? Why did they even want her in the first place? They never showed any affection for her. (She knew she liked Harold Oaks, he was a great guy, but Detective Byrnes, well, she was very interested.) She could have pondered on questions for a long time, but Carolyn's phone rang.

"Hello?"

"Carolyn, this Nancy Clark." Nancy was her supervisor.

"Hi, Nancy. I am surprised to hear from you on a holiday."

"Yes, well. We're out on the Mississippi on our boat. I think most of the boat owners in Dubuque are here to watch the air show and fireworks. Believe it or not, Judge Rawson is in the boat next to us. He told me Michael's mother is going to be released to her parents on Friday and will be leaving to go to Minnesota with them. They plan to take Michael. We're meeting in court with them and the foster parents and Michael on Friday at 10:00 A.M. His secretary was supposed to contact me tomorrow, but seeing me on the river, he decided to give me the heads up. Anyway, since you are so close, I thought you would want to give the Jacobs advanced notice.

Carolyn's stomach felt sick. Tears came unbidden to her eyes. That beautiful little boy, who was so talented and loved, living, and learning with the Jacobs, was going to be released to his drug-ravished mother and never-seen-before grandparents. What about the child endangerment charge? Basically, he would be leaving security and caring for what? Sometimes, she hated her job. Everyone was going to be devastated.

"Carolyn? Are you there?"

"Yes, Nancy. I am just crushed. Michael couldn't be in a better place right now."

"I know. You said as much. That's the pits with this job."

"But Nance, what happened to the child endangerment charge?"

"Looks like they will transfer that to Minnesota to process since, legally, Michael will be residing there in the grandparents' care."

"I just wonder how much care that will be? They haven't been in any hurry to get him."

"Yeah, I know. But I do have some good news."

"Well, I could use a dose of that."

"It seems I can get more work done out on the river than in the office. Judge Rawson also informed me that all the paperwork had gone through. If the Jacobs are willing to adopt Pedro and Silvia, the gates are wide open."

"Nancy, can you image how the Jacobs will receive those clashing pieces of news? It will tear their hearts in two!"

Now fully in tears, she excused herself and hung up the phone.

"Mommy, why are you crying?" Annie asked her.

They pulled into their driveway. Bob looked at her with concern. She unbuckled Annie from her car seat, lifted her in her arms and started to sob. "I am very sad." She looked at Bob and mouthed, "Later."

• • • • •

Late that night after watching the fireworks from one of the best seats on the hill, their front porch, and with Annie and Connor tucked in bed, Carolyn, Bob, Marilyn, and Rosa gathered in the living room. Carolyn told them about the phone call from her supervisor. It had been a difficult evening for Carolyn, getting through supper and the long wait until 10:00 when the fireworks started, then oohing and aahing with everyone, all the while trying to keep a smile on her face. Tomorrow, after she talked to Jill and Brian, and they had talked to Michael, Carolyn would tell Connor and Annie.

"It's crazy," Carolyn said, looking up at Bob, who had her securely tucked under his arm. "How can one day be filled with so many emotions? This morning I was so proud of us; you and Connor building the caravan, Mom and I helping to paint and detail it. It's a work of art! And it was so rewarding to see how many people admired it. Vicariously, they were admiring all of us. That's a good feeling, isn't it? We are so lucky.

"The horses looked beautiful and behaved so well. The kids were so excited, and Connor was giving his little gypsy spiel at the back of the caravan. He has your confidence about him, Bob, and your dad's charm. It couldn't have been a more perfect morning. I was on a happy high.

"We've made friends with the police officers who came to our aid yesterday. Everyone is so helpful. Imagine how smart Connor and Annie were yesterday. I'm so grateful and relieved that no one was hurt. Palm Reader even helped! The detective at the police station is very competent and I have no doubt, Mom, that he will be able to get you some resolution. I know you're feeling relieved about that and the fact you no longer have to claim Adele and Jasper Wallace as parents."

Marilyn nodded agreement but didn't say anything because she knew her daughter needed to talk.

"My heart is so heavy, but for the kids' sake, I have to put on a front. This morning I was in the clouds, drifting along on a wave of confidence, satisfaction, and yes, even euphoria. Now, my head is heavy with grief. I can't imagine what it will be like for Jill and Brian. I'll have to tell them that they have the best and worst to face this week."

Chapter Nineteen

Tuesday Morning

Jill awoke feeling sleepy and satisfied. She curled up to Brian. It had been quite a day yesterday with the parade, helping Carolyn and Bob with the horses, then going to Brian's folks for a picnic with all the aunts, uncles, cousins. What a lot of fun.

That afternoon was spent playing baseball in the field next to the house, where Brian's dad had just cut the hay and, for good measure, trimmed the baselines with the riding lawn mower. Pedro was in seventh heaven. He was a natural. But everyone played. It was a mixture of guys and girls, young and old. Even Michael surprised himself by hitting a ball that rolled down the third base line. He was so shocked that he just stood there watching, as if to say, "Isn't that interesting?"

Brian, who was playing catcher, picked him up around the waist and ran with him to first base. They beat out the throw because the sister-in-law playing third base "accidentally" dropped the ball and then threw wild to first. Brian set Michael on the ground, slapped him on the backside and yelled, "Run to second, Michael!" which Michael did and was safe, standing there beaming. It was hilarious. All the adults were laughing, and some of the older cousins on the other team were yelling good-natured protests. The next time Michael was up to bat, he told Brian, "I know what to do. You don't have to help." Except, he struck out. All the kids told him it was a good try.

Then his dad and brothers set up a long table next to the grills on the patio. Everyone took salads out of the coolers and placed them on the table with the condiments, paper plates and napkins for the potluck barbecue. They had two grills going. Everyone got their burgers and salads and sat on blankets and lawn chairs to eat. Silvia sat next to his cousin Rachel's girl Jodi. They seemed to hit it off really well. Jodi was showing her how to use a string loop on her hand, tangle it around her fingers, and make it magically slide free. Jill would have to remember to get a piece of heavy string for Silvia to practice with.

When they got home, the kids were all sound asleep. No fireworks for them on the farm. The noise upset the animals and the smoke was a hazard to the air quality. It had been a fun-filled day for all of them.

The kids were going to have to clean up before the library run. It had taken enough effort just getting them moving upstairs, where they got their shoes off and crawled into to bed. Forget brushing teeth. It would probably be slow going in the morning.

It must be about 4:00 now. Jill was too sleepy to open her eyes, but she snuggled closer when Brian turned toward her.

"Hello, Jilly. You awake?" he whispered.

"Yeah, just thinking about the great day yesterday."

"Mmm. That WAS fun. I don't think the kids will ever forget that."

"I don't think I will forget it. Perfect. Life has been so perfect. I like to look for the best, but I am afraid the shoe will drop one of these days."

"Well, it always does eventually. I guess it's life. But until then my little worrywart, it is essential to enjoy!"

"I agree." And they both did.

· · · · ·

Sister Margaret's phone rang at 7:00 A.M. She was relishing a few more minutes in bed before getting dressed for 7:30 early Mass, after which she would tutor her 'man from Iran' at 9:00. It was going to be a busy morning. She sat up and slipped her feet into her slippers, which were lined up on the floor. Then she shuffled over to the phone. Ouch, she was stiff.

"Hello?"

"Hello, Sister Margaret. This is Carolyn . . ."

"Oh, Carolyn. That was so much fun yesterday at the parade. The caravan was such a big hit. I can't decide if it is like a fairy castle or a treasure out of the deep woods of the 'little people.' After I left the parade, I rode up the hill on the back of the sister's float. That was a lark."

"I'm glad you had such a good time, Sister. "I am so sorry to call this early, but I thought you would want to know that Jill and Brian might need your help today. I just found out last night that they have to appear in court with Michael on Friday. Apparently, the grandparents are coming from Minnesota to take his mom and him back with them. They're going to put her in rehab up there."

"Oh, dear! I never thought this would happen. Michael is going to be devastated, not to mention Jill and Brian."

"I know. I haven't told them yet but I'm going over there this morning at 9:15. Mom said she would take Connor and Annie and pick the kids up for the library run. They're also having a juggling program at 10:00. She's going to keep them there for that. Do you think you could go over to see them this morning in case they need support?"

"Oh my. I'm tied up this morning with my 'man from Iran' at 9:00. Do you think it would be okay if I stop in sometime in the afternoon? By the time I get over there the kids would be back. I want her and Brian to have time to work through this. What do you think?"

"You know, that's a good idea. No matter who is there, it is going to crush them."

"This is really a travesty! Carrie, have you seen how that little boy has blossomed since he has been with them?"

"I know, I cried about it last night. I wish there was something we could do."

• • • • •

Brenda knelt next to Sister Margaret in the chapel. "I have to talk to you after Mass, Sister, if you have time," she whispered.

At the end of Mass, they both headed to the dining room for coffee and a quick breakfast.

"You know the crew from the *Today Show* will be arriving this afternoon. Mr. Roker called early this morning. He forgot it was already 8:00 in New York and only 7:00 here."

"His name is Roker? I've been calling him Roku."

Brenda laughed. "That's a device to watch movies and television programs on the TV"

"Oh, I have to remember that. Which one is he again? Roker?"

"That's it. Anyway, he really wants to meet you. He will be out later this afternoon. Do you think you could come to the ETC at about 4:00 if you aren't too busy? He mentioned that he wanted to interview you tomorrow."

"Oh, my. Okay. I'll have to wash my outfit. It's still in the hamper from last Friday."

"Great. Thanks, Sister."

"No problem. Now I have to go tutor. See you at 4:00 in the barn."

As she drove to the Enlightenment Center, her head was filled with a jumble of floating detritus, little boy leaving, foster parents grieving, outfit in hamper, Mr. Roku, casino win . . .."

•   •   •   •   •

At 8:00 the phone rang at Jill and Brian's. It was Carolyn.

"Hi, Carolyn. Are Connor and Annie excited about seeing the juggling show this morning? I sure am. I know Pedro is going to want to do flaming torches next!"

"That's why I called, Jill. Mom is going to be ushering the kids in at the show this morning to help out the staff. She said she would be happy to take all the kids, help them find their books and then bring them home after the show."

"That's really nice of her. I was looking forward to the show too."

"Jill, I was hoping I could talk to you and Brian when all the kids are gone. I have something good and something sad to tell you. Mom said she could pick the kids up at 9:00. Can I come over about 9:15, please?"

"Well, of course. What is it?"

"I'll tell you when I get there, okay?"

• • • • •

What an enjoyable time Sister Margaret had working with her 'man from Iran.' It helped take her mind off the morning call from Carrie. They had discussed the nuclear business between Iran and the U.S. She added that to the jumble in her head as she got into the little compact and took off. Next thing she knew, she was pulling into the casino lot. She put the car in park and removed the keys. She craved a retreat badly. Reaching into her pantsuit pocket she felt the folded bill.

• • • • •

Marilyn was right on time. Jill had put on her actress mode so that she wouldn't spread her worry among the kids who were talking with such animation about going to the library and seeing the juggling show. They had been moving slowly earlier, so she told them that they could just put on some clean socks. They were still dressed in yesterday's clothes. She would change the sheets this morning while they were gone. Most of the dirt from yesterday's activities was probably spread on the beds. It would give her something to do after she talked to Carolyn. She had a feeling it wasn't good news. She always liked to work when she dealt with bad news.

When the kids left, with her chest feeling constricted and her stomach in knots, she sat in a chair and waited. She and Brian were waiting at the kitchen table when Carrie rapped on the door and walked in from the back porch. Jill stood up and noticed the look on Carolyn's face.

"I'll get you some coffee, Carolyn. You sit down." Brian got up and went over to the coffeepot.

"Thanks, Brian. But I already had some earlier. Please come sit down with us."

"What is it, Carolyn?"

"Well, I have two items of news. The first is wonderful. You and Brian have been approved for adoption. If you choose and they are willing, Silvia and Pedro are yours."

Jill and Brian both stood up to hug each other. "That is awesome! Thank you, Carrie!"

"Well, I am glad you are happy. I know Silvia and Pedro will be excited to hear this."

Then, in unison, Jill and Brian asked, "But what about Michael?"

"That is the sad part—for all of us. I talked with Judge Rawson this morning before stopping by. This is the situation. Joan is in rehab now but in an awful state of depression. She still faces the charge of child endangerment, but the court is willing to drop it because her parents have agreed to come and get her and have committed to placing her in a program in Minnesota. They have also agreed to take Michael and care for him in Minnesota. I haven't met the parents. They didn't show up when she was arrested, or when she was in rehab. Judge Rawson had a call from Social Services in Minneapolis last Friday. They told him the Smiths would be coming on Friday of this week. That's all I know."

"But, what are they like? Will Michael like them? Do they even know him? Why didn't they come sooner? If they are taking care of Michael's mom, how will they have time for Michael? Are they old? Or are they young and working?"

"Hold on a minute, Jill. I don't know the answer to those questions. The Judge wanted them to come sooner, but they said they had some business to take care of. I'm sure that will all come out on Friday."

Brian spoke up. "So then, is there hope for Michael and for us? We love that kid! We would take him in a minute."

"Well, I would like to think so. But Judge Rawson is usually of the opinion that kids should be with family. We'll just have to wait and see."

"We are his family!" Jill told Carolyn helplessly.

They decided before Carolyn left that they would wait until evening to tell Michael what was happening. No sense in spoiling his whole day.

"I just knew the other shoe was going to drop!"

"Jill, please don't talk like that. Now we need to be positive. What if we make a plea to the Judge, letting him know that we will adopt Michael. This fostering business is nuts! We fall in love with these kids, and now they want to give Michael away to grandparents that didn't even show up for him until almost six weeks after his mom had the crash with him!"

"Now, Brian, YOU are getting upset. You never get upset. We both need to think this through calmly. I like your idea. If that's all we can do legally, then we will do it!"

•　　•　　•　　•　　•

Sister Margaret squared her shoulders and pushed the handicapped button for the casino doors. The regular doors were heavy. Ah, the sounds, the well-circulated air with a heavy hint of stale cigarette smoke, the muffled dings and songs of a potluck of colorful games, and that thick, thick, carpet. She felt like she was home.

She would not sit down by the Mermaid machine. She wasn't here to win. She was here to play and to veg out, let her mind go into space. Things would work out. She sat in front of Cleopatra and inserted her $10 bill.

"Thank you for coming," a soft, sexy voice welcomed her.

"You're welcome," she mimicked back like Jill would do and then smiled.

She hadn't been seated for more than a couple of minutes getting into the groove when a tall gentleman with slightly greying brown hair sat next to her. He was dressed in light khakis and an attractive blue polo shirt. Not the look of the usual casino goer. He had a notebook in his hand.

"Good morning. This is my first time at casino. I was wondering if you could show me how these machines work?"

"You mean how they take away our money?" Sister grinned at him.

"Oh, I already know that. You see, I am an undercover author. I am writing a book on why people gravitate to slot machines."

"Oh, so you want to look like you are just hanging out so you can get inside information? Do you have a real job? I spotted you right away for a spy."

"That's what I like about elderly people. There is a lot of wisdom and savvy in their heads." He pulled his hand out of his pocket, handed her his business card, and extended his hand. "Ray Fagan, psychologist, former drug rehab director at a facility in Chicago. Currently looking for a break from the heartbreak. Thus, the book idea."

Sister Margaret shook his hand. "Sister Margaret Sorenson." She dug into her pocket for the last of her rather wrinkled cards. She would have to see about getting more if this kept up.

"Sister. Even better. Could I interview you?"

"No, thank you. But I will show you how to operate that machine."

He pulled a dollar bill out of his pocket.

"Okay. Insert the bill into this slot." He did so.

"Now. Chose how many lines you want to bet. That machine is 1,5,10,15, or 20." She pointed that out on the keys. He chose 10 lines.

Now, these bottom buttons are multipliers. You can push the 1 and you bet 10 cents, 2 and you bet 20 cents, and so on. Got it." He indicated he was going to press the 10.

"Wait!" He heard the panic in her voice. "That means you are betting $1.00!"

"Right."

"Then you will have nothing left!"

"Or I will win a lot more." He grinned at her, his finger lingering over the 10. "Tell you what, if I win more than $10.00 will you let me interview you?"

Sister Margaret looked uncertain. "Ten dollars or more? Okay. But I have a condition too."

"What is that?"

"That you're available to me for a little drug rehab idea I have floating in my head."

"Are you on drugs? God, I hope you aren't a dealer!" He winked, and his eyes crinkled as he smiled.

"No, not me, someone else is in trouble." Now she had a very clear idea. Where did that come from? Coming to the casino sure had been good to her lately.

"So, as I understand it, if I win more than $10.00, I can interview you? And if I lose the money, I will help you?"

"No, whether you win or lose, you will help me."

"Fair enough. Okay. Ready?" She nodded. He pushed the ten times multiplier. She grimaced as she watched. Then, as if in slow motion there appeared, a wild horse, a cactus, a wild horse, a wild horse, and a wild horse. DING! DING! DING! Three hundred dollars and a twenty-five-spin bonus.

Sister Margaret sat with her jaw hanging to her collar bone. Ryan Fagan started to laugh heartily. He was pumping his fist in the air and whooping, making a real spectacle of himself.

"I see why you like to play slots now." They watched, enthralled as the money kept adding up. The casino workers began to show up because of all the commotion and the music of horses stampeding to the William Tell Overture. They thought it was kind of unusual that Sister Margaret was sitting there beside a big winner. She had just won a bundle a couple of weeks before, and of course they recognized her. She immediately withdrew her money from the machine to be safe. Winning once was bad enough. Twice would be over the top!

Ray was still laughing and joking with the casino workers telling them how the little nun was showing him how it was done. Sister Margaret's face turned hot.

When they led him off to do the taxes, he turned to her and said, "Don't take off now. You owe me an interview."

"You have my card. Give me a call at the convent. I have to get to 1:00 lunch." And she was feeling guilty that she had forgotten all about Jill and Brian and Michael's problems.

• • • • •

Marilyn had just gotten the kids all buckled into the car when her phone rang. When she answered, it was Detective Byrnes from the police department asking her if she could come to his office in the afternoon. He had some very important news for her. They arranged a time and she took the Jacob kids home. Jill looked fine and was interested to know all about the juggling.

During lunch at Carolyn and Bob's, she told them that Detective Byrnes wanted her to come to the police station. Rosa offered to stay with the kids, so Carrie and Bob could go with her. Carolyn was sure glad she had taken the week off. Marilyn was in an emotional whirlpool.

Chapter Twenty

Tuesday Afternoon

Jill and Brian had decided not to say anything to Michael about living with his grandparents and his mother in Minnesota. It was three days until Friday.

"Who knows," Brian had said. Maybe something will come up before then." Meanwhile, they decided to enjoy the kids as much as possible. Jill didn't want to do anything before consulting Sister Margaret. Both she and Brian thought they should wait to tell Silvia and Pedro they wanted to adopt them until after they knew Michael's fate. Their hearts were aching for their little family.

Jill was on a cleaning rampage. She did that when faced with a problem she was unsure how to solve. Brian had taken the kids with him in the truck to pick up some parts he had ordered for the tractor. They should be back shortly.

When Sister Margaret walked in Jill dropped her mop and ran to her, tears running down her face.

"Jill, Jill, just take a deep breath. It is going to be okay. You don't have to shoulder this alone. It's going to work out. I have an idea."

With those last words, a smidgeon of hope lodged itself in Jill's heart.

"Now, honey. This is what you do. Don't tell Michael yet. Give me a day or so to make some inquiries. There might be a way that Michael can stay with you. Promise me you will do your best to keep a happy face. This is a day to be cherished. Michael is with you. Make the most of it and trust in God." And hope he leads me in the right direction, she thought!

By the time Sister Margaret left, wondering why she always got herself into these predicaments, Jill had pulled herself together. When the kids returned the family decided to take a walk out to watch the technicians set-up for the *Today Show* before Jill left for work. The camera crew had arrived.

· · · · ·

Brenda and Harold had put the horses out to pasture to graze and find some shade before the 2:00 session began.

"Brenda, would you like to run to Hardees before the afternoon volunteers and clients arrive?"

"Yeah, good idea. It will have to be quick though because the *Today Show* people are arriving to set up this afternoon. And of course, we have twelve more clients who have never been here before, and a new group of volunteers. Harold, I am so happy that you are giving so much time to help us start out on the right footing."

They walked out to his truck and he opened the door for her.

"I am the one who should be thanking you. I am rather lost without Lucy. This is helping me stay on an even keel. And I am enjoying the work." He closed the truck door and went around the other side.

They had a quick lunch during which he asked her something that really surprised her. "How did you become so smart in so many areas?"

She laughed, "You mean scatter-brained?"

"No, I mean smart."

· · · · ·

The police station was quiet when Marilyn, Carrie, and Bob arrived and rapped gently on Detective W. Byrne's door. His office consisted of a rather sparse space, all its walls lined with four drawer file cabinets with color coded labels. There was a scuffed old desk topped with a thick piece of glass, an in/out stacker, a mug with pens and pencils, and a manila folder in the center. Nothing extraneous.

The detective stood up immediately and laid down the document he was reading. "Come in please and have a seat." He motioned to the two chairs sitting in the small space between the desk and the door, and then excused himself for a moment returning with a folding chair for Bob.

He pulled his suit jacket off the back of his chair and slipped it on. Marilyn's mind immediately started to wander. He was a good-looking man and had a nice comforting attitude. He made her feel safe. And maybe a bit interested? Face it, a lot interested.

"Can I get you a bottle of water? Or a soda?" he offered

They all thanked him and said they were fine. Marilyn was on pins and needles, wondering what he was going to tell them. He sat back down, opened a desk drawer, and pulled out a cassette player that had a tape in it. He plugged it into the outlet behind him.

"Ms. Sewell, we got a rather lengthy statement from Adele Wallace this morning with her lawyer present. It's all on tape and transcribed in this folder. The transcriptionist has made an extra copy for you. However, I'd like you to listen to the tape. I think you will be surprised, and maybe very relieved. I was flabbergasted."

He pressed the play button.

> WB: Ms. Wallace. Would you please tell me why you told Marilyn Sewell that she wasn't your daughter?
>
> AW: Well, she isn't and that is a long story.
>
> WB: Go on.
>
> AW: We needed an heir, okay? Jasper was climbing quickly up the banking ladder. We are in the upper Chicago society, you know. There are expectations to

live up to. Well, neither of us were too keen about a kid and couldn't seem to conceive anyway, so we had tests and it turned out that Jasper's sperm just didn't have what it took. Know what I mean? We had gone to Lansing, so in case either of us was the problem, no one in Chicago would know.

WB: Go on.

AW: Well, it just happened that Jasper was in Ohio on business at the time the call came, so I took it.

I got to thinking that I really wasn't crazy about losing my figure by having a baby. It would probably curtail my entertainment activities if I were pregnant. I mean, the clothes you must wear! No matter the money you spend, that mound in the front ruins the look. Know what I mean?

What if I was one of those women that puked all the time and was tired. I wasn't too sorry that he didn't have it in him.

So, I devised a plan and when Jasper came back from Idaho, I had it all figured out. It was November, the perfect time. I hate Chicago winters. He bought into my plan because he didn't really want to go through the ordeal of me being sick and getting fatter and fatter. It would kind of hamper the sex, you know what I mean?

WB: And what was the plan?

AW: Actually, it worked brilliantly. I padded my bra to look a little engorged and spent a week each morning, faking vomiting in the bathroom. I began calling friends to say that we were going south for the winter because the weather just got me down. During that time, we made plans to rent a place in Texas along the coast for the winter. I would stay there during the workweek, and Jasper would fly down to meet me on weekends. We were there by Thanksgiving. Jasper stayed a week while we set everything up. I hired a gal to check out homes for unwed mothers in the largest cities, so we could adopt. It had to be a white baby. Money can buy a lot of silence. We didn't want the stigma of an adoption. We wanted this baby to be seen as ours. All our other friends were having babies. It was a brilliant plan, having a baby without the bother and pain.

Well, Jasper was down for two weeks at Christmas and we had a blast. I was keeping a kind of low profile, so we flew to Mexico, tanned on the beach, and drank piña coladas in the pool. When we returned, we called the gal from Dallas; she had found a white woman who swore the baby would be white. We paid this gal off and sent our lawyer to take care of all the legal matters. Confidentiality, you know?

WB: Did you ever meet the mother?

AW: No, of course not. After Christmas, we returned to Brownsville. Jasper went back to work and told everyone the good news that I was already five months pregnant but was having some difficulty and supposed to stay off my feet. You should have heard the phone ringing off the hook with friends and relatives offering congratulations. I almost felt guilty for sitting by the pool every day with my margarita. You know what I mean?

A few of my friends wanted to come to keep me company. That was the only glitch. But I told the one who was really persistent that it would help us out if she would line up three of the best nannies in the Chicago area to begin working for us at the end of March when the baby was born. She was a very particular person and would interview and give me reports. My own mother and Jasper's were easy, thank God! I set them to the task of organizing a nursery. That kept them occupied.

WB: And no one else ever suspected?

AW: Listen, Jasper and I were a good team. He would work long hours and try to get a three-day weekend at least twice every month. His bosses were so sympathetic about me having to be alone. We were willing to go through all the play acting and decided at the time that one kid would be enough.

When Jasper came, we partied long and hard! Tried to spend the weekend in San Antonio or Austin. It was hardest on me. The shopping wasn't too great in Brownsville. No Macy's. The boutiques were so-so. I missed the busy social life in Chicago, the Valentine fund raiser, the St. Patrick's Day parade and gala. But I told my friends that this baby was so important; I had to take good care of myself. I told them how much I liked my doctor; he said things would be fine if I just took it easy.

WB: When was the baby born?

AW: Well, actually, she was born a week earlier than we expected. I called Jasper and he flew down to pick me up. Then we went to Dallas. I had forgotten to even ask about the baby when the contact called. We had our legal man in Dallas take care of the adoption papers. When we got there, we found out it was a girl. We were both disappointed, just kind of expected it would be a boy, but they didn't have any boys that we could nego-tiate for. In the long run, it didn't matter. We had a baby.

Although I was a little worried because she looked a bit red and shriveled, she turned out to be quite a beauty.

WB: Did you meet the mother?

AW: No, I didn't want to know who she was or anything about her. This was our baby. We paid for her. It didn't matter to me who made her as long as she had all her fingers and toes and wasn't retarded or handicapped or anything like that.

When we got home, the nannies, all three of them, were there to greet us and await orders. I think everyone was surprised at how good I looked. Our mothers had decked out the nursery in neutral colors and had enough clothes bought to get us through three years of life! Everyone was so excited.

It didn't take us long to learn that babies are really intrusive. Even with nannies, we often heard crying. I couldn't stand it.

April was really cold so Jasper and I were able to get away for a three-day weekend in the Caribbean. Let me tell you, good nannies make for easy mothering. Of course, the "grandmothers" weren't around much after the first viewing. After that, I tried to be out of the house as much as possible.

Marilyn and Carrie sat dumbfounded as Detective Byrnes leaned over to turn off the cassette player. He didn't speak.

Finally, Marilyn spoke. "Twisted."

"My thoughts exactly, Ms. Sewell."

"Please, call me Marilyn, Detective. I feel you know my life story better than I do."

"Walter." He smiled at her. "So, you are adopted. It was done legally, if sneakily. With some more prodding we should be able to trace the agency in Dallas and perhaps find the mother. That will be your call. But there is more. Do you want to hear it?"

"Yes. Let's hear everything she has to say."

Detective Byrnes pushed the play button.

> WB: Do you have anything more to say Ms. Wallace.
>
> AW: Yes, I just want to say that Marilyn has never been grateful to me for all that I did for her. She had the best nannies, the best schools, the best clothing. We sent her to Switzerland to go to school. I primed her for marrying many young men of means. She rejected all of them. Then she goes and gets pregnant. I send her to a home for unwed mothers. She sneaks off with the baby after I had told her to give it up. Then she disappears, and I end up paying for PIs for almost thirty years trying to find her!
>
> After she disappeared, I didn't have a story any more. That was humiliating. My friends started falling by the wayside. I also blame her for breaking up my marriage because she caused me to put us into debt, the ungrateful child!
>
> WB: Ms. Wallace, she is not a child. She is a mother and a grandmother, a very good one it seems. Did you help her with her homework? Did you go to her school conferences? Did you comfort her when she was ill? Did she hire the nannies, choose the schools, ask for the clothing, want you to select men for her to marry? Did she get pregnant or was she raped? It seems to me that she had no choices in these matters. She was of age to leave and to find her own life.

Marilyn smiled, hearing the controlled anger in Walter's voice.

AW: We paid for everything. She just faded into the woodwork. It was the biggest mistake of our lives to adopt her. If it wasn't for her, Jasper and I would still be together.

WB: Who is Dale Scarlone?

AW: Scum. Jasper's step-brother.

WB: Is it true you sent him to pick up Marilyn after she had her baby.

AW: Well, he came around and offered.

WB: You said he was 'scum.' What did you mean by that?

AW: Well, he had some run-ins with the law.

WB: And you sent him to pick up your daughter? Did Marilyn tell you he raped her?

AW: Well, yes. But I am sure she got pregnant in Switzerland.

WB: We can check that out with blood and DNA tests. Do you know the whereabouts of Dale Scarlone?

AW: Last I heard, he was involved with the mafia in New Jersey. We want nothing to do with him.

Detective Byrnes turned off the tape.

"We still have Ms. Wallace in custody. Since she has been charged with attempted kidnapping, any bail assigned, will be high. There will be a court date set up. Until then, I will have to listen to the jail personnel complain about her complaining. She doesn't like the jail outfit she has to wear." He grinned and turned his face away, but not before Marilyn noticed it.

"Walter, what about Dale Scarlone?"

"We have feelers out and should be hearing something today. I'll call you when that happens. In the meantime, this is the transcript of the interview."

Carolyn spoke up. "Mom, I don't care who your birth mother was. She had to be better than that witch on the tape. I have never known anyone so self-centered, so blasé about a child's life, so un-caring. I'm happy that you don't have to connect yourself to Adele Wallace any-more."

• • • • •

When Brenda and Harold arrived back to the ETC the Today crew was already setting up a large tent-like structure and unpacking cameras and other equipment. Brian and the kids were helping. That Brian was everywhere you needed him.

"Thank you, Brian. Thanks, kids. Glad you were here when the crew arrived."

She walked over to one of the guys and introduced herself and Harold to the men. "Is there anything we can do for you now?"

"Not quite yet. You have people coming in at 2:00, right?"

"Yes, from 2:00 to 6:00."

"Well, I am looking at the light. It will be ideal to film at that time. If you don't mind, we will just get as much footage as possible. Al plans to do the live interview tomorrow morning. It won't last more than fif-teen minutes. I have a note here that they will be interviewing you, Ms. Schmidt, and Sister Margaret Sorenson. Do you think everyone can be here tomorrow? I know Sister can. And Dr. Oaks? how about you? Would you be willing to say a few words about the horses, if there is more air time to fill?"

"Sure."

"Great."

Chapter Twenty-One

Tuesday Evening

Jill was so relieved that she was off work on Tuesdays. She didn't think she would have been able to work. Supper was a buzz of conversation back and forth with the kids who were explaining all the activity that went into setting up for the *Today Show*.

"Mom," Michael said. Ah, that sounded so good, and so sad at the same time. "You should have seen the cool tent house they set up to protect the equipment."

"Show her, Michael," Silvia said. "You sketched it in your notebook."

Michael left the table to get the notebook. It occurred to Jill that perhaps she should be teaching him to ask to be excused. That wasn't the priority now. He came back carrying his sketch pad with a very accurate depiction of the scene.

"Brian, did you see this? We have to get Michael some instruction. He has talent."

Michael beamed. Brian looked at her wistfully. "That would be an excellent idea. Your pictures are outstanding, Michael. I bet one of the sisters who has some artistic talent could give you some pointers."

"That's right! Sister Mona broke her hip and is in nursing care. She would love to see what you can do. She used to be an art teacher! I'll take you over with me tomorrow when I go to work. You can take your book to show her."

"My fingers and eyes just seem to know where to go," Michael told them bashfully.

Jill's high note faded in her heart as she realized that they needed to tell Michael. They would do it tomorrow afternoon.

"Listen up," Brian said to the kids. "Tomorrow morning we have to get up early so I can set up the produce stand. The sisters are going to start bringing their veggies about 7:30. We'll need you three up by the raised beds so that when they get their boxes of produce arranged, you can help them carry it to the booth. Now you're going to have to cross the road, but one of the sisters will be out with a stop sign to direct traffic. You wait until she tells you it is safe to cross. Both ways." He looked at Pedro. "That means you too, speedy."

Pedro grinned.

"Hey, kids, let's help Mom clean up the kitchen and go outside. I'll set up the volleyball net with the tree and the porch pole and we can have a game."

"But, Dad, can we use the beach ball?" Michael asked.

"Michael," Pedro said. "You have to learn some day to use the correct ball."

"I know, but I am only going to be seven and that volleyball is hard and heavy for my age." He was going to be seven. That's right. In August he would be seven and he wouldn't be with them. Jill, picked up some plates and turned to head to the sink. A tear was dripping from her eye.

"Okay. Then I guess we can use the beach ball until you are seven," Pedro agreed. "And I think it should be Mom and me against Dad, Michael, and Silvia."

•   •   •   •   •

After supper, Bob and Carolyn sat at the kitchen table. Kevin had returned at 3:00 from Arlington. Rosa and he decided to take in a movie as they rarely had time by themselves during racing season. Bob told him about a remodeled theatre that was supposed to be top of the line and might be fun to check out. They thought they would give it a try and then would go out for supper to make a night of it.

Bob was working on his curriculum. It was coming along well. It seemed that one idea always led to another. Carolyn was checking over some of the plans he had, like getting all the kids to know about the ETC.

"Gee, Bob. I would like to take this course. The part on the abuse of the horses selected for the Pony Express is really interesting. And the fact that they were half wild. Also, all the hands-on things the kids can do is something that will really stick with them. They have so many options." She flipped through more pages.

"This section on HORSES HAVE ORIGINS TOO is really a clever way for kids to learn their geography of the world. It can also get them thinking about their own origins and interconnectedness." She filed that thought to be conjured up later.

"Oh, and I like the idea for the anatomy. That is such a good way to remember. Did the saddlery place actually offer their big plastic horse in front of the store to visit the school?"

"Yes, Shadow can come to school for anatomy class. They also said they would bring equipment in a truck and talk to the kids about all the tack used to keep a horse outfitted and groomed."

It was nice having Carrie to himself. Marilyn and the kids had gone out to ride Palm Reader and play with Ouija.

"Carrie, that was some meeting with Detective Byrnes this afternoon. How bizarre."

"I know, the lengths Adele Wallace went through to fake her pregnancy. Mom is actually so relieved that she is adopted. Wasn't it pathetic to listen to that woman? She is so self-centered and was really abusive to Mom in the fact that, even though she gave her everything that money could buy, she didn't give her any attention or affection. Same with her husband. They were so wrapped up in each other and their social status. Funny now that he is divorcing her."

"And the way Adele sluffed off the fact that your mom was raped? Like it was nothing."

"She was sure that Mom was pregnant when she came home from school in Switzerland. Give me a break."

"What about this Dale Scarlone? He might be dangerous."

"Remember? Detective Byrnes said that last known, he was somewhere in New Jersey and had some connection to the mafia. He'll call when he has something more. To think I have to call him my biological father." Carolyn shuttered.

She had no more than said that then they heard a car on the gravel driveway. Carolyn got up to look out the window.

She turned to Bob. "It's him. Detective Byrnes. I wonder why he didn't just call."

● ● ● ● ●

At 7:00 in the evening, Margaret answered the phone to recognize the voice of Ray Fagan.

"Sister Margaret, it is so nice to talk to you. Our meeting has given me a block buster opening for my book on the attraction of gambling. I want to take you out to dinner. I am $5,000 richer than I was this morning."

"What took you so long to call? I have been waiting seven hours."

"Oh, sorry, Sister Margaret. I didn't know there was a hurry."

"Well, I lost the bet. I want to pay you with an interview like we agreed. And I will. But I have something more important to talk about. This is a matter of time and people's lives."

"Okay, Sister. Do you want to get a bite to eat and we can talk?"

"Well, I ate with the 5:00 group. I missed lunch because I had some other things to do. Can you come over to my place?"

"Yes, what time?"

"Can you come tonight?"

"Are you sure it isn't too late?"

"As long as you come now and I can get to bed by 9:00."

"Nine o'clock. It isn't even dark yet on these summer nights."

"Well, Mr. Fagan, when you get to be ninety-two you might be in bed by 9:00 too." And then she realized she was being a bit controlling. "By the way, if you are hungry, I can raid the fridge in the kitchen and you can have something when you get here. Sorry I didn't think about that before."

"No need Sister. I'll get something before I go back to the motel. I'll be over in twenty minutes. I'm staying at the Motel 6 on Highway 20."

"You can be here in fifteen minutes at this time of night."

He chuckled. "You sure are anxious to see me."

"Yes, I think you may be God sent and I don't want him to have to wait."

· · · · ·

Walter Byrnes got out of his car and looked around. This was a beautiful place, a bit isolated. It was two blocks from the park road. But very open and spacious. Wow! Right above the Mississippi. He had lived in Dubuque most of his life and didn't know this property was here. It adjoined the park.

As he was checking things out, he heard hooves pounding earth and yelling and laughing. He walked to the end of the five-car garage and around the corner to see Marilyn Sewell on a huge horse, her hands clutching its flowing mane. She was bouncing around on its back and laughing hysterically. The Donovan kids and a little foal were running after her.

"Whoa!" she yelled and the horse slowed and stopped. "That was thrilling!" She told the kids, as she slid down off the horse's back, gained her balance, and started petting the horse and talking to it.

"Grandma, you did really good for your first time," the little girl Annie told her.

"Maybe you went a little fast for the first time," her grandson remarked.

"It was so exhilarating! I have NEVER done anything like that. It was fun!" Just then she noticed Walter Byrnes standing by the fence and her face turned a bright red.

At the same time Walter realized he had business and wasn't there to gawk at an attractive woman, Marilyn's daughter and her husband walked up beside him.

"You should have seen her on the horse," Walter said to them as if she had done something that needed to be recognized.

Marilyn walked over to them, followed by the rest of the contingent. "My legs are still shaking," she was saying. "That was so much fun. My first time."

"Mom, maybe you should do it when Bob or I are out here. You might hurt yourself."

"Carrie, I am reinventing myself to be who I WANT to be now that I know I have no connection to the Wallace's. I'm going to live this life to the fullest! I LOVE riding. I didn't know I loved riding." She spoke with amazement.

"Well, Marilyn," Detective Byrnes said. "Perhaps you should rein in a little for now. I have news on Dale Scarlone." He looked very serious.

"Let's go up to the house," Marilyn told him. We can talk on the back patio if you want. No mosquitos out yet tonight.

"We'll take the kids in to get cleaned up and ready for bed." Carolyn told her mom. Please let us know if you need us."

"I will. Thanks."

Marilyn and Walter sat down by the patio table.

"This is really a beautiful place."

"It is, isn't it? Carolyn and Bob inherited it from a distant cousin of his through his great-great grandfather who was a gypsy in Ireland. An interesting story."

"I'd like to hear it sometime. But I think you will want to know that Adele Wallace was covering up for Dale Scarlone. I talked to Jasper Wallace on the phone. He is so fed up with her. He didn't know that you had told Adele that Dale had raped you. He said that she told him you got pregnant in Switzerland and she had decided to send you to a home for unwed mothers. Since he hadn't had much input in raising you, he just took her word for it. Very uncharacteristic reaction of a father."

"Like you say. He really wasn't much of a father either."

"When I approached Adele about this, she said she was just trying to protect the family name, she thought it might hurt their social status."

"What a disaster of a 'mother' I had."

"At any rate, she never let on to Scarlone that she suspected he really HAD raped you. Actually, she was a bit afraid of him. And she was afraid when he showed up and wanted to pick you up from the home for unwed mothers. She was afraid to say no. So, she lent him the chauffeur and the family limo for the task. To her credit, she did call the Home to let them know they would be coming for you."

"Can you believe that?"

"No, I can't, but it seems that woman will do to anything to protect her 'status.' It baffles me why Scarlone wanted anything to do with you. He must have meant you harm, didn't want you to go to the police. He and the chauffer were jailed in Davenport when they were picked up for dangerous driving and fleeing from a police officer. Scarlone was carrying a gun without an Iowa permit. They were sentenced to six months. Apparently, he was determined to find you, but you had done a good job of disappearing. I guess you had practice."

"Practice and a lot of help."

"Well, he told Adele she should hire an investigator to find you. He didn't have money himself because Jasper, had cut him off when he was picked up by the cops. Your mother said this exactly. 'I thought it was a good idea to keep up appearances.' And then she said that after twenty-eight years of trying to satisfy Scarlone's obsession with finding you, she had spent a fortune. By then Jasper was involved with his 'bimbo.' Her word. Jasper is suing her for a divorce. Dale Scarlone has been letting Adele Wallace do his stalking of you all these years."

Marilyn was speechless.

"Marilyn, Adele Wallace will be going to jail. The incident on your property will put both her and the chauffeur behind bars for a while. Now we have to worry about Dale Scarlone stalking you."

•　•　•　•　•

She was right. It did take only fifteen minutes to get to the convent where Sister Margaret lived. It was about 7:30 when Ray parked at the new building and walked in through the main door. Sister Margaret was standing there waiting for him with an 'I told you so' look on her face. She invited him to sit in a large deserted lounge area with comfortable chairs.

"Sister, I can't tell you how happy I am that you taught me how to gamble."

"Stop teasing me, Mr. Fagan. I have some heavy stuff on my mind that I need to talk to you about."

"I'm listening," he said as he made himself comfortable in a well-padded wing chair in the lounge. "Can you please call me, Ray, Sister. 'Mr.' sounds so strange."

"All right, Ray. I have a problem. It has to do with a precious and talented six-year-old boy named Michael. His mom was high on drugs and had him in the car in the middle of the night when she had an accident. He is okay. He was bruised up a bit but perfectly healed. My friends, the Jacobs, are fostering him. His mom has been in the police station since the accident and charged with child endangerment. She is also in rehab. On Friday they will release her to be taken to Minnesota to live with her parents and continue treatment there.

"The thing is that the grandparents never once came to visit her or ask after Michael. The one visit Michael had with his mother was reported as non-fulfilling, no physical contact between mother and son, and no communication attempted on the mother's part."

"Poor kid. Unfortunately, there are a lot of poor kids in this world. Mom sounds like she is in deep."

"Exactly. So, if you want to know, I was at the casino to figure out what I could do for Michael and the Jacobs who love him dearly. I go to the casino to decompress. It works a miracle on my over-taxed mind, untangles my entanglements and helps me help others. You can write that down."

"Well, I have never even considered that angle. I am getting really excited about my research, but totally bummed about your little guy. That sounds like a very depressing situation for him."

"Yes, well, let me tell you my plan and see if you can help me out. As a little extra incentive for your help, I can tell you quite a story of how the casino has changed many people's lives for the better."

"Sounds interesting, lay it on me." And she did.

Chapter Twenty-Two

Wednesday

The sun was inching up behind the barn casting an early morning light across the field, the hillside still in shadow by 4:30 A.M. Four horses stood quietly in the pasture waiting for their big television debut.

Many others were up early in preparation for the big day. That didn't mean they had slept well.

The night before, Marilyn and Walter had sat together in the kitchen to update Bob and Carolyn, as well as Kevin and Rosa, on Marilyn's continuing saga with the Wallace and Scarlone factors. Walter said they might be in danger, the whole family. He already had a plainclothesman stationed by the property entry and one camped out in the trees along the public road.

"Bob and Carolyn, I feel so badly that I have put you and your children in danger. I had no idea that looking into my life would have played out like this." Marilyn apologized to the family.

"Well, be assured that I am taking the 'better safe than sorry' attitude," Walter told them.

"We appreciate that.," Marilyn smiled at him.

"Mom, nothing that is happening is your fault. It was bound to come out sometime." Carolyn gave her mother a hug.

Marilyn turned to detective Byrnes. "What should we do now, Walter." She liked using his name.

"Well, things should be fine for tonight. If you don't mind, I would like to stay here at your house, just to make sure I'm close if I should get a call from one of the guys. Tomorrow, Marilyn tells me, you had planned to be at St. Francis on the Hill to help out with the produce and see the taping of the *Today Show*."

"That's right," Bob said. "Do you think that is dangerous?"

"No, that will work out. We don't want to alarm anyone. I have guys over there tomorrow anyway patrolling traffic. They'll have a picture of Scarlone and will be warned to be on the lookout. I'll be there too with you, Marilyn. I think you should warn your friends, the ones with the children? Jacobs?" He looked toward Marilyn. She nodded.

"Another thing," Walter addressed Carolyn and Bob. "I assume your horses are valuable, right?"

"Well, they're like family to us," Carolyn told him.

Walter, pulled out his phone. "Then I am going to get another officer up here while we are gone tomorrow to keep an eye on the horses and your property, Mr. Donovan."

"Thank you. I appreciate that. It still doesn't solve the problem, though, does it?"

"No, but they're working on it in my office."

Another sleepless night ensued at the Donovans.

They insisted that Walter Byrnes have a blanket and pillow and stretch out on the couch. He accepted graciously but spent the time in touch with his men and surveying the view from the window that overlooked the garage where the horses were being kept inside tonight, even though in the summer, they were used to being outside in the field. He also called in the plans for protecting the convent and the taping of the *Today Show* activities. It was unlikely that a man like Scarlone would do anything at a big event, but they had to cover all possibilities.

News came through during the night that Scarlone was on the move, last seen in Chicago two days ago. He would know about Mrs. Wallace's arrest. Things were bound to start happening soon. He would update Marilyn and the Donovans in the morning. Bob's folks could be with Annie and Connor at all times. Walter would be with Marilyn and Bob wouldn't let Carolyn out of his sight. But Bob was supposed to work with a client tomorrow, and then Carolyn would need someone to watch out for her. He laid awake getting all his bases covered.

• • • • •

Brian and Jill were already stirring in anticipation for a busy day ahead but were grieving about talking with Michael. They had decided that no time was a good time to inform him that his grandparents were coming for him and his mother. The excitement of the new produce stand and the television stars coming to film this morning, instead of a way to mask the inevitable, sat more like an exaggerated heartbeat marching toward finality.

Jill woke up with an upset stomach, not her usual excitement to greet the day.

"You want to sleep a bit longer, Jilly?" Brian asked her as he slipped into his work clothes to go out to bring the horses in from the field.

"No, honey," she said smiling. "I am putting on my happy face for everyone. This will work out. I know it will. Sister Margaret is on it. She has come through for us before. But I think we need to let the kids know what is going on. They're our family. Maybe at lunch time?"

He bent over to kiss her smiling face, then sat next to her on the bed, pulling her into his arms. "Did I ever tell you how special you are?"

"Oh, you have, and it always makes me feel so good. You make me feel good. The smile is real now, Brian. I'm filled with hope and thankful for this day."

"I'll put the coffee on before I go out."

"Thanks! Breakfast will be ready at 6:00. Brenda said the sisters will be out by 7:00. Bob and Carolyn will have their kids over to help too. She told me yesterday that Kevin and Rosa are coming along with her mom. We'll make this the best time ever! The kids will be distracted with the produce stand and won't even know something is amiss."

Brenda was so excited she couldn't sleep. Al Roker had showed up last night and given her and Harold a copy of questions they might be asked for the interview this morning. It turned out that Roker would be doing the weather report from Dubuque, Iowa. The other stars would be hosting in New York, so they would be volleying back and forth. Giving an interview so early in the morning was a little off Brenda's schedule. But actually, her schedule was changing to fit into this busy lifestyle she led. She found herself ready to go to bed at night as soon as it got dark.

After tossing and turning until 5:00 she decided to get up and dressed. She put on the coffee pot she kept in her apartment so she could get a jolt or two before going out to the barn. Brian was going to get the horses in, settled and fed.

At 6:00 the phone rang.

"Hope I didn't wake you. This is Harold."

"Are you kidding. I couldn't sleep. I am dressed and ready to go. I've been stewing over the questions for the interview. The sisters have everything lined up for the produce stand and Bob and Brian are going to work with them. We have the clients and volunteers all scheduled. Mother Superior has asked for some more police presence to handle the traffic of sightseers and getting them to stand behind the rail fencing so that they don't get in the way. Whew! So much to think of. I have become a list maker and that is helping me. Oops! Sorry, Harold. Are you still there? I was spewing at the mouth. I do that when I am nervous. How are you?"

"Well, excited. Can I come over? Will the sisters feed me breakfast?"

"Oh, please! Angel will be at the main door of the new building. Just tell her to give me a call. See you soon!" There was a smile in her voice. She sounded like a co-ed in college.

Harold was grinning and shaking his head as he hung up the phone. That Brenda was a talker. But she filled up his empty spaces. She was interesting and interested at the same time.

•   •   •   •   •

Sister Margaret couldn't sleep. She really liked Ray Fagan, even though he was a terrible tease. He reminded her of a fifth grader she had taught many years ago. The kid was a charmer but was such a distraction, and so witty. But she needed to talk to Mother Superior first thing this morning. She had a plan that might temporarily keep Michael with Jill and Brian. Ray was willing to help. What were the odds that she would sit next to a drug rehab expert at the casino? He was really excited about his book. They had actually stayed up past her bedtime talking about what people saw in pushing little buttons and losing money.

She didn't know what she had started here but life was non-stop. It had all begun at the casino, she told him. She didn't know how long she could keep it up. It sure was simpler when she got up, went to Mass, interviewed her sisters, or went to tutor her 'man from Iran,' and then the hour at the casino, a nap in the afternoon, typing up stories…Like she told Ray, her life was so full to overflowing, she had a hard time keeping up with things. He was coming over to the taping today to be introduced to her extended family. She would be happy for them to meet him.

Her phone rang at 6:30. It was Marilyn.

"Sister, I have some disturbing news." Margaret listened quietly getting more and more alarmed.

"Thank you for calling, Marilyn. We needed to know this. I am glad you already talked to Brian. I'll go see Mother Superior to let her know that there will be police protection here. And Brenda, like you say, I'll tell them not to panic and go on as usual. Are you're sure this Detective Byrnes can be trusted?"

"Oh yes, Sister," she gushed.

Sister held the phone away from her ear with a quizzical look on her face. Marilyn sounded almost like some of those infatuated teens. Now what?

Things were sure changing around the convent. Mother had even changed Mass time to 11:00 so all the sisters, working in their various capacities, could be helping with the produce and at the ETC.

•   •   •   •   •

Bob and Carolyn got up early to let the horses out and get the kids up. Detective Byrnes had communicated the latest to them. He saw the Donovan parents, grandparents, and children safely in their cars and then, with Marilyn accompanying him, led the three-car caravan off the property for the ten-minute drive to Saint Francis on the Hill. They arrived to find a police officer standing in a reflective vest at the bottom of the drive. He stopped them and greeted the detective.

"Good morning. Welcome to St. Francis on the Hill. The *Today Show* is taping this morning so we are asking all viewers to stand behind the fence to the right of the barn. You can park along the road, in front of the two buildings or in the field out back. There is a produce stand ahead on the left. The sisters will be donating proceeds to the ETC project today. Your help is appreciated. Please drive carefully."

"Good job, Davis. That's exactly what I wanted. That will give you time to check the cars as they come through. After the Donovans' cars behind us get through, ask all the others to park out here on the main road and walk in, unless they have their ETC ID. Those people will need to drive up for their sessions. Also, if they have a handicapped sticker, you had better let them through. Most wouldn't be able to make the hill."

"You got it, boss."

He pulled ahead and noticed the produce stand.

"That's Brian with one of the sisters and Silvia, his daughter."

"Where are the boys?" he asked Marilyn.

"Probably out getting produce to carry down. Oh, look. Here they come. My goodness."

Surrounding two proud looking young boys carrying plastic crates of produce were five elderly sisters, scanning the area around them. A sister sitting on a lawn chair across the street stood up and stepped out into the street in front of Detective Byrne's car, which he had already stopped. She was wearing a reflective vest and holding a STOP sign, almost as big as she was.

The procession crossed the street.

"Silvia! Pedro! Michael! We'll be right there!" Connor was yelling out of the car window behind them.

The sisters ushered the children under the produce tent where they tenderly began to arrange their radishes, lettuces, green beans, peppers, chard, spinach, and kale in an artful display. Brian and the boys waved as they headed back to get more produce, crossing the street in front of Sister 'Stop Sign.'

Detective Byrnes and the Donovans parked in reserved spaces right out front of the main chapel. Connor was about to take off to meet his friends until his dad took him by the shoulder and told him to wait.

"But, Dad…"

"I know. You can go help but take Annie and stay with Grandma and Grandpa. Mom and I will be out here helping the sisters. I see Jill and Silvia are there too."

"Okay, Daddy." Bob noticed that Marilyn went with Detective Byrnes, who was walking around back to meet up with his other men. He had his walkie talkie.

People were beginning to arrive. They were walking up the hill even though there was still plenty of parking. The officer had followed directions well. It seemed everyone was stopping at the booth asking directions to the filming area and inevitably, leaving with neatly packed bags of produce and smiles on their faces knowing they had gotten a bargain in freshly picked greens and happy to leave a donation behind for it.

Silvia was showing Annie how to sort the money from the donation can into the correct slots of a metal cash box. Mother Superior stopped by but not Sister Margaret. She was first up to talk and it was almost time for the live taping to begin.

Brian and the others came back to the stand twice. Each time a contingent of sisters swapped places with the ones at the stand. It was just like an army doing maneuvers. They were all having a good time except Sister 'Stop Sign' who complained that they didn't wait for her to hold up her sign, even though few cars were being let in.

At 7:50, Detective Byrnes came by with Marilyn to suggest that they should go watch the live taping. He had everything checked out and police presence so he was confident all would be well. Ten sisters took over the stand saying they would watch the taping on the computer later. Bob went to meet his first client as he was scheduled to do the 8:00 session. He made sure Carolyn was with his folks and the kids.

• • • • •

Al Roker, being a meteorologist, started the taping with a large weather board of the United States. It did amazing things to show what was happening all over the USA. Sister Margaret got to thinking that if teachers had something like that when she was teaching, the kids would have been very smart!

She was dressed in her only special outfit, red top, white skirt with the big red poppies. Good thing it was washable. Her long-sleeved top felt good this early in the morning. It looked just as good as it did the day they did the opening of the ETC. She, on the other hand, looked a little nervous and tired.

Brenda had bought a cute top with sparkles to dress up her jeans. Harold was wearing cowboy boots and a nice clean new Stetson. He really looked the part of a horseman.

All three of them thought the interview went really well. It turned out that Harold had a good sense of humor and a really good broadcasting voice. He didn't mind answering questions as he had been around the operation since its inception five days earlier. Only five days.

That was hard to believe. Brenda thought they did a good job telling how important it was that they had well-trained volunteers who were paired up with people they could help the most. She mentioned that they would have another volunteer training session in August and hoped that if there were people in the area who hadn't heard of them yet, that they would sign up.

As a volunteer, Harold told how he was a retired vet and worked with the horses. He said it was so fulfilling to see the connections that their clients made with the animals and the therapist volunteers. He also wanted to stress that the four horses were rescue animals and it was amazing that even *they* seemed proud of the work they were doing.

Sister Margaret emphasized how the Equine Therapy Center was providing a service for people with physical, mental, social, and emotional problems. They also stressed that they were completely non-profit and relied on donations to keep the program going. Before she gave up the microphone she mentioned:

"We would also like to invite the visitors to St. Francis on the Hill to be sure to stop at our produce stand on the way out to get your fresh veggies right out of the garden this morning, if you haven't already."

And then it was over. Al Roker thanked them. The program was switched back to New York. He seemed to be in no big hurry and invited Sister Margaret to sit for a while. They watched the crew breaking down the set around them, packing the equipment into a van, and heading down the drive. Al told Sister that yesterday afternoon they had gotten a lot of footage of clients and volunteers in action. That would be airing now on the TV

Ray Fagan walked over and Sister introduced him to Al. Ray had the gift of gab and had them all laughing.

Bob came over to see Sister Margaret and meet Al Roker when he finished with his session. She also introduced him to Ray.

"Bob, this fine man is Mr. Roker. Mr. Roker, my talented friend, Bob Donovan." They shook hands as Sister also introduced him to Ray. "Ray is a new friend I am becoming very fond of, Bob." Then she asked him, "Well, how was your first volunteer session?'

"I really enjoyed this, Sister. My client was a former horseman. He lost a leg in Afghanistan and is also suffering from PTSD. He wants to come to see the Gypsy Vanner horses and is interested in the curriculum I am developing."

Annie and Connor and Carolyn joined them. Sister Margaret introduced Ray and said that they would be seeing more of him around the place. Carolyn looked at Bob knowingly, another person in trouble. Bob offered to take Al to the airport to catch his 12:00 flight to Chicago. Al took him up on the offer.

The trip to the airport was filled with conversation. Al wanted to see Palm Reader and Ouija and thought some of the plans Bob shared for the Curriculum he was developing were fascinating. And he was so curious about the little girl who told him that horses talked to her. Her brother backed up her assertion. In fact, he thought that might make a good show some day. Carolyn was pleasant but quiet.

• • • • •

Brenda was so glad this was over. Now she could get back to the regular work. She planned to work with at least one client a day in the ETC and to watch that all went well. She would also fill in if someone couldn't make a session they were assigned for. On top of that, she was itching to continue researching greenhouses, keep up with the big garden, and make this produce business a twice weekly option. Then there would be harvesting, canning, washing, and carding wool, perhaps a pumpkin patch for area schools…All this went through her mind when Harold walked up looking so fine in his duds.

"Harold, you are one handsome retired guy!" she smiled at him.

"Thank you, ma'am. Don't suppose you have time to grab a bite to eat?"

"I think I need that." Before they could get into the car, Sister Margaret walked up with a new fellow, Ray Fagan. "Ray is a new friend and he'll want to talk to you tomorrow sometime, Brenda."

"Sure. What time?"

"Whatever is good for you." They made arrangements. Brenda gave Sister a hug and kiss on the top of her head and watched as she trundled off holding onto Ray Fagan's arm.

"What do you suppose is going on there?" Brenda speculated.

• • • • •

Dale Scarlone sat in a cheap motel in a Chicago suburb watching the *Today Show*. He'd just gotten off the phone with Adele Wallace. She was in jail. Good. What the hell was she doing calling him from jail on his private cell number! Marilyn had evaded him for almost thirty years! At least he knew where she was. As long as she was alive, he knew he could be implicated. Damn DNA business.

• • • • •

Walter and Marilyn drove back to the house. Kevin and Rosa followed them because they had to be on the road to Louisville. They had said goodbye to their son and daughter-in-law and grandchildren who had taken Al Roker to the airport.

It wasn't more than a few minutes when Walter's phone dinged in a text.

"Marilyn, will you read that please."

She picked his cell phone up from the console of the car and read, "Adele Wallace called this number from the jail phone: 1-578-378-2476. We think it was Scarlone. She addressed him as Dale."

She was still holding the phone when it rang. She handed it to him. He listened. "Good. We can take it from here." He pushed the button and laid it back on the council as they pulled into the driveway.

"That was Chicago PD. Scarlone just checked out of a Motel 8. He is probably on his way to Dubuque now. That would be about three and a half hours. We have to get set up. Let's go in and get Bob on the phone. They should be on their way back from the airport in half an hour or so. We'll get his parents on the road. It will be much better the fewer people that are here if Scarlone shows up. You can be sure we'll take good care of your family." He looked at Marilyn with confidence.

They helped Kevin and Rosa load their bags into the truck.

"Marilyn," Rosa said to her as she climbed in beside Kevin. "Please call us as soon as you know anything. We won't be easy until that man is behind bars."

Marilyn gave her a hug and promised she would call to keep them updated. "I trust the police to watch out for us."

It was never easy for a parent to drive away from danger, but there wasn't much they could do.

● ● ● ● ●

Wednesday afternoon, Jill and Brian decided that they couldn't wait any longer to talk to Michael and decided to include Silvia and Pedro also in the conversation. The kids sat down for lunch, excited about their busy morning with the produce stand, watching the taping, and helping Brian and Jill take down the portable stand and store it in the garage out back.

"Did you see how bossy Sister Stop Sign was?" Pedro asked Michael. "She even made us stop when there were no cars coming!"

"Pedro," Michael told him. "She was just trying to do a good job because she didn't want anyone to get hurt."

"Yeah, but, bro, I mean, come on!" Pedro protested but realized Michael was right.

Jill listened as she opened a couple cans of soup. "Pedro," she said. "Her name is Sister Honoria."

"Nobody told me." Then he tried to redeem himself. "That Ray Fagan guy Sister introduced us to was really funny. He knows some good knock, knock jokes. Hey, Dad. Knock, knock."

"Who's there?"

"Cows go"

"Cows go who?"

"Cows go moo not who."

"Very clever," Brian grinned.

At that point, the kids began to repeat them, trying to decide which one they liked best. They had all liked the man.

Silvia set the table, the boys carried over the fixings for sandwiches and some bananas. It would be a light meal. She had taken a lasagna out of the freezer for this evening. She would have to work tonight and decided she would take Michael with her for an hour or so to introduce him to Sister Mona. She was immobilized with a broken hip but loved to look at her art books and would enjoy seeing Michael's sketches.

Jill was counting on Sister Margaret to come through on Friday. She said she was working on a plan. Jill wondered if Ray Fagan was a part of it. That woman got things done. And she was such a sweetheart.

During the meal, Brian brought up the subject they both had been dreading, because he knew how emotional Jill got, especially lately, now that she was a mother.

"Kids, Mom and I have some news we want to talk to you about. We think you all should know. First of all, and this is very exciting news. We received word that we were granted permission to adopt you, Silvia and Pedro. That is, if you want to be our children legally."

Before he had the words out of his mouth, they were high fiving each other and Michael, who looked really happy for them. Then they started to hug Jill and Brian.

"Can we call John and Martha?" Pedro asked.

"Yes, you can call them this afternoon."

"What about me, Dad?" Michael asked him hopefully.

"Okay. Michael, that is the part I am not happy to talk with you about because we can't adopt you yet."

"Michael, your real mom is getting help with her drug problem. In fact, your grandma and grandpa are coming on Friday from Minnesota to take her back with them. They want to take you too. But I want to tell you right away, that Sister Margaret is working on a plan so that you can stay with us." She just had to say that when she saw the devastated look on his face. "We're going to try very hard to make it work because the five of us are family now, and we don't want to ever break us up!"

She started to cry. Brian stood up to pull her into his arms.

"Sorry, sorry," she said. She smiled through her tears and motioned to the other kids to come to them. They had one big hug with Michael in the middle.

"Don't worry, bro. We'll take care of it," Pedro told him with certainty.

"You're our brother, Michael. We love you. You;re a good boy," Silvia told him.

•　•　•　•　•

In the lounge, Sister Margaret sat down in the chair across from Ray Fagan.

"Ray, I can't thank you enough for consenting to do this for us. It was really exceptionally fine of you. And you'll talk to everyone tomorrow?"

"No, problem. I have to repay my casino mentor in some way. I have already found a little place across the road so you're handy to interview. I met this elderly couple who have a basement in their condo that I can use. Then when they go south this winter for four months, I can have the whole place for free, just to watch it, shovel snow, salt the sidewalks, etc. It will be great for writing."

"That sounds good. Now if you don't mind, I am going to put my feet up. Get out your notebook or tape recorder. I am going to tell you a story."

•　•　•　•　•

Bob, Carolyn, and the kids dropped Al Roker off at the airport and turned right back around having gotten Marilyn's call. Carolyn also called Bob's parents who were on the road south to assure them that they would be careful and would let them know what happened.

Detective Byrnes suggested that Carolyn and the children should perhaps stay with at the Jacob's house in the afternoon until they got things sorted out. Carolyn called Jill.

"Of course. Come over, Carrie." And then she whispered, "We told them. I sure hope Sister Margaret comes through with her plan."

Carolyn's phone rang, "This car has become an office," Bob commented.

"Carolyn, its Sister Margaret. Is there any way you can stop by sometime this afternoon?"

"Yes, Sister. The kids and I are going over to Jill and Brian's. They told Michael. He's one worried little boy. Also, we had news that Scarlone is on his way to Dubuque. We want to keep the kids away from the house."

Annie and Connor looked at each other. What was going on.

"Oh, my. So much happening. Let me know if something comes up that you can't make it, okay?"

"As long as I am connected to my phone, it will be okay." She hoped. What did people do before phones? It seemed that she lived with one in her hand some days.

· · · · ·

Carolyn knew Jill was feeling good about having Connor and Annie over. The kids had gone outside and were playing in the yard and going to collect eggs before the 2:00 session started at ETC.

She walked over to the convent and greeted Angel, who buzzed for Sister Margaret. She called on the phone from her room and asked Angel to direct Carolyn down the right hallway. When she reached the door, Sister Margaret had it open and was peeking out. She gave her a hello and a hug.

"Come in and sit down. I am going to call Michael's grandparents in Minnesota. I got their number from Nancy in your office. She knows me from the adoption board and said it was okay. as long as I didn't make any waves."

"What are you going to say?"

"Well, that is why I asked you to come. I want you to listen. Don't say anything in case it makes a difference. Just listen and tell me what you think."

"Okay." She didn't know if she could just listen but she did.

Sister Margaret sat down in her recliner. "Hello, Mr. Smith?"

"Yeah."

"This is Sister Margaret from St. Francis on the Hill in Dubuque."

"Wait a minute. Stacy!" he yelled. Margaret had the phone on speaker and jerked it away from her ear.

"Hello," said a tentative voice.

"Mrs. Smith. This is Sister Margaret from St. Francis on the Hill in Dubuque."

"What do you want?"

"Well, I just want to tell you what a happy little boy Michael is with his foster parents, the Jacobs. You must be so proud of him. He is such a great lad."

"I wouldn't know."

"Oh, he was probably a toddler when you met him. He is going into second grade now."

"Is he?"

"Yes." No response. Then…

"So why did you call?"

"Well, I am friends of the Jacobs, Michael's foster parents? All of us who know Michael want only the best for your daughter and her son."

"She has always been a bitch, wimpy child, moody teen. We weren't sad when she left. Can't say I was surprised to hear last year that she had a kid and needed help."

"Oh, so you haven't met Michael."

"No, she didn't even send a picture. We told her she was the one who got herself in trouble, she could get herself out of it."

"You did? Mrs. Smith, would you be offended if I said that we have a plan here in Dubuque to help your daughter and to take care of Michael?"

"I would say, go for it. Then we don't have to make that long trip and listen to each other bitching." And she hung up the phone.

•   •   •   •   •

Carolyn came back into the house smiling at Jill and the kids. Jill, was all dressed for work and had Michael in tow with his sketch pad under his arm and a sharp pencil behind his ear.

"Where's Brian?" She asked.

"Don't worry. He'll be right here."

"Call him and tell him I will stay with the kids if you want. I can't go home until I hear from Bob."

"Oh, thanks, Carolyn. That would be great. He is working on some project for Brenda."

She gave Brian a call, hugged each and every kid, and then with Michael in hand, headed to the kitchen door. Carolyn stopped her and whispered into her ear. "I think things will be okay."

Jill and Michael walked up the steps to the second floor a little before her shift started. At room 202 they stopped. Jill knocked on the door and a pleasant voice said, "Come in."

The room was hung with beautiful works of art of all manner of genres, *The Girl with a Pearl Earring* by Vermeer, *Forrest of Beech Trees* by Guztav Klimt, *Sunflowers* by Van Gough, *Spring Flowers* by Norman Rockwell. There were others too.

"Hi, Sister Mona."

"Jill, dear. I missed you last night."

"My day off, Sister. I brought someone to meet you. This is, Michael."

"Hello Michael"

"Hello Sister Mona." Michael was enthralled with the artwork hanging on the walls. Everything was so different. But it was all really good. He was especially interested in a small painting that was taped to the closet door. It showed a boy and a horse and was not in pencil or paint but crayons.

"Did you paint those?" Michael asked her. "My mom said you are an artist."

"I didn't paint those. They're copies from artists I like." She pointed to the closet. "But I did that crayon one on the closet door. Do you like horses, Michael?"

"Yes, I do. I like to sketch them."

"Sister Mona, I don't want to tax your energy, but if you and Michael would like to visit for a bit, I have to clock in and get to work."

"I would love to visit with Michael and talk art." She smiled at the boy.

Jill looked at Michael. "Okay?"

"Sure, Mom." Ah, she loved to hear that word. She felt things would turn out all right.

"Sister, if you get tired, just tell Michael. He can turn on your call light and I'll come to get him. Otherwise, I will stop in at 4:00 to send him home."

"Absolutely. Come here, Michael. Let's see what you brought."

Michael stepped up to her bed and opened his sketch book to show her a drawing he had done of Brenda's horses grazing in the pasture.

Sister Mona gazed at the page. "Now I like this," she said. "You have a really good eye for filling the space. And your picture isn't flat. You are making shadows that gives your work depth. That is the good thing about working with pencil." She pointed to a large art book on the table. "Have you ever seen any artwork done by other artists in pencil?"

He shook his head.

"Open that book to page 48. That section is dedicated to pencil art."

Michael was quiet turning page after page, drinking in the beauty. After a while, Sister Mona said, "Someday, Michael, you will be in a book like this. God gave you a great gift to see things in their entirety and to capture them on paper. I would love to sketch with you."

"I'll ask my mom." He smiled at her. They looked at the art hanging on the wall and he told her what he liked about each one.

"I don't have anything in charcoal. Turn to page 102 in that book. You can see what that looks like."

"What is charcoal? Is it what Dad uses on the grill?" And the conversation continued until Jill showed up an hour later to check on him.

"Michael, Dad is coming over to meet you. He has supper on and Annie and Connor and Carolyn are staying."

"Okay, Mom. Sister Mona, do you want me to put this book back on the table?"

"Yes, please, Michael. And come over any time. I'll be here for a while and sure enjoyed talking with you about art. Next time, I'll get out my sketch book and we can draw."

"Great!" He tucked his book under his arm and followed Jill to the door. She stopped to look back over her shoulder at the grinning nun. They both mouthed 'thank you' at the same time.

• • • • •

When Brian walked in with Michael, Carolyn told him that Bob had just called and said it was all clear to come home. Scarlone was at a small motel, and they had surveillance at both entrances. Walter had gotten a search warrant and they were going to take him in for questioning.

Chapter Twenty-Three

Thursday

Everyone was sound asleep when Jill got in from work. After showering she climbed into bed trying not to wake Brian. That man was so hard working and so patient with the kids. She had read in the *Guinness Book of Records* that the record for the longest marriage was eighty-six years. The man was one hundred and six years old when he died. She would happily stay with Brian that long. He understood her so well. She was so hopeful that Michael would remain with them. Oh, how she wished that they could adopt him, but she would be just as happy if he could stay with them forever.

Brian moved to put his arm over her stomach. She rolled over to face him. and he wrapped her securely and pulled her close.

"I'm glad I woke up. I was supposed to tell you something," he mumbled.

She quieted his mumbling mouth with a kiss. "Was it that," she asked?

"That I love you, I think? Or was it something else?"

"I'm sure it was the first and the second probably."

"Oh, yes. Sister Margaret called tonight to say that she and her friend Ray would like to come over for a bit in the morning. Have you met him yet?"

"Yesterday. He was at the taping. Seems like a nice guy. Sister really likes him."

"Yeah, I met him too. He has a good handshake. And he's kind of laid back."

"I wonder why they want to come over?"

"I don't know but Sister did say it was part of her plan for Michael."

"Then I am all for it? What time?"

"After breakfast, 8:30. It's going to rain so I plan work on the tractor and the lawn mower."

"Have any plans for now?"

"Why, Jill. I am sure I can think of some."

"Good, because I have a few of my own!"

•　　•　　•　　•　　•

Bob and Carrie were having a serious conversation. They had gone to bed late after talking with Marilyn. Walter had called her earlier to say that they had Dale Scarlone in custody. He was carrying without an Iowa permit, so they could hold him for a while. He would have to get a lawyer.

Marilyn had made the decision that since almost thirty years had passed since the rape, that she could leave it go. She didn't want her family to be involved in anything messy, especially because of Connor and Annie, who were too young to understand. They didn't have to worry about Scarlone for now, and hopefully never. He and Adele were in adjoining cells driving each other nuts. Walter thought he would probably find out a lot more by morning. He also had mentioned that Marilyn could have a *no-contact* order put out against him if he was ever on the loose again.

"I'm worried about you, Carrie," Bob said to her after Marilyn went to bed. "You haven't said much, being as busy as we have been. But, I know you. These things bother you. You are wondering what part of you is your father."

"You're right. I've been thinking about it a lot. One thing that I am happy about though, is that Mom seems okay with things. She trusts

Walter when he says that all is going to be okay. I think she has accepted that what happened, is over, and perhaps now she won't have to worry anymore about Scarlone showing up again. Although it worries me that a man can be obsessed with a woman for that long. Unless he is behind bars, I won't feel safe.

"But you know, Bob, I think Mom is interested in Walter. The attraction seems mutual. Did you pick up on that? It's something I've never seen happen to her before. She has always steered clear of friendships with men."

"I've noticed that too. It would be great if she had someone she could share her life with. She's really a wonderful woman, Carrie, and she had a terrible upbringing. I admire her for how well she took care of you and managed her life in hiding."

"Thank you, Bob. I know she feels that and appreciates it."

"And what about you? How do you feel about a man, your father, who raped your mother?" Carolyn liked the fact that Bob always said it as it was. There was no going around and around.

"I feel diminished. Knowing that your dad raped your mom isn't the best thing to think about."

"No, I don't imagine it is. Does it help any if I say to concentrate on what you do have, a husband who has known you for almost ten years and thinks you have such a caring heart and a giving personality, not to mention that you are beautiful and everything he has ever hoped for?"

"I am feeling a lot better." She smiled at him.

"Well, take this into consideration too. We have produced two healthy, happy children who show signs of being very good assets to humanity, and who are bright and interested in life."

"They are outstanding children. My heart is feeling lighter. Keep talking."

"You have a mother who is brave and who brought you up to be independent and to make the proper choices in life...like an awesome husband."

"You got that right on all accounts."

"Need more?"

"I wouldn't mind."

"You're great at your job and make a difference in the lives of so many people. You are important."

"Ah, I think that is enough. I feel my head swelling."

"I have another thing I want to say. You are not only my life partner, you are my business partner and my sounding board. I would be so much less without you in my life, Carrie."

"Bob, thank you. I am going to let go of my past now. I am what you say. That isn't to brag, but a statement of gratitude. Having you keeps me balanced. If there is a heaven, it is with you, and the kids, and the relatives, and all of our friends. And I am so grateful for our good mentor, Sister Margaret. She has enriched our lives so much, getting us involved with the Jill, Brian, and Brenda, and helping with the ETC."

"What about that Ray Fagan? She has just picked him up. I like him. He seems very genuine and light-hearted. I wonder what her plan is for him,"

"I just met him briefly," she responded with curiosity. "Yes, why is he hanging around with our feisty little nun?"

"I think we might find out tomorrow. They're coming over at 10:30. Ray texted me before bed. Sister has some things to discuss he said. They were hoping all of us would be here."

"I bet it has to do with little, Michael. Did I tell you that Sister called the grandparents? She really laid it on about how great Michael is. You should have heard the Smiths, Bob. They absolutely cannot abide their daughter and have never met Michael! It was so sad. And Joan, that's Michael's mom, is just so damaged."

"So, are the grandparents coming?"

"Don't know. They just said they didn't think it was worth it if things were going so good here. If that judge rules that Michael goes, it will be the worst. But I have faith in him. He is a reasonable man.

And, I'm going to give him an earful, if I need to. But we don't want it to come to that in front of Michael."

• • • • •

Brenda woke up to the sound of rain plopping on her window. She checked her phone. Seven. There was a text from Brian. HORSES IN BARN. READY FOR INDOOR WORK. That guy was always a step ahead of the game. This rain was coming at just the right time for a lot of their produce. She texted her thanks.

There was another text. It was from her oldest daughter. They were on the day shift now and since Jenny had some extra time at night, she was hoping to volunteer at the ETC. She missed working with the horses. Eric was good for watching the kids one night if she could be with them on his poker night with the guys. Well, that was cool. She texted: YOU WILL BE GREAT! I'LL LET YOU KNOW WHEN THE NEXT VOLUNTEER TRAINING SESSION IS.

Another text! At this rate she would be late for work. Actually, this was all work related. This one was from Ray Fagan. Nice guy! New friend of Sister. Wonder if she found him in the casino too, she thought. Sister must have given Ray her number. BRENDA, SISTER MARGARET WOULD LIKE TO MEET WITH YOU AT 9:30 IN THE LOUNGE. CAN YOU DO IT? RAY FAGAN.

YES, she texted back. Sister Margaret. She was a wonder. Had she hired Ray as her secretary? Usually she was the one directing traffic. It was uncanny that she made you feel like you were the center of her universe. I love that woman, she thought.

Brenda was just about to get dressed when her phone actually rang. She smiled. Harold. They just got along so well.

"Good morning, Harold."

"Good morning Brenda. Did I wake you?"

"No, I have just been clearing off some messages. What's up?"

"Well, if you're interested, I just heard on the radio that the Dubuque Brass band is playing at Eagle Point tonight at 7:00. I was wondering if you wanted to go check it out if the rain ever stops."

"Absolutely. They are good. And LOUD!"

"Great. I'll pick you up at 6:30 if that is okay. The Lounge?"

"Sure. Enjoy your day off."

"Actually, I'll miss working at the ETC but I do have a good book to read that Bob loaned me. I might just prop up my feet in the recliner and get started, unless I fall asleep.

She laughed. "Well good luck. I'll see you tonight! I wanted to discuss an idea for a greenhouse that I came across in an environmental magazine. But I won't start now because I know I will run off at the mouth! See you later."

A date. Made at 7:10 in the morning. She shook her head and smiled.

•   •   •   •   •

Brian, Jill, and the kids had finished breakfast and cleared off the table. Silvia was washing the bowls and silverware. Michael and Pedro were drying. They were waiting for Sister Margaret and her friend, Ray Fagan. "I think they want to talk about court tomorrow, Michael," Brian told him.

"Well, Silvia and I are coming with you, Michael. You're our brother."

"Of course, you are," Jill said. "We'll go as a whole family."

"Here they are!" Michael shouted hearing the bang of the screen door. His dad had fixed it so it didn't squeak any more. It just banged. He ran to the kitchen door to open it.

"Good morning, Michael," Sister Margaret said. "This is my friend, Ray."

"Nice to meet you," Michael said holding out his hand for Ray to shake.

"Knock, knock!" Ray was grinning.

"Who's there?" All three kids sang out in a chorus.

"Ketchup."

"Ketchup who?" They responded

"Ketchup with me and I'll tell you!"

"That's a good one," Pedro told him as he and Silvia lined up to shake his hand.

The older children took Sister Margaret by the hand and led her to the recliner where she usually sat when she visited. Michael went ahead to get the afghan that she sometimes liked to wrap around herself when the air conditioning was too cool. Although the air wasn't on, it was a chilly, rainy morning.

Brian and Jill shook hands with Ray and led him into the living room. The three adults sat on the long couch across from Sister Margaret. The kids sat on the rug in front of the adults facing Sister.

"I feel like I am looking at the peanut gallery!" She was laughing.

"We're really curious, Sister Margaret," Brian said.

"Well, let's get right to it," Sister said. "Michael, you know your mom, Joan, is very sick, right?"

He nodded his head.

"And you know that your grandparents have offered to take care of her and you, right?"

He nodded again looking distressed.

"Well, perhaps that isn't the best idea. Now, my friend Ray here is helping me with a plan I have. I think your mom needs protection and care to help her get better, but we need your help Michael, and Pedro and Silvia's, and your mom and dad's help too. Listen to what our friend Ray has to say. We think you all can help."

•　•　•　•　•

Brenda came in out of the rain, her umbrella dripping on the rug outside the main door. Even though the weather was wet, all the clients and volunteers had shown up this morning. Marilyn was keeping everything running smoothly. If someone cancelled, she filled in the space with someone else. Maybe Brenda should set her up with a little office of her own. She would have to talk to her. She went inside and greeted Angel.

"Hi, Angel. Is Sister Margaret here yet?

"No, but Ray just called to say they would be right up. They are at the Jacobs but he had the car so Sister won't get wet."

Just then the doors slid open and they walked in. Brenda gave Sister a hug and a kiss on the head.

"Did you meet this guy at the casino, like you met me, Sister," she teased.

Margaret gave her a little push on the arm. "Shush, Brenda. You know that is our secret. And yes, we did. Ray is helping me out with a plan that I hope will help Michael be able to stay with Jill and Brian. Sit down and he'll tell you."

•   •   •   •   •

When Ray and Sister Margaret pulled up to the barnage at 10:30, Annie and Connor were standing on the pavers in the rain wearing their red raincoats and rubber boots, waving wildly. Ray rolled down his window.

"Hi Sister Margaret. Hi, Mr. Ray Fagan. Don't get out yet."

Just as they said that, the garage door opened and Bob came out pulling Annie and Connor's red Radio Flyer wagon, holding a golf umbrella over it.

"Hey, Ray. Help me get Sister into the wagon. We don't want her to slip on the pavers."

"Oh, for heaven's sake! I haven't ridden in a wagon since I was a kid."

"Well, Sister, you get to relive your childhood."

"Don't be afraid, Sister Margaret. Connor and I use it all the time. It's safe. Just put your feet in and hold on."

It was quite a procession. Ray lifted Sister Margaret out of the car with no effort and placed her directly into the wagon that Bob was keeping dry with his huge umbrella. Marilyn and Carolyn were standing under the awning on the patio with big grins on their faces.

"Good thing I didn't wear my good outfit!" Ray was pulling the wagon with Connor and Annie on either side, walking sideways to make sure Sister didn't fall out. Bob was leaning over her with the big umbrella.

"Hello, Carolyn. Hello, Marilyn. Well, this has been quite an interesting arrival." She was laughing as Ray picked her up by the waist and lifted her out of the wagon under the awning. "What a hoot! I hope no one was taking a video to send to *American's Funniest Videos.*"

"Well, Sister. Too bad no one thought of that. You could have won $10,000 dollars for the ETC," Ray told her.

"Oh." She seemed a bit disappointed. "Do you think we could have won?"

They all laughed, including Sister Margaret.

"Come inside. We want you to stay for lunch with us when you finish telling us about your plan, Sister. You always have the best plans," Marilyn said. "Carolyn told us about the call to Minnesota."

All seven of them went into the living room to get the information. They were all in agreement with the plan.

"Let's have lunch," Carolyn invited. Sister and Ray were happy to.

While the ladies set the table and made sandwiches for the lunch, Connor read his new library book to Sister and Annie told her all about Annie Oakley. Bob took Ray out to show him the two horses they were keeping in the barn during the rain, not that weren't hearty enough but because it was a lot of work to get their wet tails and manes untangled.

•   •   •   •   •

After lunch, Jill mentioned to the kids, "Sister Margaret is our special friend, don't you think?"

"Yeah, she's going to try to help me to stay with you and Dad and my brother and sister, Mom."

"And she's going to try to help your other mom too, Michael."

"Yeah, and Mr. Ray is going to help too."

"And do you know," Jill put in. "Sister Margaret helped Dad to get this job on the farm. And she and Carolyn helped Dad and me to get all of you kids because we can't have kids of our own. We love you kids! Sister Margaret has done some incredible things for us."

"I think I should make a special picture to thank her, Mom." Michael ran for his sketch book.

"She'll really like that Michael. I am going to write her a thank you note for Daddy and me."

"Well," said Silvia. "I think we should all write something and put it in a big envelope. But Mom, I'll need some help with spelling."

"Let's all sit here by the table. It's a rainy afternoon, a perfect time to write a thank you."

"I think I can make mine with all different kinds of balls drawn around the edges. Do you think that would be good, Mom?"

"Absolutely. Whatever you do, Sister will appreciate."

• • • • •

When Ray and Sister Margaret returned at 2:00 in the afternoon, Angel Grace had a large envelope for Sister Margaret. Ray walked her to her door because she really looked about ready to wilt. It had been a very good but tiring day for her. The rain didn't help any. She had dozed off on the couch after lunch. Then they gave her another wagon ride out to the car.

"Thank you so much, Ray. I think this plan is a winner."

"My pleasure. We make a good team."

"Indeed, we do. I think I need another nap."

"Okay. I'll pick you up tomorrow morning at 9:30 for the court appearance. Meanwhile, I am going to track down a few more of your sisters and finish this off."

"Thank you for everything, Ray." She gave him her biggest smile as she closed the door. Sister knew that he didn't fully realize how vital he was to her plan yet.

Ray was so happy he had taken a break from the stress of the rehab job in Chicago. With Sister's plan, he would still be able to keep his fingers in his profession but would have the added enjoyment of trying his hand at writing, something he had always thought he might be good at.

*   *   *   *   *

Sister Margaret sat down in her chair and opened the large envelope addressed to her from the Jacobs. The missives brought tears to her eyes.

Sister Margaret is on the Ball. Your friend, Pedro Jacob

Clever Pedro. He was such an athlete. The picture he drew was framed with every kind of ball imaginable. He had learned how to juggle watching it on YouTube with Brian. He was always moving but he took enough time to sit and write this for her

And Silvia. She was a big help to Jill and a good sister to Pedro and Michael. She struggled with school now, but she had a lot of common sense. She loved the note, even with its errors.

Dear Sister Margaret,

Thank you for finding us the best mom and dad. Now we have the most ausom home becuz we have are brother, Michael to!! Luv, Silvia

Jill had written the most beautiful letter. And Brian had signed it. Brian wasn't much for oral communication but what he said was genuine. They were so lovely together. Sister read it over and over.

> *Dear Sister Margaret,*
>
> *There isn't a card or a piece of paper large enough to express our gratitude to you. If you hadn't taken an interest in Brian and me, we might not have our beautiful family, home, and jobs we love. Most importantly, we may never had made your acquaintance. God bless you as we do.*
>
> *Gratitude always! Jill   Brian*

Michael. Michael. Clearly an old soul and open heart. He was talented beyond imagination. Jill said he and Sister Mona talked art now. He had drawn her a picture of a bunny rabbit that looked like it might just jump off the paper.

She just had to see this plan through. It *had* to work. These people deserved it, and Joan Smith deserved it too. She had to hold on. Sister fell asleep happy.

Chapter Twenty-Four

Friday

Judge Rawson did a doubletake when he walked into the courtroom on Friday morning. Besides Joan Smith, the woman charged with child endangerment and drug abuse, who sat at the defendant's table with the county attorney, the courtroom was crowded to overflowing with well-dressed men, women, and children. Lots of children, all spit and polish with shiny clean faces and neat, crisp summer clothes. He checked the docket as everyone sat down, just to make sure that this was the case. He was supposed to release Ms. Smith and her son to the grandparents from Minnesota.

In the front row, behind Ms. Smith sat, two middle-aged people who looked rather dour. Next to them was a very elderly white-haired lady in an impressive red and white outfit. He recognized the woman, the nun from St. Francis on the Hill who had something to do with the Equine Therapy Center. Next to her sat another middle-aged man who looked alert but relaxed, wearing a light summer suit and a neat tie

Behind them was Carolyn Donovan, a well-respected social worker for the county. The handsome dark-haired man next to her had to be her husband. Then it dawned on him that he had met them at the Fourth of July parade on Monday. The slightly older woman, who had to be Carolyn's mother, had been on the driver's seat of the splendid gypsy caravan at the parade. There were two children sitting quietly next to the grandmother. The boy had been giving his own spiel from the back door of the house on wheels, which was a work of art. He had talked to the Donovans after the parade for only a bit because there was such a crush of people.

Next to the nun and her companion, sat a very young couple with three neatly dressed children, one sitting between them and one on either side. Behind them were all kinds of kids with their parents and grandparents. And then there was a group of about twenty older women, neatly attired. He also recognized the woman who worked for the nuns and ran the Equine Therapy Training Center. She was accompanied by an older gentleman who had a Stetson sitting on his knee.

Where was the little boy that was supposed to go with his mother? There were so many kids, it was hard to tell. He banged his gavel to signal the start of the session but there was no need because you could hear a pin drop.

"Joan Smith, will you please stand."

The county attorney whispered to Brian's mother and she stood slowly, obviously terrified.

"Ms. Smith. The county has been in contact with your parents. They have agreed to take you home to Minnesota where they will assume responsibility for you, make sure you finish your drug rehabilitation and will take care of your son Michael until you are able to. Are you aware of this?"

She looked around, rather dazed, spotted her parents and Michael. The country attorney told her to say 'yes.' She nodded her head. He repeated that she should say 'yes.' "Yes," she whispered.

"Will Mr. and Mrs. Smith, the parents please rise?"

Michael's grandparents stood up. Michael, sitting between Jill and Brian, hid his head in his dad's shirt. Brian and Jill both put an arm around him and the another around Pedro and Silvia, who wore worried expressions.

"Mr. and Mrs. Smith, do you agree to take your daughter home and to enroll her into the Minneapolis Rehab Center for treatment, to get her there daily and pay the fee for the rehabilitation?"

"Well, Your Honor. If the court insists," Mr. Smith grumbled out the answer.

"You don't seem too sure of that, Mr. Smith."

"We can do it."

"Thank you. Will Michael Smith please stand up?"

Jill was wondering when Sister would make her move. Both she and Brian stood with Michael tucked between them.

"Hello, Michael. How are you?"

"Frightened, but I trust in Sister Margaret," he spoke out clearly. The grandparents looked at him. This was the first time they had seen him.

"What do you trust Sister Margaret to do?"

"To take care of my mom so I can stay with Jill and Brian and my brother and sister, Pedro and Silvia."

"Well, let's all sit down then and hear what Sister Margaret has to say. Sister Margaret?"

Sister Margaret stood erect. She had had her hair done the day before and was wearing the outfit that she had thrown in the wash yesterday.

"Your Honor. When I found out about the plan to send Michael away with his mother and grandparents, I was worried. You see, I was responsible for his placement with the Jacobs
. We figured it would be terrible to take a boy away from his foster family who loves him like a son, to go with grandparents he has never met, with his mother who still needs time to heal."

"Michael, do you like where you are living, with the Jacobs?"

"Yes, sir."

"And why is that?"

"They love me."

"How do you know that?"

"Because they respect me. They listen to me. They laugh a lot. They let me collect the eggs. They like my pictures."

"That certainly is love," he nodded at Michael.

"You can feel it...love," Michael had the last word. Jill and Brian hugged him when they sat back down. Pedro reached over for a high five and Silvia squeezed his hand and smiled at him.

"Sister Margaret, would you continue please?"

"Yes, Your Honor. I would like to introduce Mr. Ray Fagan, a certified drug rehab therapist, who will be directing the plan which includes all the people gathered here with us. You see, we want to help not only Michael, but his mother who needs intensive care if she wants to become a contributing person who is confident enough to someday take care of herself and her child as he deserves...as he is now being cared for by Brian and Jill Jacob. Mr. Fagan will explain it all."

Ray stood up, looking very professional. When he began talk, it was evident that he was a professional.

"When I met Sister Margaret, she was wrangling with how to help Michael who was happily living with the Jacobs but about to be sent to live with his grandparents and his mother, who still is recovering from drug and alcohol abuse and is not able to care for herself, let alone her child.

"Sister has come up with a plan that involves all of Michael's extended family as well as the sisters at St. Francis on the Hill.

"The plan is this: Michael will continue to live with the Jacobs. Joan Smith will be provided with a room at the convent of St. Francis on the Hill. She can live there and must earn her room and board. I will manage her drug rehab as I am qualified. I have just relocated to Dubuque for a period of one year while I work on a book. I have my papers and references."

Given permission, he walked over to the judge and handed him the documents.

"The next piece of paper I will hand you, Your Honor, is evidence of our commitment to helping Joan Smith. Our goal is to aid her to find purpose in her life and to eventually be able to care for her son. Michael will help in this effort. We think it will be a long process because the drugs and alcohol have done a lot of damage. Everyone in this room has offered to provide care for Joan Smith. She will be under supervision every day and learning skills along the way."

He passed out a sheet of paper containing the schedule of Joan's life from July through August, giving the first copy to Joan, one to her parents, and the next to the judge. Joan didn't even look at the paper.

"As you can see Your Honor, there are a lot of people involved in trying to help Joan turn her life around. Even Michael will spend supervised time with her each week, to try to get to know her and help her become the mother she should be. This is difficult for him, since she is a stranger to him because of her disease.

"As you notice, this is just a two-month schedule. The children will be going off to school at the end of August and so this schedule will change. I have assured Sister Margaret that I will take care of that. By then I will know everyone better and will tweak the plan as needed. You can also see that it includes off campus interaction with a Dubuque support group. There are seven sisters who have volunteered one day a week to be in charge, helping Joan to arrive in time to her appointments with various other people who will include her in their lives and teach her different skills by working alongside her. That includes Brenda Schmidt, the Jacob family, and the Donovan family as well as the aunts, uncles and cousins."

Ray was standing next to the judge, having presented him with the plan. Judge Rawson stood up and shook Ray's hand and asked Sister Margaret to come up. Pedro, Michael, and Silvia hopped up to help her. They looked like a miniature honor guard escorting the tiny queen. Connor and Annie came too. Then they turned around and marched right back to sit with their parents. The judge came around the bench to shake her hand.

"Sister Margaret, where did you come up with this idea? It is brilliant!"

"On retreat." She blushed bright red as she lied. Well, kind of lied. She wasn't under oath, and after all, the casino was where she cleared her mind of clutter, so she could be a better person.

"Well, we all should go on more retreats. In the process of helping one young boy, you didn't leave his mother out, and you included so many people. I always think, that if people are told how they can help, a lot more problems would be solved in this world. I can see how respected you are. Even these little children love you."

"She is our grandma. What's not to love?" Pedro piped up from his seat, and then slapped his hand over his mouth, realizing he had spoken aloud.

Judge Rawson laughed. Then he asked them all to sit down. When things had quieted down, he addressed the Smiths.

"Mr. and Mrs. Smith, I hope you will agree with me that the generosity of these good people will be the best for your daughter and your grandson. Joan will be offered the opportunity to learn useful skills and social interaction. She will also be in a loving, structured environment. I am ordering that this Plan be put into effect, that Michael should stay with the Jacobs and that perhaps you would communicate with Mr. Fagan, who now will be running the operation, about how you might play a role in their lives."

Mrs. Smith had tears in her eyes. "I would be happy to, Your Honor. We live far away, but I'll try to call and become more involved in their lives." Mr. Smith was quiet, his head hung, embarrassed and glum. *Probably relieved too*, Sister Margaret thought. Then she chastised herself for having a mean-spirited thought. Sanguine and salubrious, Margaret!

At that Michael stood up and crawled over the top of Jill and Pedro and carefully around Sister Margaret. He stood on his tiptoes and whispered into his grandmother Smith's ear, "You can call *me* too." She patted him on the head, nodding, and sat down while Michael retraced his steps to the place he belonged. Joan sat still and damaged, seeming unaware of her surroundings. It was going to be a long haul.

"This case is concluded, very happily and positively, I think. And now, as long as we are all here, and I know this will be a surprise to everyone but Mrs. Donovan, I would like to announce some wonderful news. Pedro and Silvia, could you please come forward."

The surprised children stood up in time to see John and Martha enter through the back doors. Pedro did a large wave, Silvia a small finger wave. Pedro turned back to the judge and said for his information, "Those people are our other grandpa and grandma."

Jill and Brian turned around to see John and Martha and waved to them. What was going on? Could they possibly be signing the adoption papers today?

"We also have Sister Margaret and Grandma and Grandpa Jacobs," Silvia pointed with an open hand. "And Grandma and Grandpa Higgins, Mom's parents, are over there." Silvia finished with an accentuated flourish that looked so much like Jill. Brian and Jill looked at each other, surprised that Silvia had taken the initiative to speak up.

"Well," Judge Rawson continued. He loved this kind of court case. "It is so good they could all be here today. You have quite a family."

Then he turned to Michael, "Michael, and your other two friends," He looked at Pedro. "Connor and Annie," Pedro whispered loudly.

"Connor and Annie, you better get down here too."

Annie looked so funny swinging her little hips as she walked between her brother and Michael. She was wearing her fringed Annie Oakley skirt with her white beaded cowgirl shirt. All she was missing was her hat, which her mother said she couldn't wear.

Then he looked at the cousins waiting expectantly. "All right. Now, all the cousins better come down here too."

There was the patter of feet as the gallery emptied of kids.

The judge stood up tall behind his desk and pulled two papers out of a folder and motioned for Jill and Brian to come forward. Each placed a hand on Silvia and Pedro's shoulders and held hands with each other.

"This almost feels like our wedding," Brian whispered to Jill.

"And now Silvia and Pedro, I want to ask you if you if you want Jill and Brian Jacobs to be your forever parents."

"Yes," Silvia said immediately.

"That's a given. Thumbs up. A-Okay," Pedro reiterated. Brian and Jill looked apologetically at the judge while they tried not to laugh.

The judge held up two papers. The kids all craned their necks to see. "These papers say that the court approves the adoption of Pedro and Silvia to Jill and Brian Jacobs."

He looked at the brother and sister as he signed both sheets. "They are now your parents."

Annie started cheering like a cheer leader. Carolyn and Bob sat in their seats trying to keep from laughing. Carolyn had tears rolling down her face. Sister Margaret was shaking in her seat trying to stay dignified and crying at the same time.

Brian and Jill, pulled their two children in a hug that included Michael and Annie and Connor.

"One more thing, before all of you leave. I need to stress how important it is that Michael and Connor and Annie and all your cousins are family. And family looks out for each other. They try to be good to each other and help each other grow strong. And the mothers and fathers and grandmothers and grandfathers love you all. Take care of each other. Court dismissed."

"Excuse me, your honor," Ray Fagan stood up from where he was sitting next to Sister Margaret.

"The next Plan is this. I would like to announce that tomorrow at noon, there will be a big bash at Eagle Point Park to celebrate this wonderful occasion. Pedro and Silvia were adopted legally, and Michael can stay to be their brother. Joan Smith will get the best help we can give her. Everyone, please come to the first pavilion on the left to celebrate. It's a potluck. I will bring the drinks, plates, napkins, cups. Everyone else, please bring a dish to pass. Judge, Mr. and Mrs. Smith, you are invited too."

Sister Margaret looked at him with wonder in her eyes. "You must be the archangel Raphael," she said to him quietly.

He laughed. "No, just a lucky guy who sat next to a lucky old woman at the casino, whose ways kind of rubbed off on him."

"Shush," she said.

• • • • •

Later that day Bob and Carolyn were standing out by the fence watching Connor atop of Palm Reader and Annie sitting in the grass talking to Ouija who was frisking around beside her.

"Carrie, what would you think if I were to quit my high school history job and start at the middle school. The superintendent of the district called before we left for the court house this morning. The principals at the two middle schools had shown him my outline and suggestions for the Hoofprints in History program. They would like me to teach it, particularly because I have good background and good connections with people who could really make this program come alive, like Brenda and Harold. They think it could be a showcase that, perhaps, I could sell to other schools when it is completed."

"I would be very happy with that if that is what you want, Bob. I've read what you've completed so far and you know I was impressed. I think the kids would be very fortunate to have you for their teacher."

"They said they would give me a travel allowance to travel between schools. It would be an adjustment. But I think I would like it. I've become so engrossed in the research this summer. I'd like to see it through. Of course, there will be tweaking."

She smiled at him and grabbed his hand. "Bob, I think you would be great!"

• • • • •

The phone rang in the house. Marilyn picked it up thinking she needed to do some checking on the schedule for the weekend at the ETC. With the party tomorrow, she had to get one more volunteer.

"Hello? Equine Therapy Center."

"Hi, Marilyn. It's Walter."

"Oh, it's so nice to hear your voice. I have been thinking about you." *Well, actually, quite a lot.*

"That's good to know." She could hear the grin in his voice. "I am just calling to let you know that I have good news at this end for a change. Accusations have been flying between Adele and Scarlone, and they are revealing a lot of dirt that will do neither of them any good.

"Also, I just got a call from the New Jersey PD. They want Scarlone shipped out there. Something to do with money laundering. That will put him away for a good long time. And Chicago is interested in Adele Wallace, something about embezzling from one of her husband's funds."

"Holy smokes. That means they will both be out of the way. Just don't tell Sister Margaret or she will be thinking of a plan at one of her retreats to rehabilitate them."

He laughed. "As we speak, they are both being cuffed and shackled for the trip to Chicago. The county will drop Scarlone off at O'Hare to meet a special charter that New Jersey is sending out for him. Then we'll deliver Ms. Wallace to Cook County Jail."

"Well, it sounds like things are wrapped up on this case for you in Dubuque."

"Yes, but I sure hope I get to see you again, Marilyn. All work and no play, makes for a dull boy."

"I would like to see you again too. Just want to ask though. Any attachments for you?"

"Nope, free and clear. Never been married. No special friends. Kind of a loner."

"Well, then. I would be very happy if you would take me to Eagle Point Park tomorrow at noon, that is, if you are free. We are having a big party for the Jacobs who have just adopted two children and for Michael, their foster son who gets to stay with them, and also for Michael's mother Joan who we are going to try to rehabilitate."

"Interesting kind of party. What should I bring?"

"Oh, nothing. It is just potluck. I am taking a hot chicken and dumplings so that will suffice."

"Yum, that sounds good. But did you know that I am an excellent cook and baker? I'll bring a strawberry cake that you are going to love."

"I didn't know you could cook! I don't know anything about you?"

"Ditto here, Marilyn. Hope you have the time to take a nice long walk around the park to tell me about yourself tomorrow."

"Great! You need some fresh air after being stuffed in that little office all day."

"Well, mam. I must tell you that I run at least two miles every day. Outside. Trying to keep my expanding gut at bay."

"Ah, there will be so much to learn." She was smiling when she hung up.

•   •   •   •   •

On the way home from the court, with a carload of excited kids, Brian and Jill just smiled and smiled. And then Jill thought of something.

"Oh, Brian. Can you stop at Walgreen's for a sec. I have to pick something up. I will just run in and out. No need to bring the kids in."

"Okay. He pulled into the lot and Jill ran in for her purchase. She was back in three minutes with a small bag.

"That didn't take long."

"Nope. Got what I needed."

Chapter Twenty-Five

Saturday

What a day to remember, news to tell the kids. Wait until she told Brian. The evening seemed to drag on forever for her, whereas it usually flew by with all the activity of getting the sisters washed up and tucked in for the night. They say that time marches on but tonight it felt like it was stuck in mud. Just a state of mind she guessed. She had been watching the clock all night, determining how long it would be until she could punch out.

Now it was midnight and she was ready to climb into bed. Her kids—ah how good that sounded—were tucked in and sleeping securely knowing they were safe with Brian and her and anticipating a big celebration tomorrow. What would they say when they found out?

She slipped into bed beside Brian, trying to make it jiggle a bit so he would wake up. No luck. What was with him? Usually he woke up when she came in. It was about the only time they had to themselves any more.

She sighed loudly. Nothing. She cleared her throat. Nothing. She ran her hand down his arm and he rolled over, hooked his other arm around her and pulled her close. "You should have done that the first time," he teased her. "What do you want, Jilly?"

"You! You were just pretending."

"I was gauging if you would be in an amorous mood but didn't want to get my hopes up now that you are a mama for real."

"Don't think that will stop me, Papa."

"Didn't think it would."

"But Brian, I have something to tell you. You'll never guess."

"Want to bet?"

"No, I am dying to tell you."

"That you're pregnant?"

"What! She sat straight up in bed. How did you know?"

"Well, I have been living with you for four years now. You haven't had your usual zip lately although you've been trying hard. And I noticed little body changes. And I peeked in the bag on the counter in the bathroom."

"You! You…sneak! You stole my thunder!"

"Ah, Jill. I would never do that on purpose. I was so antsy lying here. I even tried to stay up until you got home but I was so tired. I knew you would wake me. I saw the strips weren't opened yet. So, you did? And you are?"

"Yes."

"Does it get any better, Jill? Can you do it all?"

"Yes. It gets better. And I will do it all or ask for help if I need it. Brian, I am so excited. A fourth child. The house is already getting too small! I'll ask Sister Margaret. She'll know what to do."

"You know, Jill, I love that woman. But I think she gave us some training wheels, and we're riding along pretty darned good. Maybe it's time we take off those wheels and try to stay up on our own power. Let her enjoy watching us coasting along or taking a spill now and then."

"Oh. You're right. We never wanted to be dependent on others. Thanks for reminding me. Now let's talk about how we'll tell the kids."

•　　•　　•　　•　　•

"You'll never guess," Jill said to the kids as they finished their breakfast the next morning and Brian cradled his coffee mug in his hand, enjoying the dramatics.

"We are going to have a brother or sister!" Michael shouted.

"Of course. I checked out the box in the bathroom last night," Silvia added dramatically.

"And I read the instructions. Uggh! Pee on paper. I hope you didn't get your hand wet, Mom."

"Pedro!"

"Well, just saying."

"I hope it is a girl for Silvia. Then there will be two boys and two girls," Michael told them.

"No, bro. A boy would be better for the teams."

"Well, Pedro. I play ball." Silvia sounded offended.

"Yeah, I know. But you are different."

"Well, let me tell you," Brian interjected. "Your mom and I will love this baby no matter if it is a boy or a girl. And it would be nice if you congratulated us, because in one day we now have four kids."

"Congratulations!" Three pair of arms flung around their parents' necks.

• • • • •

After talking to Ray, the Donovans loaded up early to go to Eagle Point Park taking a big cushiony lounge chair in the back of the truck, and the cooler filled with fruit pops for the kids, and Carolyn's fruit salad. Marilyn's chicken and dumplings entrée was in a roasting pan. Carolyn would plug in when they got to the park. They were going to help Ray set up. Walter was picking Marilyn up a little later.

It was only 11:00 so the park was very quiet. They were able to get the small pavilion overlooking the Mississippi with a view very similar to the one in their own front yard.

Annie searched out the best spot for Sister Margaret to sit, at the head of the sidewalk on the top of the little rise with a clear view of the Mississippi, where everyone would be passing through to drop off food. She could talk to them.

Ray arrived with Sister Margaret shortly after.

The Donovans went to greet them and take Sister's hand to help her up the sidewalk to her chair.

"This chair is for you, Sister. Mom, said we need you to greet the people as they come."

"Oh, that's a good job for this old lady."

"No, you're the queen," Annie said. So that's why Sister Margaret found herself sitting in a comfy chair in the shade on a sunny day, the birds singing and the children whooping in the playground behind her, the Mississippi twinkling in the sunshine.

Next to arrive was the convent van with twelve of her sisters.

"Margaret, who crowned you?" Sister Julia joked as she led the contingent of sisters up the walk. They were carrying various lawn chairs, coolers, and bags of goodies. Bob and Ray hurried over to help, emptying their hands and setting up chairs around Sister Margaret.

When Marilyn and Walter arrived, they sat down in two vacated chairs next to her.

"Sister, I'm glad we got here a little early before it gets crowded. I just wanted to tell you that you really ARE the queen. I am so grateful to you for helping me to purge myself of bad memories and to find out the truth about the Wallaces."

"Well, I am glad it helped. Carolyn came over earlier to tell me that she is good with things. Grateful and going forward she said. I think that is a good attitude."

Walter also expressed his appreciation. "You know Sister, if all this hadn't have come out, I never would have met Marilyn, and I consider that would have been a very unfortunate loss."

Marilyn smiled at him. He got up and held out his hand to her. "We promised each other a walk around the park before lunch. Remember?" Sister Margaret felt a wave of joy wash over her. It was about time that Marilyn got a break.

After that people started to arrive in droves. Brenda came up with a large basket containing a hot dish that smelled wonderful. She sat next to Margaret at the top of the hill to rest. "I had to haul this thing from over in the other lot. Didn't realize it was so heavy."

"Where is Harold? I thought he might come with you."

"He's coming but his daughter and her kids are here and he is going to bring them along to meet everyone. He had to wait for them. But he just texted that they are on their way. I'm a little nervous about meeting his kids. He's really a nice man, Sister."

"Well, I think so too."

"You know, Sister, you have made such a difference in my life. I am a changed person. I used to be so dissatisfied and kind of bitchy. Now I'm happy and excited and so grateful to have all you have offered me. I hope I'll be able to have your convent mostly self-sufficient in a couple of years. Mother and I have been talking about looking into installing some solar energy panels on the hillside where they just tore down the old boarding school for girls."

"That sounds interesting."

"Well, Sister, if I hadn't met you at the casino, and you hadn't taken an interest in me, I have a feeling that I would still be that unsatisfied woman I once was. I'm trying to be more like you, looking for solutions and not whining about problems so much."

"You're doing a wonderful job, Brenda. It is amazing the difference you have made in such a short time."

"Thank you, Sister." She looked up. "Oh, there's Harold. I'd better get this up to the table. Looks like Bob and Carrie and Ray have things under control."

Ray came over carrying a large glass of lemonade with ice cubes for Sister. "I'll take your basket for you Brenda if you want to go meet Harold."

"Thanks, Ray! You're my knight in shining armor."

The minute the chair next to her was emptied, someone else filled it. All of the Jacob kids had to tell her that she would be a grandma again because their mom was having a baby but adding, "Don't tell her I said so. She wanted to tell you herself."

Then Jill and Brian both stopped to tell her the astounding news. They were so elated.

"I suppose that house is getting a little small," Sister Margaret smiled at their happiness.

"Perhaps, but not for a while. We'll figure it out, Sister," Brian told her. "There are always solutions. You taught us that."

Ray disappeared for a while and came back with Joan, Michael's mom. He sat her down next to Sister, and shortly returned with a glass of lemonade for her. She was mute but included because Sister and whoever sat next to her, made sure to draw her into the conversation with their eyes and hands. She didn't have to say anything, and she didn't. She just wasn't ready to talk. Sister Margaret noticed that she looked all over, taking in everything, and then got up and wandered off to a bench by the playground to watch the kids. Good for her! She noticed one of her sisters went and sat next to Joan. They were already taking on their responsibility. Ray was brilliant, the way he had planned her rehab and did all the legwork to get the schedule put together.

The judge came with his wife bringing chips and dip. Last to arrive were all the Jacobs and Higgins clans with more food. John and Martha showed up chauffeured by their son. Pedro and Silvia helped Martha up the hill to sit by Sister. There were no tears or shouts of anger, only the sound of kids having a great time and adults enjoying one another's company.

The Smiths didn't come. They went back to Minnesota, but Sister Margaret knew that Jill would take the initiative to have Michael call them. They seemed to need rehab as much as Joan.

After lunch. Pedro convinced Brian that everyone should go over to the baseball field for a good game with all the cousins and aunts and uncles. So, they all packed up cars with coolers and chairs.

Bob drove Sister Margaret over to the ball field, her lounge chair in the back of the truck. Mrs. Higgins and Mrs. Jacob the elder, got her settled under a tall oak tree where she watched a lively game, visited with the sideline coaches, and enjoyed a lot of "I remember when" moments.

Chapter Twenty-Six

Sunday

Brenda found Sister Margaret sitting in her recliner. She wasn't sleeping. In her cold hand she held a piece of computer paper. It read:

Carry On!

P.S. I sure would like to ride in the Donovans fairy chariot one more time.